Judy Howard

To Dan
and Marie,
you are my
best cat's
fRiends.

Going Home

With

A Cat

And

A Ghost

Judy Howard

ISBN: 1479167983

ISBN 13: 9781479167982

Library of Congress Control Number: 2012915659
CreateSpace Independent Publishing Platform
North Charleston, South Carolina

Other books By Judy Howard

Coast To Coast With
A Cat And A Ghost

Dedication

THIS BOOK IS DEDICATED TO THE BABY BOOMER
GENERATION. TO THOSE WHO HAVE DREAMED AND LOST,
AND YET STILL DREAM—ENJOY THE RIDE.

JUDY HOWARD

Acknowledgements

There are three aspects to the creation of GOING HOME WITH A CAT AND A GHOST and the list of people involved is long.

First, the physical process of critiquing and editing a manuscript is brutal and never done.

To my critique group at The Village in Hemet, California, you encouraged me to let go of my love for long, flowery sentences and misplaced modifiers, and cheered me on: Anne Dunham, Denver Howard, Bill Fleming, Susan Squier, Gila Shabanow, Norma Garwood, Brenda Grelock, and Natalie Flikkema. Without all of you, I would never have embarked on this incredible literary journey.

My humble appreciation extends to: Jim, Vicki, and Carrie Hitt, Lynne Spreen, Jim Parrish, JoLynn Buehring, Kathy Shattuck, Mary Jane Kruty, Peggy Wheeler, Howard Fiegenbaum, and Harlee Lassiter. Thank you all for your endless hours of support. I could not have done it without you.

Secondly, an author needs readers, the people who read the manuscript before it ever goes to press. Vicki Andreotti, May Sinclair, Mark Sickman, and Kristi Zeiders, thank you for the time and attention to detail you invested in me. And Sandy, I asked you so many times I am ashamed.

And thirdly, the most critical aspect of the writing process is the spiritual element. The people who take up residence between the lines, the "water boys" who keep the author trudging along, one word, one page, one chapter, and one book at a time.

My sister, Sandy: You are my best critic—loyal, honest, loving—and my best friend. What will I do without you?

Vickie Andreotti: How can you always come up with the boost I need to scale the latest writing, marketing, or publishing block? Everyone needs someone who believes in them. I have found that with you.

And my readers: Without your rave reviews, your excitement, and desire for a second book, I would not have had the courage to continue. Thank you for cheering me on. I hope you will not be disappointed.

Many organizations contribute to an author's success: the Inland Empire California Writers Club, Sisters in Crime, Shirley Wible of the Sun City Library, and Sandra Brautigam of the Grace Mellman Community Library. Also, the many members of the RV community: the Escapees and the Winnebago, Good Sam, FMCA, Roadtrek, and the Gypsy Journal.

Thank you all for your invaluable contributions, physical and spiritual, and your belief in me as I continue on this great adventure.

Author's Note

GOING HOME WITH A CAT AND A GHOST is a work of fiction. The character Judy Howard is purely a fictional character I created from my imagination.

Names, characters, places, and incidents either are the product of my imagination or are used fictitiously. Any resemblance to actual events, locales, or persons, living or dead, is entirely coincidental.

GOING HOME WITH A CAT AND A GHOST portrays a dream that lurks in all of our imaginations as we consider...what if?

Best regards,
Judy Howard

Chapter One

Alone inside the comforting confines of my motor home, I watched as the world scrolled past my windshield. The dawn illuminated the eastern horizon and I felt as if I sat in a darkened theater, watching in anticipation as the credits rolled across the screen, the title yet to be announced. The motor home hummed its soft but steady song of power and strength while my playlist of country music two-stepped down the road, skipping over asphalt cracks and do-si-doing through the California traffic. As I drove, I settled into the rocking motion of travel while the wheels of my mind spun in reverse, two thousand miles, back forty years to a night I couldn't remember but changed my life forever.

On that Saturday night in January 1965, I hadn't turned seventeen. My youth's short life stretched behind me. My life's path had been smooth and the future bright for a girl of my age, but I still had the shallowness of a sixteen-year-old, unaware of the thorns hidden along the way, destined to wound my future.

The last vestiges of Christmas had been unwrapped and taken to the trash along with the tinseled tree. I felt let down at this time of the year. Advertising promised a hoopla of the holidays that never came close to my experience. I hadn't been swept away on a romantic or snuggled with a sweetheart sipping cocoa by the firelight wrapped in my grandmother's afghan. What I wanted was never under the tree and, though I tried to become fired up about the magic and wonderment, when the New Year arrived, people returned to their everyday lives. They went back to work, trying to make a living, treating each other with the same mundane attitude as they had during the rest of the year. At sixteen, I questioned the point of it all.

I spent most Saturday nights at the skating rink with my friends, talking of clothes and boys. It was there I nursed my hopeful heart with promises of a chance encounter with Brad, the boy of my dreams, the boy who confused me with looks of desire but, like a skittish thoroughbred, shied away when I returned a look of my own. It was at that skating rink—a colorful, musical world of its own—on that Saturday night that my future became poisoned, tainting my innocence and changing my life.

The huge building spread low in a gravel parking lot filled with teenager's hot rods that today are considered vintage. With the holidays forgotten and the Midwest's bitter winter settling in, I crunched across the frosty parking lot after Dad dropped me off. Bundled in my new Christmas coat and snow boots, I hurried through the cold to the rink's entrance. When I opened the door, I felt like Alice in Wonderland, the outside world forgotten, overcome by the roller rink's atmosphere. Inside, loud, live organ music reverberated against the walls, causing the building to tremble while the rotating mirrored sphere, hanging from the ceiling, reflected and sprinkled dots like colorful snow. The confetti lights swirled in the air, racing around the polished hardwood rink, keeping pace with the skaters.

The music, along with the clicking of wooden wheels across the floor, muted the voices of teenagers who exchanged gossip and popped gum while they bent over benches, tying shoelaces. I paused after entering, allowing my eyes and ears to adjust to the dimness and the din. My friends Jackie and Carrie stood by the benches that circled the rink. Approaching them, I noticed the room, standing apart from the crowd. I watched his expression morph into gentleness when he saw me. Fantasizing about him in the privacy of my bedroom when the lights were out was my favorite way to fall asleep.

A Clorox-white T-shirt showed off Brad's farmer's tan and his faded jeans slung low and snug on his hips. He combed his blond hair with a practiced sweep into a ducktail. Long sideburns framed his clean-shaven, baby-soft cheeks, and his blue eyes that caused the girls to swoon now penetrated my heart as he gazed my way. He hung back in the shadows, always the bystander, cool and aloof from the social froufrou that went on among his peers. Girls continually approached him, shuffling, swooning, and hanging on his arm, but he stood unaffected as if he were a proud stallion switching his tail at annoying flies. At times I noticed him leave with girls of questionable reputation, but I always felt they were toys he quickly tired of. I never saw him with the same one twice.

He was my heartthrob and had probably parted earlier with his buddies who, full of rutting energy and bravado, had gone on to the bar to further inflate their male egos. Brad was "too cool" to skate, but came to the rink because he knew I could be found giggling and gossiping with friends as we verbally journaled every moment of our teenage week. I enjoyed watching Brad's controlled, tight expression go warm and soft when my eyes met his. Averting my gaze as he did the same, I focused on my friend Jackie.

Jackie was my best friend. I envied her stylish clothes and would have traded my house-dressed mom and flannel-shirted dad for her cool, sophisticated parents. Carrie was my next best friend and the opposite of Jackie. Her outfits were stylish, too, but shorter and tighter. Carrie balanced out the Threesome, as we called ourselves. She looked up to me for guidance while I in turn looked to Jackie who grounded our circle of friendship.

I approached, raising my voice over the rumble of skaters passing by.

"Hi."

"What's up?" Standing up on her skates, Jackie whirled around to face me. Her wool pleated skirt remained hugging her hips and her eyes looked mischievously past me. I followed her gaze, which settled on Brad in the distance. She knew of my bad crush on Brad.

"Nothing much." Acting nonchalant, I turned my back. Trying to dismiss her teasing grin, I removed my coat and sat down on the bench she'd vacated.

At that moment Carrie swept up, braking suddenly, her short skirt flaring with her movement. "Did you talk to her, Jackie?"

I looked up. "About what?"

Carrie wore the shortest style and the reddest lipstick. I focused on the bright color of her lips. I thought she seemed to overdo everything. She often complained that her father abused her mother, and I was sure he mistreated Carrie as well, although she never breathed a word of it. She played the role of the obedient daughter, but was anxious to get married and leave home. I would never call her boy-crazy to her face. That was my analysis.

Carrie stomped her foot like a child asking for candy. "About that new guy. He goes to Lanphier with Brad's buddy, Bob. I want to meet him."

"I don't even know what the new guy looks like," I answered.

"But Brad and Bob are friends. Bob must know the guy if they both go to Lanphier," Carrie whined.

"I don't know Brad well enough to ask him that." My face flushed from embarrassment.

Reaching over to finger the small gold locket I always wore, Jackie chimed in. "You know Brad has a thing for you. You haven't taken that locket off since he gave it to you at the fair."

"Come on, Jackie," Carrie interrupted, pushing Jackie's hand away. She rescued me from Jackie's teasing. "We'll catch up with you later, Judy." Anxious to get out on the floor, the two hunched down and pushed off from the railing.

"Yeah, okay. Later." They both swirled off hand in hand onto the floor, melting into the multicolored crowd. After removing my boots and loafers, I proceeded to lace up my skates.

"Would you like to skate?" I jumped as I turned to the voice and away from my friends, who had already disappeared into the moving crowd. It wasn't Brad; he never asked me to skate. Only when I manipulated the timing for our paths to cross would I receive more than the gaze from his bedroom eyes. Only then would he invite me out to his car, where we'd sit in the backseat of his '57 Chevy, talking until the rink closed. But that night the timing was off because I watched him go outside with his friend Bob.

"Sure," I answered. It was a guy I hadn't met before. He seemed nice enough. I didn't know his name, but I had seen him around. I finished lacing up my skates and we made our way onto the floor. He took my hand and we moved to the rhythm of the music as we glided around the arena. He didn't say anything, but his look was intense as he watched me skate, and it baffled me how he avoided clashing with the other skaters. After several songs I thanked him, released my hand, sweaty from his grip. Cringing, I wiped my palm on my jeans and caught up with Jackie and Carrie. After skating a few more songs with them, I opted to sit out. From the sidelines, I watched couples and singles move to the music, laughing, talking, holding hands, and swirling. Everyone seemed to belong. I felt distant, as if standing on a hill looking down on the scene.

"Hi." It was the new guy again. Only his mouth moved in a smile. I realized I hadn't asked his name. I still didn't ask. His light green eyes burned like lasers when he looked at me, and I turned away from his piercing gaze. His dark brown hair was cut like my father's, too short on the sides and back. His jeans hung loose, hiding muscular thighs that pressed up against me when he sat down. A blue flannel shirt covered a black turtleneck sweater that seemed to hinder his thick neck from turning.

"You look awfully nice tonight. That's a nice sweater. Is it new?" But he looked through the sweater and I sensed his interest in what I wore under it. "Can I get you a Coke?"

"Okay."

He skated away but returned in minutes with a Coke in each hand.

"Here you go." I reached for the cold drink in his left hand, but he shoved the one in his right into my extended hand. I took a gulp as he sat down, again crowding next to me. "I've noticed you the past couple of weekends and always wanted to ask you to skate. You are a good skater."

I didn't respond. Twenty minutes passed as we watched the skaters in silence.

The new guy hadn't spoken but I felt him shifting, unable to sit still, anticipating something. I turned to face him when he tapped my shoulder. "I'm going out to my car and have a cigarette. You wanna come?"

Brad popped into my head, but I quickly pushed his image aside after I glanced across the room to see him surrounded by several girls from Lanphier High. Brad watched as his buddy, Bob, lit a redhead's cigarette. I imagined they too would be going out to their cars with the girls.

"Sure." The fresh winter air would be welcome after working up a sweat on the rink, and anyway, I felt a little lightheaded. We put on our street shoes and coats and stepped out into the crisp January air. The coldness slapped my flushed face as someone grasped my arm, both sensations becoming my last clear memory of that night.

Feeling wobbly, I staggered as the grip on my arm led me to a glossy black car with dark tinted windows. The car's image remains embedded in my mind's shadows to this day. Several boys stood around smoking and drinking. Darkness engulfed me while they joked and talked loudly; their tinny voices resonated in my head. I tried to make sense of the scene through blurred vision as the boys punched one another in angry gestures.

Someone must have opened the door and pulled the front seat forward to allow access to the backseat. "Go ahead, climb in." The words drifted into space and disappeared, replaced by a thick spicy scent that made me queasy. The figure held my Coke as I climbed in, handed it back, followed me, and sat solidly beside me. "Drink up," he said. I heard chants and cheers, disconnected, as if from a pep rally far away. The taunts and lewd remarks twisted into lyrics to a song blaring on the car's radio. The blurred, shadowy ghost figure next to me laughed like a colorful clown in a house of horrors. The rest of the evening played out like a bad horror movie. Lips sought mine as crude hands probed under my blouse. A hooded shroud covered my consciousness. I floated in and out to a rhythm much like the skaters inside.

"I'm your bad boy. You like bad boys, don't you, bitch?" The words, in contrast to the fuzziness around me, rang like a trumpet sounding a sharp alarm. A lurid song I never heard before, but could still hear, filled my head. Dull, off-key notes wrapped in cotton absorbed my brain's drowning demands to flee.

His hands moved to my jean's zipper and soon my body was forced to a rhythm that could not be stopped. It was over as fast as it had begun. He climbed off before I was aware he'd been on top of me. Moving back to the corner of the seat and lifting his hips, he zipped up his jeans. His voice pierced my stupor. "Let's go back inside and get another Coke. Tuck in your blouse. Fix your hair."

Stunned and weak, I stumbled from the car's dark interior as ordered, straightening, tucking, and zipping. When I entered the building, Jackie came skating up.

"What have you been up to?"

I glanced around. The dark figure had vanished. *Hadn't there been someone with me?* I was confused, disoriented. My head spun and I thought I was going to be sick.

Jackie looked on as I shuffled over to the bench and sat down. "I don't feel so good," I explained. Thoughts and memories disappeared into a black hole before I could make sense of them.

"What's wrong? Are you sick?" Jackie glided over and plopped down next to me.

"Oh, I'm just a little queasy. I'm okay. I'll just sit here for a while. You go ahead."

"You sure?"

"I'm sure, go on."

She rose as if in slow motion and floated off into the crowd.

I didn't know how much time passed when I felt Brad by my side.

"Hey, how're you doing?" When he looked into my unfocused eyes, his lip drew into a thin line and his brow creased.

Unable to keep up my façade, I said, "I don't feel so good." I leaned over into a ball, holding my stomach.

" Let's go outside. You'll feel better with some fresh air." He supported me as I stumbled out to his car. "Get in." I did as I was told.

'I'm going to be sick." He crouched down beside me and held my head as I leaned out into the parking lot and heaved.

Brad smoothed my hair back from my eyes, touching my chin and tilting my head up. I tried to focus. "Have you been drinking?" he asked.

"No, I just had a Coke but it tasted salty." I didn't under-stand why Brad's expression turned to ice.

"Where'd you get the Coke?"

"At the snack bar, I think. I don't know. I mean, I don't remember. Maybe I went outside. Yeah, I think I did. There were some guys outside. I think I got it from them."

"Who were the guys?"

"I don't know. *I don't know!*" My thoughts swirled like smoke caught by the wind. Dread prickled the back of my neck as flashes from the backseat penetrated my senses. I shivered at the shadowy scene that revealed patches of horror. "Oh my God!" I lurched forward again. My body shuddered with dry heaves, this time from the realization of what had happened rather than from the drug in my Coke.

"Oh my God!" Aware of soreness and throbbing, I hunched over into a painful ball. Brad pulled me close. I buried my face in his sheepskin-lined coat.

My sixteen-year-old past, that laid out behind me like a well-worn path, now stretched into the future, alive with ghostly shapes. Brad held me and the sinister images dimin-ished. I inhaled cool air, replacing the hot fear within me. Brad said nothing.

"Come on. You've got to get it together. I'm going to get you some coffee. You wait here. Lock the door when I get out. I'll be right back. Then we'll talk."

Teens laughing and talking broke the silence in the park-ing lot. I watched when Brad returned but still jumped when he climbed in and slammed the door. "How are you doing? Better?"

"What am I going to do?" I tasted my salty tears. How could I remember nothing and yet know such humiliation, shame, and aching agony? My unconscious knew what my consciousness only guessed.

He leaned over, took my hands, and curved them around the coffee cup. "Take a sip. You'll feel better."

His eyes met mine and I felt an unfounded ray of hope.

"Tell me what happened. Who were you with?"

"I don't know what happened! I remember talking to Jackie and Carrie. I got a Coke after I skated for a while. I think I went outside for some air. I remember feeling sick. But maybe I didn't go outside, maybe I just sat there. *I don't remember!*" My breaths came in short gasps and tears stung my whisker-burned face.

"I'm sorry. I need to know what happened." I felt the rage in his taut muscles as he once again struggled to bind up his emotions. With calmness I knew he didn't feel, he said, "You're going to get yourself together and call your dad to come pick you up. I'll check with you Monday." His words conveyed confidence and control. I sat up straight and inhaled deeply. I wiped away my tears and fumbled in my purse for my hairbrush. Maybe everything was going to be fine.

"All right," I said. My fingers reached up to stroke the delicate gold locket I cherished as if it were an amulet. I had not taken it off since the day Brad gave it to me. It was gone.

Nothing was ever going to be fine again.

Chapter Two

"Come home, come home, I've been waiting for you for so long, so long..." Faith Hill's song on the radio rescued me from my musings. Her silky voice rang like a fine crystal bell, its perfection sent goose bumps up and down my arms, while the deep familiar sound of the Winnebago's power and strength soothed me.

This voyage was going to be a trip back in time, not because my itinerary was to follow the historic Route 66, but because the journey was a trip to a place I couldn't reach by motor vehicle. No asphalt road would lead me to my goal. My quest was a place where the blacktop ended, where dreams lay broken, unfulfilled in the dirt, waiting to be dusted off and examined—that was my destination.

Anxious yet hesitant, I worried if I were doing the right thing. The interstate's lines stretched into the distance and became my yellow brick road because I was going home—home to Springfield, Illinois, and my fortieth high school reunion; home to the murky memories and the source of enduring nightmares.

My motor home, which I christened "The Wizard of Winnebago," was loaded to the windowsills with everything I might need for the long trek home. Examining the tiny closet and fridge, both stuffed with all the clothes and food they could hold, an observer would conclude there was no Wal-Mart along the route. I packed sweaters and shorts, the food processor and frozen dinners. The twenty-four-foot Wizard was considered small in the RV family, but it suited me and my "travel crew."

My entourage included a polyester-stuffed, life-sized doll named Cowboy Jack, who rode shotgun, and my cat, Sportster. The two shared the small space that was going to be my home, my woman cave for the next couple months.

I flinched and jerked the steering wheel left when a semi roared past. My small rig swayed to the right and then shuddered in the wake of the big rig's air draft. The rocking motion brought me back to the present as I again tried to remember what happened forty years ago. The semi shrank into the asphalt as it disappeared into the distance. The engine's steady hum sang a song of travel to the road stretching before me. *Clack, clack,* over the asphalt cracks it sang. The melody lured my mind into wandering again and, like a magnet, my thoughts drew back to those life-altering minutes that transformed my life. Patches of the nightmare remained, cutting in and out like a bad cell call.

A car eased silently past me, its deep black paint glistened against the blinding reflection of its chrome bumper. It was vintage, probably headed to a car show. I felt my neck prickle as the vehicle disappeared into the distance and was swallowed by the asphalt. It reminded me of my dark past and shadowy memories.

Monday after the rape, I trudged to my locker. In two short days life had become a chore. There was no joy. My hands, trembling since Saturday night, fumbled with the combination. The metal door jerked open with a clang and I gasped at the message taped inside: "You tell, you die, bitch." I ripped the paper from the door. Now my entire body shook. Crushing the paper into a ball, I shoved the wad into my pocket and slammed the door. I gathered every ounce of control to hold back my tears and found my way to first period.

Brad and I skipped last period to keep the doctor's appointment he had insisted on making. It was not my family's doctor and Brad was elusive when I asked how he had found the man. I tried to assure Brad I was fine but he dismissed my false bravado.

In the exam room, I sat stiff and numb with Brad as we listened to the doctor's diagnosis. I suffered tearing and bruising, and the possibility of pregnancy still loomed but was too early to diagnose. I went home with pain pills and antibiotics, forced to wait and think.

With the doctor's words still reverberating in my head I grabbed Brad's arm to stop him as we walked to the car, "Oh, God! What if?"

"We'll deal with it if we have to." Brad pulled me close and we continued to the car.

"But I can't be pregnant! It would kill my parents! I just can't be! And what would everyone think? About me? And about you, Brad? Everyone's seen us together. You know what they would think."

"We'll deal with it if we have to. Let's just take it a day at a time." His voice was serious, confident. Grown-up.

How could I be burdening him with all of this? But I pushed the subject. "How would I get rid of it? I would have to. I would just *have to.*"

Brad sighed heavily. "There are doctors who will do it."

I stopped. Grabbing his arm again, I jerked him around and stared at him. "You know someone?"

"This doctor will know someone. Are you sure that's what you want to do?

"I don't have a choice."

Brad said nothing, just opened the car door. I collapsed inside and watched him walk around the front of the car. His back was straight, face grim, lips tight when he got behind the wheel. I moved over next to him and he cradled me under his arm. We sat, silent, staring ahead.

"We could get married." His voice was low, almost a whisper.

I jumped away from his side as if his words had burned me. "We can't do that! You can't do that! How could I do that to you?" The significance of each word pounded down my dreams. "Absolutely not." The two words filled the car's interior and hit their mark, the final death blow to my heart.

Brad said nothing. He stared at me. Was he thinking, *Should I say I love her?* or *Thank God she refused?* "We'll figure it out." He said. "Try not to worry."

The weeks dragged by in a fog. Every morning, harsh sunlight pierced my bedroom window. With reality's glare came my first thought of the day—*Oh, God! What if?*

Carrie tittered through the following weeks with questions, addressing my subdued behavior, but she was sixteen, too, and I was able to distract her easily with shallow questions.

"So, Carrie, Jackie tells me George took you to the drive-in. How did that happen?"

Gushing with excitement, she answered, "Last Saturday night he asked me to skate. He told me he'd wanted to skate with me since the first time he saw me. He said I was a good skater. We spent the entire evening together. He didn't skate with anyone else. He drives a neat car with dark windows so no one can see inside, if you know what I mean."

"So you like him?" I didn't have to ask, but I did.

"Well, we didn't see much of the movie." She giggled.

She sensed my mood was not just from the monthly curse. At the Cozy Dog one afternoon as we shared a shake, she said, "Are you okay? Ever since Saturday night you've been acting weird. Did I do something? I was just teasing you about the locket. Is that why you aren't wearing it anymore?"

I choked on my Coke. This was my best friend, but the wad of paper with its threats burned in my memory. Tears welled up and began to trickle down my face.

"What's wrong, Judy? You can tell me. What did I do? I'm sorry." Jackie grabbed my hand. Her touch was warm against mine.

My tears began to flow and I watched them drop soundlessly onto the napkin, each droplet embedding a damp circle in the linen. "It's not you, Jackie. You haven't done anything." I looked up. How could I tell her? I again thought of the threatening message from my locker. And what would she think of me? Would she ever talk to me again? Desperate for someone to confide in, I blurted it out. "I was raped. And now I might be pregnant."

"Oh my God! Did Brad do that to you? He wouldn't do something like that? I know he wouldn't."

"No, Jackie. No. It wasn't like that. I don't know who it was." I told her everything. I didn't take a breath until my miserable story was laid out on the table. My tears dried as I recounted what I could remember, drawing my friend into my reality of guilt, shame, and fear.

"Oh, Judy. What are you going to do? What does Brad say?"

"He says he knows someone who can take care of it. A doctor." I studied her reaction. I saw the worry as her brows raised and her eyes welled with tears. Her hand, still clutching mine, squeezed even more tightly.

"Brad wants you to do that? Would you do that? Could you?"

"No. He said we could get married."

"You're going to get married?"

"No. Absolutely not."

"You're going to get an abor..." She looked around, lowered her voice to a whisper. "An abortion?" She pulled her hand away as if she might catch my affliction.

"What else can I do, Jackie? I can't marry Brad because I'm pregnant with God-knows-whose baby. I couldn't ask him to do that. Anyway, maybe I'm not."

She reached over with both hands and held mine. "You're right. You probably aren't. We're probably worrying over nothing." Her voice didn't ring with the lilt of confidence I wished, but my heart twisted with love for my friend when she said "we" and rubbed my hands in comfort.

"Yeah, probably."

The following Sunday, I was reluctant to go to our family picnic, but suspicions would arise if I didn't. The gathering included each and every family member bringing a special potluck dish. Washington Park's frozen pond was full to brimming with bundled-up ice skaters, all family and friends I had known all my life. Throughout the year, the park was a meeting place for birthdays and anniversaries, fishing in the spring, swimming in the summer, and sledding in the winter. My cousin John came around and we skated the length of the pond, under the bridge and back again. He was like a brother to me. His folks recently divorced and he now spent a lot of time at our house when his mom worked. Tall and lean, he carried himself with a fluidity and control, making him an accomplished skater on the ice as well as in the rink. On weekends, he frequented the roller rink as much as I and saw to it I never felt left out. Where had he been that night?

"How's everything?" With his hand on my back, we wove though the crowd and I tried to enjoy the crisp afternoon.

"Everything is fine," I lied.

"Did you see Sadie's new baby boy? She and Chuck are bursting with pride." He waited for my response but I couldn't find words. He continued. "Your friend Carrie is going with that new guy from the rink. What's his name?"

"You mean George?"

"Yeah. They're always together."

"He's all right, I guess." I didn't sound convincing. Something about him made me uneasy. But most guys made me anxious since that night.

"I talked to Brad Friday night down by the river road. He and Bob were drag racing with their friends. George was there, too. Have you seen much of Brad?" He knew I had a crush on Brad, though I never told him. "I don't see you as often at the rink these days." I knew he was probing, trying to get me to open up.

"I see him now and then." I was never going to open up. I had shared my secret with Jackie, but never would I share it with a male, no matter how good a friend. My heart wept at the distance I was creating between me and my cousin.

"I know you already know this, Judy, but if you need to talk, I'm always here to listen."

"I know, John. I'm fine, really." I felt the distance between us, but steeled myself to its emptiness. Ashamed and embarrassed—and, after the threatening message in my locker, terrified as well—I was certainly not going to reveal anything. I yearned to draw comfort from family and friends, but instead wished only to escape the questioning looks and comments.

Two months later the waiting game was over; the score was in. I had lost. Brad answered the call from the doctor, who never questioned dealing with a seventeen-year-old since he "specialized" in taking care of "unwanted matters." There would be no chance of my parents receiving the news. When Brad and I met at the café across from school, I knew without asking. His face did not melt at the sight of me. He confirmed what I already knew and gave me the date of the appointment that was supposed to fix everything.

Again at the Cozy dog, Jackie and I sat in the shadows at the corner table.

"What do you think I should do, Jackie?"

"It has to be your decision, Judy. I'll understand and support you, however you decide."

"What would you do?"

"Gee, that's a hard one. I don't know." She whispered, "Abortion," then raised her voice back to normal. "It's illegal. And some say you'll go to hell."

"I'll worry about hell when the time comes. I really don't believe in it, anyway."

"I just can't imagine having a baby, you know...at our age. We're too young. I hate to say it but it I think it would ruin my life. You know, if it were up to me."

"Yeah, that's what my dad would say."

"And you've already been accepted to USC. How can you turn that down? But then being married to Brad, well, that would be sweet. Maybe it would be worth losing everything to take him up on his offer."

I ignored her attempt to lighten the discussion. "I can't ruin his life, too."

"You're right. I know how much you love him. Enough to let him go. You are special, Judy. Just remember you'd be doing what's best, not just for you, but Brad, too. You'll have a chance for marriage and a baby when the time is right. You have your whole life ahead of you."

"Somehow that doesn't feel like a good thing."

"I know you, Judy. You'll get to the other side of this. You're gonna be okay."

There had been no more discussion. Brad accepted my decision and found the doctor to perform the procedure. I could not tell if Brad was angry or relieved and did not have the courage to ask. Whatever he felt, I could not have handled knowing. I trusted he had found the best doctor and hoped the illegal procedure would be safe and professional.

Brad picked me up after school and drove me to the appointment. After Brad parked the car, I glanced at him while I clutched my purse like a life preserver. Our eyes met. The kindness and understanding in Brad's gave me the courage to open the car door and take the first step toward my future, and the last step for the unknown life inside me struggling through its first months of survival. The irony of it all struck me, even at sixteen. I could feel the entire world's pulse and nature's promise of life at the same moment I prepared to interfere with it. I swallowed hard, shoving down the bile that rose in my throat as Brad gently took my elbow. The doctor's office wasn't downtown, but at its edge. It wasn't in an office building, but its basement. We walked the walk to the doctor's dungeon.

A question screamed inside my head as we descended the steps to the doctor's basement office. *How difficult would it be climbing these same steps an hour later?* The dim light in the office revealed little equipment and I wondered if the musky odor was from the dingy linens that lay on the old stuffed chair in the room's corner. A dust beam emanated from the one small window, forming a small rectangular patch of sunlight on the gray concrete floor. Once I had undressed and climbed onto the cold, stainless-steel table, I was surprised by the speed and efficiency of the procedure. The doctor, in a crisp white lab coat, illuminated the room. Not what I expected. He talked in soothing tones and explained he was giving me a bright future instead of taking something away. I heard his words but they did not penetrate the demoralizing gloom enveloping me.

As quickly as it had been created, my condition was sucked into oblivion with surprisingly little discomfort. I expected excruciating pain to punish me and alleviate my guilt and shame. It didn't happen. So when we climbed those stairs that led only the two of us back into the sunshine, the weighty load of emotions became almost too much to bear. Without Brad's strength, I never could have scaled the steps that brought me up into the daylight and a broken future.

Brad studied me closely, trying to see what I hid within me, the fears, the sadness...regrets? His tortured expression made me wonder, *Could this entire ordeal be hard on him, too?*

"Are you okay?"

"Yes, I'm fine."

"Do you want to go somewhere? To the park? Maybe we could talk?"

"No. Just take me back to school. My dad will be there to pick me up. He'll wonder where I am." I saw his broad shoulders slump. He looked as depleted as I felt.

Only an hour had passed when Brad dropped me back in front of school so my father could pick me up as usual, unaware of his daughter's new mark of maturity.

"I'll see you Monday at school. Call me if you need anything." Brad leaned across the front seat and pulled me into his arms. What little bravado I had stored up crumbled in his embrace. I knew it was over. I would not see him again, not like this. He would not hang around to fend off the demons that would surely haunt me. And how could I ask more from him? Although he had acted as my savior, I wondered if I meant anything to him. Were my feelings one-sided? And it didn't matter anyway. I was unable to face him on any level. Yes, he had stepped up to my rescue without my asking. I could not have asked for his assistance and, certainly, I would not ask for more. I felt the fullness of what I thought was his love as I sank into his arms, but it may have only been the kindness of a friend helping a friend.

In ten seconds flat, I convinced myself I deserved nothing more. The deed was done; I was on my own. We would pass in the halls, sharing our secret in silence. I opened the car door, climbed out with my empty heart and heavy feelings. Brad told me he hated to leave me alone, but I decided it best. If word ever got out, I didn't want anyone to connect Brad to what had happened or what we had just done. I stood at the curbside clutching my purse to my chest, staring forward as I watched him drive away. The tires squealed and he burned rubber vanishing around the corner. I turned away, squeezing my eyes shut to contain my tears.

Chapter Three

Brad watched Judy's timid image fade in his rearview mirror. When he reached the farm, he sped down the driveway, the rearview mirror reflecting a tunnel cloud of dust in his wake. Inside the barn's shadowy interior, he saw his father busy with chores. Brad found his mother fussing in the kitchen, waiting to feed him his after-school snack before he helped with the feeding.

Everything was normal. He ate the same snack, answered the same questions about school, and performed the same chores. The chickens pecked the same spots while the horses snorted vapor clouds into the afternoon's cold air. Everything appeared normal yet oddly different. It would never be the same for him or for Judy. Brad was young but he knew the impact of the secrets they now shared. Nothing would ever be the same.

His mind tossed around the "should haves" and "shouldn't haves" as he stonily went through the motions of his chores.

I should have made a move on her back on that first day in English class, he thought. *I should have stopped her in the hall all those times she looked at me. Maybe all this wouldn't have happened if I hadn't been such a macho ass. But she probably isn't interested in me. She's a nice girl. Why would she be interested in me? But maybe she is. Especially now. Maybe she needs me. She doesn't have anyone, at least anyone who knows. How can I just walk away?* A sharp pain jabbed his stomach while his mind wrestled with his regretful heart, wrenched with the unbearable facts of their miserable situation. He kicked an empty bucket and sent it clamoring across the barn floor. His dad looked up. "Something bothering you, boy?"

"No. I'm okay."

"Well, pick up that bucket and hang it up."

The quiet at the dinner table became unbearable. Brad played with his food and finally excused himself, escaping to his room away from his parents' questioning looks. He stretched out on his bed, thinking on a normal night he would have been showered and changed, heading out the door, mounting his motorcycle, and high-tailing it to a party with his friends. But that seemed inappropriate. He picked up the police academy brochures from the guidance counselor that lay on his nightstand. As he glanced over them, his spirits lifted. *It would be satisfying to be a cop,* he thought. *I know first off I'd find the guy dealing the Mickey Finns. I'd make sure what happened to Judy would never happen to another girl. But what about my arrest record? All the times I've been pulled in for fighting and drinking? I'd never be accepted. It's useless.*

He finally dozed off, fully dressed, until his mom tapped on his door. "Brad? It's nine o'clock. You'd better get ready for bed. Do you want some pie before you turn in? Your dad and I are having some."

"No, I'll pass." When she quietly closed the door, he rose and began undressing. He wondered how Judy was doing. He turned off the light as he began the first of many sleepless nights. A tear leaked onto his pillow.

Chapter Four

I stood at the curb waiting for my father to pick me up as a couple of friends passed by shouting hello. I forced a smile and yelled "hey" back. Wrapped in my troubles, I was thinking that without Brad, I didn't know what I would have done. He carried me through to the other side of this horrible life-changing affair. I saw Dad's Jeep coming around the corner, sucked up my emotions, and tried to relax. I grabbed the door handle as the Jeep came to a stop. Dad said nothing, as usual, put it in gear, and we headed home.

Once home, I escaped to my room and collapsed on the bed. I wanted to cry my eyes out but that seemed childish. I had passed through the youthful corridor and now my bare feet felt the cold concrete path of maturity. Shedding tears over things that could not be changed had no place.

I lay there thinking of Brad and wondered what he was doing. Did he think of me and the impact of what I had done? Of course he did. He knew. That explained why he squealed rubber when he left, glad to be done with an obligation he wished he had not taken on.

I rolled over and reached for the college pamphlets. My parents and I had decided on the University of Southern California and I had been accepted. Suddenly, going away sounded like a wonderful idea. Leaving memories and reminders behind and starting anew might rid me of the heaviness of the loss that was seeping into my soul. No one would know what I had done. Although no one knew now, somehow it was important that I did not know them. The thought of anonymity gave me peace.

The aroma of dinner crept under my closed bedroom door and I decided to make an appearance lest questions arise. I pulled my leaden spirit out of bed and checked the mirror, startled to see not a girl but a woman blankly staring back. I rewrapped my ponytail and made my way to the kitchen. "Here, I'll do that," I announced as I took the silverware from my mom and finished setting the table. I ignored her questioning glance at my unnatural behavior. Dinner was Swiss steak and mashed potatoes. I went through the motions of eating and hoped they did not notice my small portions and food fiddling. I looked up and watched them eat, passing the potatoes, seasoning their green beans, unaware of each other and thankfully of me, too.

I stared at the scene, overcome with a feeling of blessing that I had done the right thing today. They would have been devastated knowing what I had done. It would have killed them to know what had happened to me. I helped with the dishes after dinner, causing more questioning looks.

I found solace in the everyday routine of my family's love that I had never appreciated before. Eating dinner, doing things for each other, caring for one another's feelings—this was what family and life were all about. Nothing spectacular, no fireworks, maybe not even passion. I marveled at the fact I had never noticed it before. Had it been only a month ago I had been robbed of my teens and forced into the wisdom of adulthood? I knew what I had to do.

And although I convinced myself that Brad had only come to my rescue out of some unfounded feeling of obligation, I knew I would always love him. But I was convinced that he would never be attracted to me now, if he ever had been. No one would want me if they knew the baggage I now carried.

Any doubts I entertained about leaving town were washed away as I tidied up the kitchen and sent Mom into the living room to watch the news with Dad. I would go to the university and make them proud. I vowed they would never discover my secret.

Chapter Five

A big rig crept up behind me, pulled out into the passing lane, and proceeded to bellow past. My thoughts barreled forward with the trucker, into the present. When he was clear, I courteously blinked my lights and steadied my little rig while it shook off the semi's powerful draft.

"Can you believe it, Sportster? Forty years? I can't." I glanced down at the cat in my lap. He lifted his head, nudged my arm, purred, and went back to sleep. Contrary to my recollections, today everything seemed fine. I watched the desert scroll by and the asphalt reduce to a thin black ribbon in the rearview mirror. My future continued to approach my past, one mile at a time.

When I scanned the road ahead, California's golden day contributed to the illusion of well-being. The motor home's engine purred, the mini-blinds click-clicked, while a cup in the cupboard matched the rhythm with its tink-tink. Near Needles, California, I coasted into a truck stop and eased up to a gas pump. My own gas tank also rumbled, "Hungry."

"Hang tight and check out the scenery. I'll be right back." I patted Sportster's head and lifted him to the dash. Stiff muscles protested when I climbed out of the cab. Six-wheelers puffed and bellowed, drinking diesel from the pumps on either side of me. Sliding my credit card, I began the long expensive process of refueling.

I watched an older couple standing in front of the gas station, sipping coffee and making small talk as they took a break from the tedium of travel. The man held her coffee while she fished for something in her purse. A napkin. She wiped his mouth with the expertise born of years of devotion. Unmoved by her mark of tenderness, he continued his dissertation that I could not hear over the big rigs' rumblings. Their togetherness caused me to deliberate. I'd only returned home a handful of times in all these years. My memories of family were still warm when my mother passed away shortly after I left for the university. And Dad, without his bride, remained living in the house where I grew up, nursing his memories.

My sister Sandy shared the West Coast with me, residing only ninety miles away in Los Angeles. Our lunches were sacrificed to L.A. traffic, with neither of us wanting to spare the time to inch along the freeways in order to meet. Sandy made regular trips home to check on Dad while I always feigned an excuse not to go. Over the years, contact with my cousin John had dwindled to Christmas and birthday cards. The family had scattered. What was I hoping to find, anyway?

I studied the man and woman as they stood, him straightening her collar. The pair kindled a yearning that flickered less and less these days. What was I doing? Chasing a dream? Or confronting a nightmare? Was I ready to face what I ran away from forty years ago?

I topped off the gas tank and twisted the cap two clicks tight. When I stepped on the accelerator, several seconds elapsed before the motor home, loaded to capacity, reacted and crept slowly away from the pump.

Five hours ago, when I had climbed into the driver's seat, I was ready to embark on this questionable journey, eager to begin the first mile and stop the last flutters of anticipation. I recalled my sentiments from the trip a year before, when I had also left everything familiar behind. The trip occurred after my husband's death, when I had set out on my first solo journey from the Pacific to the Atlantic. Now it seemed like a lifetime ago.

Cowboy Jack, God bless his polyester soul, occupied the seat next to me. The life-sized doll I had stitched and stuffed, glued and gleaned, posed as my perfect man. His bald head donned a Stetson while the toe of his snakeskin cowboy boots tapped to a two-step rhythm. I had slipped a rodeo ring I discovered at an antique store on his fabric finger, and cinched his waist with a belt buckle in the shape of a longhorn steer's head. His Western shirt glistened with silver thread woven into its plaid pattern, while pearl snap buttons formed a line down his chest. He had "gone country." I had created a perfect, rough-hewn, easygoing traveling companion.

"I hope you live up to my expectations, Cowboy Jack. I don't want you complaining, worrying at every bump in the road, or pointing out all that might go wrong on this trip." I pushed him upright.

"I don't want to hear you saying,"—I lowered my voice to a baritone—"'Do you know what you're going to spend just for gas on this trip? It's not going to be the same when you get home. You know the old saying, "You can't go home again." High school reunions are always big disappointments. What do you expect, Brad Jones to be waiting with open arms after forty years? You're foolish to traipse off across the country like this.' We don't want to hear that, do we, Sportster?"

At six a.m., pulling away from everything familiar, with the sun peeking over the hills, I had glanced over at Cowboy

Jack riding shotgun. He remained silent but stared forward with a mindless smile on his linen lips. I hoped he was as excited as I.

I finished with the refueling task and climbed into the driver's seat. Cowboy Jack slumped against the passenger door and gazed at the comings and goings of the gas station, a hubbub of activity. The travelers moved like ants in and out of the swinging doors of the restaurant/store. Several bikers stood beside their Harleys as they smoked cigarettes and nursed cold beers, while other motorists paced with cell phones to their ears. Ready to add more miles and with trail mix on the console for nourishment, I pulled away from the pump. All of us—The Wizard of Winnebago, Cowboy Jack, and Sportster—felt the V10's pulse and movement, the sway and anticipation, as we headed back onto the interstate to continue our new adventure across the country's wide expanse.

The motor home rattled and rumbled, galloping across the miles, gulping gas as Arizona's warm afternoon sunshine overcame California's early morning's coolness, but the radio's volume did not overcome my off-key voice. Regardless, I sang along with Glen Campbell's "By the Time I Get to Phoenix." My left foot tap-tapped the floorboard along with the vibration of Cowboy Jack's boot, while Sportster, his eyes lazy slits, observed my antics from an upside-down position on the dash. His soft tummy absorbed the sun's warm rays. The doll's polyester head nodded in sync. Everything appeared normal as the miles increased and the day shortened.

Chapter Six

I blinked. I wasn't dozing; my thoughts were somewhere far away. The motor home's engine whined in chorus with the lament of a semi's tires as it nudged past. The truck's noisy invasion ended my recollections.

I noticed a chill when Sportster switched his position from the dash to the warmth of my lap. The sun had completed its westerly trek across the sky, and touched the Pacific somewhere hundreds of miles behind as I inched across the map on my easterly trek. Peering in my rearview mirror, I saw sundown painted in undulating waves from a palette of pinks, blues, and lavenders. The colors filled my bedroom window.

The desert landscape captured my loneliness born from leaving California and all that was familiar. The desolation of sand and sage stretched as far as I could see, straining my mood. As the isolation of the area caused me to question my purpose, I evaluated my concerns.

"I don't need anybody, do I, Sportster?" My hand stroked his soft fur. "What do you think, Cowboy Jack?" The doll nodded in agreement when the motor home bucked from a dip in the road. "My life is perfect now," I continued with my one-sided dialogue. "I don't have to explain or make excuses. I don't have to care about anyone. Well, except you, Sportster. I will always care about *you*." He stretched as I continued to rub his back. "I miss my marriage but it was work. Marriage is hard, you know? I want easy now. I'm not going to sacrifice anything anymore. Not my time, not my feelings—nothing. And what happened, what I did forty years ago, that's over and done. How can that possibly affect me now? I'm an old woman now, for God's sake! The past is just that—the past. Whoever it was has probably moved away, or is even dead by now. A lot of things can happen in four decades. I'm sure I have nothing to worry about."

When I pulled into The Meteor Crater RV Park a few miles before Winslow, Arizona, I found a man in the registration office dusting and rubbing the counter with a spice-scented polish. For no reason, the odor sent a chill up my spine, even though the man's rotund appearance reminded me of Santa Claus. He filled the small space behind a desk cluttered with papers. We exchanged the necessary information and after he efficiently finished my paperwork, he said, "There's free coffee after six in the morning. I'm writing the gate code on your receipt. Don't lose that, and here are your discount tickets for the Meteor Museum." He glanced out the window. "Are you and your husband going to the crater in the morning?"

"Oh, it's just me. He isn't real. That's Cowboy Jack, my perfect man. He's a great traveler and never complains."

The man's belly jiggled along with the keys on his belt as he chuckled and moved around the counter, stepping closer to the window. "I'll be. It's just a doll!" He scratched his head and turned to me. "What a great idea. Not the perfect-man idea, but that you appear to have a companion."

I smiled. "I think the perfect-man idea is good, too."

"You know there's no such thing, don't you?"

"Yes, I know, but it doesn't hurt to dream, does it?"

The man smiled, tilted his head, raising his eyebrows as he shrugged. His demeanor reassured me he was harmless. I gathered up my paperwork. I couldn't wait to settle in for the night.

When I reached my space and shut off the engine, Sportster stirred, picking up his travel habits from our first journey. Whenever we stopped for the night, he'd be lured by the "call of the wild" that only he heard. To satisfy his cravings, I snapped the leash to his harness, and tied it to a ten-pound boat anchor that served as a tie-out. I carried him and the weight out into "the wild"—just outside the RV's door. There my ten-pound feline transformed into a prowling predator. He played the part of a two-hundred-fifty-pound Bengal tiger, sinewy muscles strung taut under glistening fur, ready to pounce on...any unsuspecting bugs.

Cowboy Jack did not offer to help with the setup, but mentioned his cotton butt was pressed flat from the long day of travel. When I finished plugging in the electrical, hooking up the water and sewer hoses, I settled at the picnic table and observed the hunting habits of my delusional cat while I subtly guarded him from coyotes and chicken hawks.

Darkness drifted in and washed out the sunset's southwestern colors, leaving only the rushing sound of the distant freeway traffic. My heartbeat faltered when I noticed a figure standing behind the bushes several spaces from my campsite. The waist-high landscaping edged the road, partially hiding him. The man stood several moments, gazing toward the ground as if trying to appear casual. I watched as he moved a few yards, paused, then moved a few more yards. He again paused, hunched over, and shuffled a few paces, first to one side of the road then again to the other. He rarely looked up but I felt he knew I was there. Each time his approach brought him nearer.

I was sure he had been watching since I arrived. He knew I was alone. *Does he think I didn't see him? Why is he lurking like that?* My heart pounded and my hands shook. I glanced at Sportster, who was sniffing the shrubs that separated my campsite from the next. He appeared unconcerned, but he was a cat. I continued to worry. *Am I over reacting? No, he walked erratically and he knows I am alone.* The image of my .38 tucked away in the closet flashed in my mind.

Suddenly the man moved at a quickened pace as he rounded the curve in the road. No longer obscured by the hedge, he maintained a steady stride with one arm stretched out in front of him. His extended hand held a leash. A Shih Tzu was dragging him to the next tree. The dog inspected every sagebrush and clump of prairie grass along the way. I exhaled, unaware I had been holding my breath. I chastised myself. *Just a man walking his dog.* When the pair passed under my campsite's lamppost, Sportster rushed the duo, chattering a greeting, and switched from hunting mode to campsite greeter. Before the black-and-white puppy could process he was dealing with a cat, Sportster had confronted him, nose to nose.

"What's your puppy's name?" I asked, laughing in relief.

Startled, the man hesitated to answer, unsure of Sportster's eager approach. "Joe Shih Tzu," the man said.

The puppy crouched, deciding a cat could be fun. He set his elbows to the ground, tail straight up and vibrating, and greeted his new friend with loud, incessant barking. Sportster, having succeeded in getting the puppy's attention, now moved away with a princely dignity to prove he was undaunted by the gushing display of emotions. Confused, the puppy collapsed onto the ground, plunked his head between his paws, and whined a plea of forgiveness. *Please come back! I'll be quiet.*

Turning gracefully, Sportster heeded his plea and also flopped to the ground, rolling onto his back. *Okay, then, let's play.*

Oh, goody! Joe Shih Tzu was now up and dashing for the fur ball gyrating on the ground.

The man and I both laughed at the antics of our pets.

Sportster sprang up and padded back to his hunting grounds. *Come on. I'll show you what I've found. Over here! Look!* He spoke a chirping language that invited Joe Shih Tzu to follow. The puppy, a quick study, skipped inquisitively behind as they headed over to a grassy area.

"Where are you from?" The man kept his eyes on his dog.

"Sun City, California. I'm headed to Illinois for my high school reunion. How about you? Where're you headed?"

"My wife and I just sold our house and we're going to travel full-time." He tried to reel in his puppy, who was engrossed in aiding Sportster in an examination of the dirt's bug population. "We'd better get back. My wife's fixing dinner. I'm Moe, by the way."

"Nice meeting you. I'm Judy, and this is Sportster." I reached down and patted the puppy. "Nice meeting you too, Joe Shih Tzu."

As the pair headed home, I gathered up Sportster and went inside, still feeling foolish about my near panic attack. I drew the curtains and switched on the water heater, listening as the pilot roared to life. I opened the freezer door and examined the meals I had frozen into little Tupperware squares. The menu varied from chicken noodle soup to baby back ribs. There was only room for ice cube trays. I ordered stew and cornbread.

The Tupperware square rotated in the microwave while I plugged in the coffee pot and flipped its switch. The sounds of civilization—the urn's gurgling, the microwave's ding, and the low rumble of the water heater—contradicted what lay beyond my drawn drapes. Outside, coyotes sang to a desert moon, an owl's eerie hoot hung in sage-scented air, and, as I peeked past the curtain, I was privileged to catch a bobcat's shadow steal a silent path through the scrub.

Sportster crunched his own delicacies of cat chow while I devoured my comfort food and turned my attention to the anticipation of a hot shower. An hour later, unwound from the tensions of travel, I snuggled in my pink flannel pjs printed with kittens that would warm me during the cool desert night.

I reviewed my day, filled with mountain vistas, diesel smells, and the wind's whistle. The constant challenge of controlling twenty-four feet of metal and fiberglass left me achy and exhausted. I buried my head into my pillow and smothered any thoughts as I slipped into a deep slumber that dug up disturbing dreams.

I was racing to reach the fabric-padded door and yet it was right in front of me, but I couldn't get near enough to turn the chrome handle. A group of men blocked my flight and surrounded me. They laughed at my efforts and shoved me to the ground. Scared and crying, I begged for help, but no one cared. I was on hands and knees and my right hand shook. I wiped away tears, feeling mud smudge my face in their place. Gravel and red clay cut into my palm as my left hand supported my weight. My heart constricted so tightly I thought it would stop. The men wore no faces and yet I knew who they were. To add to my terror, a dog snarled and barked in the distance. Although the darkness blinded me, I tried to reach the lever that would open and free me from the panic and pain wracking my body. I watched my special golden locket float from my neck, disappearing into a deep crevice. I screamed hysterically until sweet unconsciousness enveloped me.

In the morning I woke to sweat-soaked sheets and unidentified feelings that lived just beyond the curtains of consciousness. The sensation from last night's nightmare hovered, floating like a mysterious shadow behind the closed curtains of a theater's stage, an emotional ghost shuffling, lurking in the wings. I struggled to access the recurring nightmare but, true to its nature, the images evaporated, leaving only a lingering dread.

When I woke, Sportster was sleeping at the foot of the bed, curled into a ball. His soft paw covered his eyes so he wouldn't be disturbed by the day's beginning until he finished his own sweet feline dreams. Gazing upon his deeply contented little form, I knew his fantasies entertained only catnip, mice, and feathers flying at a stick's end. Soothed by his serenity, the blissful hush of the dessert, and the sage and sandy scents, I tossed back the covers and rolled out of bed, almost flipping Sportster to the floor. He took the disturbance with dignity, repositioned himself, and quickly returned to his feline pastures. I smoothed the bed to perfection with only a cat lump remaining, dressed, and, coffee in hand, stepped outside.

Chapter Seven

My antidote for the nightmare's residue of darkness and doom was exercise. I headed toward the outskirts of the campground overlooking Canyon Diablo. A once-dry creek bed trickled from a late summer's rain. I hiked the steep trail until a familiar tingling sensation began to creep down my arm. In reaction, my breathing shortened and came in jagged breaths. My gait faltered as I picked my way down the narrow path.

I was not sure—had the tingling turned into numbness? My legs felt like stumps. What if they buckled and I skidded to the gully's rocky shore below? I froze, staring at the loosened rocks scattering down the embankment, clattering and grabbing sticks and larger stones in their descent. I wanted to run but my unfeeling legs refused my brain's demands. I wanted to escape this panic. I pictured someone discovering my battered, broken body in the ravine, pecked beyond recognition by the creatures ruling the desert.

I pried my eyes away from the massive landslide of imagination, and focused on bronzed clouds edged with blues and reds decorating the sky's ceiling. Morning sunbeams streamed from behind the clouds, spotlighting the sage dotting the landscape, the scene proof of the earlier summer storm. I heard a bird call to his mate as he swooped downward with grace, and lit upon the rocky shore of the stream's banks. As quickly as my panic had begun, the electric frenzy released its hold and I felt the healing of nature take over. An onlooker would have noticed only a slight hitch in my step, but I felt the entire world had witnessed my anxiety attack.

I continued my descent as the breeze lifted my sweat-soaked hair. The dry wind rustled the grasses and mixed with squawks of birds chasing dragonflies, creating a cacophony. When I reached the creek's flow and gazed into the depths, I marveled at strange creatures busily darting through invisible mazes in their delicate, mystical world. I lingered long enough to gather my composure and then set a brisk pace back to the campground.

The hike erased the last trails of tension, allowing me to focus on the day and the road ahead. My goal was to find the remnants of the famous National Trails Highway, Route 66. The Meteor Crater and Two Guns ghost town would be my first discoveries on the Mother Road. Leaving Sportster and Cowboy Jack to their naps, I unplugged the Wizard and drove to the Meteor Crater. As I took the walking tour around the rim, the ruins of the museum and gift shop that had operated until the mid-fifties triggered my memory. The guide's words faded into the crowd as I drifted back.

It was 1957 and I nursed the active imagination of a ten-year-old. On one family vacation, our mode of transportation was a Willy's Jeep, our home, a travel trailer. Like what I was doing today, we'd peered into the vast hole formed by the one-hundred-fifty-pound meteor over fifty thousand years before. The crater was large enough to encompass twenty football fields.

Campgrounds were few and far between, so Dad often found a tree alongside the road to park beneath. That night, after the excitement of visiting the crater, my sister and I snuggled in the fold-down bed that served as a couch during the day. We giggled and talked until a strict scolding from our folks quieted us. It was then, in the silent darkness, that my child's imagination began to create the possibility of a tragic, five-star, science fiction, and meteor catastrophe. My ten-year-old thoughts worried the night away, wondering how my family could sleep so soundly.

The town of Two Guns had been established along the Mother Road after a bridge over Canyon Diablo was built in 1910. The bones of the town lay next to the remaining chunks of Route 66. I parked, uneasy with the isolation of the place.

Further down the road, two men leaned against their truck, its hood colored in blotches of bare metal, and its bed contained a cattle dog that stared at my arrival. They parked next to the rusty gas pump, the only vestige left of a Phillips 66 station. The stillness of the ghost town carried pieces of the men's conversation my way. They talked casually, sipping beers and laughing as they punched one another playfully. "You gonna share her number?" Far enough down the road, I felt safe in wandering around the remains of the town, but I kept them in sight and hoped they could see Cowboy Jack waiting in the motor home.

I approached the skeleton of a building. Only its front and one side wall had withstood the sands of time. I read the wind-worn letters MOUNTAIN LIONS, on the crumbling façade.

The mysterious words alluded to an illustrious character known as Indian Miller, who claimed to be an Apache and called himself Chief Crazy Thunder. He constructed a wild-animal zoo housing bobcats, coral snakes, porcupines, and a variety of other creatures. The attraction lured motorists to Two Guns, making the town a popular tourist stop.

The nearby Apache Death Cave was known for the legend of a mass execution. After committing a series of raids and murders against the Navajo, a band of Apaches hid in the cave. When discovered by the Navajo, the Apaches were trapped and burned alive for their crimes. Miller renamed the tomb Mystery Cave, and built pueblo-like structures presenting the buildings as ancient Indian cliff dwellings. He arranged guided tours, and hawked native wares and refreshments to the passing motorists.

I snapped photos of the ruins silhouetted against the evening's skyline. Spooked since I had arrived, I heard voices from the past, Apache death chants along with Miller's declarations of last-chance deals on Route 66, or maybe only a damp draft from the cave's interior whispered in my ear. Dusk hurried to settle over the high desert, so I finished my photo session of the collapsing sienna structures, now only shadows.

With ghostly impressions dancing in my mind, I arrived back at the campground and tried to shake off the shroud enveloping me. I made a light dinner and perused brochures. As I attempted to relax, the day's apparitions floated in my head, pulling my thoughts astray. As my mind wandered to the days ahead and conversely to the past, the pamphlets sat untouched in my lap and I considered the impact of what lay ahead. I felt the evening's breeze swirling through the open window as it rustled the pages, causing them to fly into the air like discontented ghosts of days gone by.

I looked at Sportster perched on the chair, observing me like an enamored boy while Cowboy Jack gazed out the window. I reasoned with myself. "I'm going home to revisit my childhood, exhume ugly, unrevealed secrets, and see my high school sweetheart, Brad. I'm no longer the insecure teenager fearing exposure." I picked up Sportster and cradled him in my arms. "When I left home, I boxed up my past along with my dolls, tea set, and hair ribbons. I sealed that bulging box tight and shoved it into a dusty, cobwebbed corner of the attic." I patted his head and kissed it. "So, what am I worried about, Sportster?"

I stretched out on the couch, and the day's impressions and yesteryear's memories settled around me like a thick blanket. Saturated with attention, the cat squirmed and leaped to the ground. Outside, darkness spread through the campsites. Despite not knowing what might linger for me down the road, it was time to move on and find out. Morning would come early.

After dinner, I cozied up with a book and Sportster, refusing to think of the skeletal images at the Apache Death Cave, or even of the warm memories of family vacations. I woke with my book on my chest and the light on. Turning out the light, I slept a wonderful dreamless sleep.

Chapter Eight

At five a.m. I surveyed the campground. Drawn shades proved no one had pushed the "pause button" to reactivate the activities of dog walking, children's play, and the aroma of breakfast wafting through the air. Until someone depressed the button, the serene stillness hung in the morning light. I climbed into the driver's seat and turned the ignition. Breaking nature's code of silence, I shifted gears and joined the fast freeway lifestyle thriving just beyond the campground's gates.

Mentally I bid goodbye to the Meteor Crater and Two Guns. I caught Cowboy Jack glancing at the crater's rim, and Sportster's gaze followed as I pulled onto I-40. I felt my folks' spirits hovering nearby. I thought of the two men at Two Guns and wondered about the girl they had discussed and how they had spent their night. Back on the interstate, I settled in for another long day as I thought of lost opportunities.

After graduation, Carrie and George continued to be a hot item at the skating rink, and were married after only six months of dating. The June wedding became the fairy tale event of Carrie's dreams. Thrilled for her, I kept my suspicions to myself that she might be pregnant. If she orchestrated the situation to cinch her ties to George and ensure freedom from her abusive home, it would not be me who questioned her motives. She was ecstatic, and although George made me uncomfortable, he always acted like the perfect gentleman, causing me to doubt my feelings. The bridal shower marked our last time together as the Threesome. During the endless summer, Carrie busied herself with the wedding and afterward with her new husband, and I saw less and less of her.

As the summer dragged on, I still met up with Jackie, but not often at the skating rink. Usually it was for lunch at the Tops Big Boy or McDonald's.

"Have you seen Carrie lately? I haven't seen her since the wedding." Jackie popped her gum and removed it from her mouth, jamming it on the edge of her plate. I watched her drown her fries in ketchup.

"Me, neither. Do you think she was PG?" I reached over and grabbed a fry she'd missed with the ketchup.

"I don't know. She'll be showing pretty soon if she is. I don't like George, do you?"

"No. Never did. There's just something about him." The thought of him sent a prickly sensation up my spine.

"How are you doing? How's it going with you and Brad?"

"I see him once in a while, but it's not the same. He wants to talk about what happened. I don't. I don't know why he keeps coming around."

"Maybe he loves you."

"I doubt that. How could he, anyway...after all that's happened? I told him he didn't have to keep coming around. I'll be gone in September, anyway."

The heated months crept by and I became more with-drawn, waiting for summer's end. All I thought about was escaping to California and leaving my nightmares behind.

Once in college and away from familiarity and questions, I attended classes and kept to myself. Only a few months passed before, disjointed and depressed, I dropped out of college and bounced from one job to the next, struggling with the demons that refused to be ignored.

My friend Jackie called regularly.

"What happened? Were the classes too hard?" I heard her gum popping and it made my sad heart smile.

"Not really. I just can't seem to concentrate. I can't seem to care."

"Have you thought about counseling? You've been through a lot. You should get some help."

"I'm all right." But my lack of enthusiasm worried me, too. I considered avoiding her calls and thought maybe she would give up the effort. But the loss of her friendship would only compound the aching that already consumed me. The more withdrawn I became, the less I could muster any feelings at all.

The intensity of feeling nothing at all finally frightened me enough to seek out help. Although unable to recall the details of the rape and the abortion, I never forgot their con-sequences. Endless hours in self-help groups and repeating my new philosophy like a mantra—Grant me the serenity to accept the things I cannot change and the courage to change the things I can—restrained me from selecting the exit my mind longed to take.

I began dating a member of my twelve-step group after a short courtship.

"What's he like? You gotta send a picture."

"He's very attentive. He said he knew he loved me the first time he saw me. You know no one else has said 'I love you' to me? I believe him. And you know what, Jackie? I think I love him, too. He makes me feel wanted and, I don't know why, but he says he needs me."

"Did you tell him?"

"No. And I never will." I knew what she was talking about. "That's in the past. I've buried that."

"I guess you know best."

"I rented office space to convert into a grooming shop. Jack's a contractor so he's helping me on the weekends. He and his buddy already installed the tub. And Jack put all the lettering for the sign on the windows. He wants to get married. I already told him yes."

"Wow! Is that the way to tell your best friend, 'Oh, by the way, I'm getting married?' Are you coming home to do the deed?"

"We're going to Vegas next weekend. He's a contractor and can't spare the time off. And I'm trying to get my grooming shop up and running."

"Well, darn. At least send pictures. I miss you. I wish I could be there but I'm so happy for you. I told you your time would come. Have you talked to Brad?"

"No. Not since I left. I told you I let that part of my life go."

Jack and I married. We both lugged emotional baggage into our marriage. He brought dominating and controlling issues that took advantage of my vulnerability, but our problems distracted me from the past that plagued me.

My cousin John called once a month, filling me in with news from home. John, five years older than I, was more than a cousin. I considered him the brother I never had. He became a part of our family functions after his mom and dad divorced. Dad, who would never admit he had wanted a son, took him into our fold. John attended our birthday celebrations, as well as Dad's household projects when he needed a strong back. My cousin's loose, lanky form towered over me, while his casual attitude disguised a deep caring attitude. No matter how down I felt, I always took John's calls that stirred memories from home. My cousin's reports became a lifeline that kept me from giving up on life entirely.

"Carrie's like you. She's 'too busy' for her friends. I rarely see her at the rink even though George shows up regularly.

Since she and George got married, I never see Carrie. Have you heard from her?"

"She called a few weeks ago but I guess I got busy. I'll have to call her back." But I knew I wouldn't.

John continued. "Jackie skates almost every weekend. She got a job at Bob's Big Boy. Her folks gave her a brand new Buick Special convertible for her birthday and she loves it. She's got a heavy foot leaving the stop signs, but otherwise she's a pretty good driver. She's started junior college at night to become a therapist."

"She sent me pictures of the car. She was so thrilled. She's going to be a great therapist." I didn't elaborate as to how I knew that.

"Brad's doing what he always does, having a good time. I see him at the rink, but not as often as I used to." John never mentioned Brad's love life, if one existed, and I dared not ask.

A few months later, when John called with the news that he and Brad enrolled in the police academy together, I was surprised not only at John's career choice, but more so at Brad's. I knew Brad's record included numerous episodes in jail, for reasons ranging from public drunkenness to misdemeanor assault charges that his dad magically made disappear, probably with payoffs and bribes. Brad implied to me his dad had connections. John explained that Brad had quit drinking and was straightening his life out.

"The two of you? Cops?"

John laughed. "Brad convinced me it's like the buddy system in the army. You know, you join together. When Brad got sober, his AA sponsor, Ken, was a detective. Ken pulled some strings, removed some yellow tape—as they call it on the force—and got Brad's application approved. Me, I had no trouble. I've always been a good boy."

I laughed in spite of the ache from the longing I always felt when John spoke of Brad.

"We both graduated with honors, too."

"I'm so impressed."

"And Brad is already taking on extra classes. He jokes about being Chief one day. Personally I think he's a workaholic. Me, I like my rank. Since I married Kate, I like my time at home. You know she's pregnant?"

"Oh, John. Congratulations!" My heart swelled with pride and then twisted with shame and guilt. I fell silent.

"One of these days you'll have your own family. Things always have a way of working out." I wondered how he knew my torment. He went on. "How's married life? When do we get to meet the guy?"

"It's fine," I said too quickly. "He never wants to take any time off. I tried to get him to come along the last time I came to see Dad, but he's a workaholic, too." I wanted to discuss my life even less than I wanted to talk about babies. "Anyway, I am so happy for you and Kate." When I hung up the phone, I felt lonelier than ever.

A month later when John called, his first words sounded clipped as he attempted small talk. His voice, deeper than usual, carried a sense of dread. He hesitated when I asked, "What's wrong?" I thought of Brad first, aware of his dangerous new career.

"It's your friend Jackie."

"What about her? Did she get in an accident with that new convertible of hers? She was always a careless driver." After a long silence, I heard John take a deep breath.

"She's dead, Judy." My cousin choked on tears; his voice wavered. His lack of composure frightened me.

"What happened?" I cried in disbelief.

"They found her body out on Peoria Road, three miles from the skating rink."

"What happened? Did she have an accident? Did she skid on the ice? There's a curve right there. It's not a bad curve, but if there was ice..."

John interrupted me. "She was raped and beaten to death, Judy. We found her body in old man Crosby's cornfield. It wasn't an accident. It was Brad who got the call and found her." It was as if pain and fear shot through the phone line like an electric shock, and consumed the bright yellow breakfast area of my apartment. Silence stretched into minutes. The moment became etched in my brain, every detail, every sound—forever. I brushed toast crumbs to the floor. My legs felt dead. The door to the apartment across the hall slammed shut.

In that instant I knew how my friend died. My imagination recreated every second of her dying moments. I knew what happened. I instinctively felt her desperation, her fear, and her dying breath. I sat frozen. I touched my cheek when I felt a puff of warmth feather my eyelash, and then I shivered with a coldness that made my bones feel brittle.

John told me the date of the funeral I knew I wouldn't attend. I knew who had done this. Although I didn't know, I knew that the same dark shadow, with the same spicy scent, accompanied by the same song that echoed in my nightmares, now lurked somewhere in old man Crosby's cornfield.

As I drove, I thought of all the yesterdays that had rolled by like the scenery across my windshield. The years had increased the distance from my past but now, the tomorrows and miles decreased, bringing me closer to that same past.

Chapter Nine

The hum of the tires blended with the engine's purr. I was headed home. I couldn't believe I wanted to go back there. I had only gone home a handful of times since I left for college. I existed in anonymity, denying my past, and survived in the absence of a close, satisfying relationship. I drifted in shallow waters that demanded little self-examination.

My thoughts drifted to the day Dad called, explaining Mom was in the hospital and not expected to make it. "Your mother's had a heart attack. You need to come home."

"I'll be on the next flight." There was no need for questions; I heard the sadness in his voice. With my husband out of town on business, I flew home alone. My cousin John picked me up at the airport.

"How is she?"

"She's still hanging on but she's very weak. She wants to see you."

I steeled against the despair that began to encompass me.

"We'll go right to the hospital. Your dad's with her. I don't think he's left her side since she got there." Visibly shaken, John's shoulders slumped. Closest to our family, and more of a brother than a cousin, he reached over and took my hand.

When we arrived at St. John's Memorial, he dropped me in front and parked the car. Joining me at the elevator, he pulled me next to him as we waited. I had been born here. My sister had been born here. My grandma died here, and now my mother was going to die here, too. Nuns floated noiselessly through the dimly lit halls. The sun streamed through the one window at the end of the corridor and reflected onto polished linoleum that had not been replaced in fifty years. I leaned into John.

An oxygen tent surrounded my mother's bed and tubes seemed to crawl in every direction from her body. I heard a machine breathing in the room's corner. I had no sooner stepped across the threshold and absorbed the scene when I spun around, pushing John out of my way. I ran down the hall, burst into the bathroom, and, falling onto my knees in front of the toilet, I heaved. When the violent reaction subsided, I sat back on the cold linoleum, closed my eyes, and sobbed uncontrollably. It occurred to me I had not cried like that since my dog Boots died when I was ten. But now I cried. I cried for the dog, I cried for my grandma, and I cried for the unknown soul I had refused life. I thought I was never going to stop crying. What seemed like a lifetime had only been twenty minutes when I looked at my watch and heard John's voice outside the door. "Are you okay, Judy?"

I pulled myself up off the floor. "I'm okay. I'll be right out." After splashing cold water on my face and blowing my nose, I inhaled deeply. Patting my face dry, I noticed the tiny window near the ten-foot ceiling, the only connection to the outside world. It sent me back to the doctor's office where I felt I had made a deal with the devil. Suddenly I hated this place. A fierce rage welled up inside of me and surrounded my sorrow. With another deep breath, I grabbed my anger and headed back to my mother's side.

I hadn't noticed my sister sitting in the room's only chair. She rose and cradled me in her arms but I didn't cry anymore. We held each other for several minutes. Dad stood stoically next to her chair. He looked so old in this damned, dimly lit, death hole of a place. Dad put his hand on my shoulder and said, "She's been asking for you. We'll wait outside." Even his voice had aged. They left me alone as I moved my leaden feet to the bedside, slid the plastic back, and stepped into the tent. Mom opened her eyes halfway.

"I'm so glad you could make it." Her voice was a raspy whisper and my stomach began to hurl again, but I drew on a strength I didn't know I had.

"It's okay, Mom."

"I just wanted to see you one more time and tell you how much I love you."

"It's okay, Mom. I know."

"I just wanted you to know. You're the one I've always worried about. Your sister's always been able to take care of herself, but you...I always worried."

"Oh, Mom, I'm okay." My throat tightened until I hardly breathed.

"No. I want you to listen to me. I know something happened to you last year. I don't know what, but I know something happened. I want you to know that whatever it was, it is not as bad as you think. Nothing ever is. I just want you to remember that. You have always been my special one, full of life and adventure. Don't waste your life on regrets."

"I won't, Mom. I'm okay. Really."

"Good, then. Send your dad and sister back in."

She passed that night in her sleep. Just stopped breathing, even though the machine continued its rhythmic inhaling and exhaling until the nun came in, mumbled some words to God, flipped the switch, and sealed the room in silence.

In Springfield, the grieving process can be prolonged up to three days, and because my folks had lived in the community all their lives, the maximum period was needed for friends and family to pay their respects. The funeral procession would then transport Mom to her eternal resting place, where she would sleep with Abraham Lincoln in Oakridge Cemetery.

Back at the house, people came and went all day. Dad held it together in his quiet, stoic manner while Sis and I kept busy serving food, washing dishes, and straightening the house between offers of condolence. Leaning over the sink, I heard footsteps enter the kitchen. "Just set it on the counter here." When I heard no response, I glanced up. Brad's frame filled the kitchen's entrance. No longer a teen, his build commanded a physical supremacy as he stood at the door. Our eyes locked and my breath quickened, then stopped. After an imperceptive pause, he crossed the room. I nervously went back to scrubbing the pot in the suds.

"I'm sorry about your mom." He rested his back against the counter.

"Thank you. At least she didn't suffer long." *God, that's what everybody says!*

"I lost my dad in October. It's rough."

"Yes, I heard. I'm so sorry. I know how you feel. I also heard you're a police officer now. You and John both. Wow!"

"Is it true you got married?" The question hit like a sniper's bullet, fast and deep. Brad watched, waiting for my answer as I scrubbed the pot beyond clean. Finally he reached over and took the pan from my hands, rinsed it, and began to dry it. He wore no cologne but I recognized his scent. I stepped back and snatched up another dishtowel, rubbing my wet hands so hard my skin turned red.

My stomach twisted. "Yes. I did."

"Are you happy?" I felt the heat of his stare bore into me, exposing my doubts, my regrets, and my reserve. His mouth formed a tight line.

"Yes, I am. I tried enthusiasm but it came out more like a whimper. I saw a flicker, a tic, drift across his controlled façade.

"I'm happy for you. You deserve the best." And then he looked right through me.

Desperate to change the subject, I said, "I also heard about Jackie. Have you caught the guy?"

My brows raised in question, my breath held, I waited for the answer. After a long pause, his jaw muscle pulsed. "No, we haven't."

"Oh." Unable to say more, I looked down, trying to hide the disappointment and fear as I twisted the dishtowel tightly.

"Oh, I'll get him. If it is the last thing I do, I'll get him." His voice cut like sharp ice. Hardening his eyes, he clamped his jaw even more tightly.

Bursting into the kitchen, hefting another tray of dirty coffee cups and plates, my sister, Sandy, announced, "Carrie's here." The tray's contents rattled as she placed it on the counter. If she noticed the electric tension in the room, she ignored it. Relieved for the excuse to escape, I rushed out of the room.

I had to search for Carrie in the small living room and found her hovering in a corner. She seemed shyer than in high school. I thanked her for coming, and as we made plans for dinner, I glanced out the front room window in time to see Brad's '57 Chevy pull away and disappear down the tree-lined street.

That night, when Carrie picked me up, she explained her husband's presence. "George told me he wouldn't pass up dinner with his two best girls. You remember George, don't you?" Carrie giggled but her voice was tense. As the glossy black Mercury idled, Carrie slid over closer to George and I climbed into the front seat.

The instant I slammed the car door, I felt a panicky feeling that set every nerve on edge. Used to controlling my unexplainable reactions, I clamped down the urge to run.

A sickening scent filled the car, and the night became even darker as my eyes tried to probe the blackness of the tinted windows.

The unbearable evening lasted too long. When George held the restaurant door, his hand slipped too low on the small of my back as he guided me inside. He sat close in the booth, with his elbow constantly grazing my breast. He smiled a slippery smile each time Carrie looked the other way.

"George bought that old Texaco station on Ninth Street. His repair work is doing well, and he added on another bay to do body work. He makes a lot of overnight trips to Chicago and St. Louis for parts. I don't mind, though. With the baby coming and all, we need the money."

"He doesn't take you along? For a night in the big city?"

"No." Again, she tittered, a laugh that would transform into crying if someone said "boo" to her.

"How about you, Judy? I'll bet you get a lot of action out there in California." George stared at me. The question made my skin crawl.

"She's married, George." Carrie's childlike scolding tone only made his leer more prominent.

"I need to get home. It's been a long day." I pushed out of the booth.

Carrie took my hint and handed George the bill as she began to slide out of the booth as well.

"Yes, I'm sure George is tired, too. Aren't you, honey?" She didn't wait for an answer because he ignored her, still focused on me.

"Before we go, let's get some pictures. You did bring the camera, didn't you, Carrie?" His leer made me think he'd like porn.

"Oh, sure, George. Why didn't I think of that?" Carrie rustled through her purse.

After George snapped a picture of Carrie and me, he insisted on one of him and me. He put his arm around me and his cheek touched mine.

"Come on, Judy, you're not smiling," Carrie encouraged. I felt my grimace and hoped it translated into a smile.

Somehow I climbed back into George's car and held it together, though I could hardly breathe. I jumped out as it rolled to a stop in Dad's driveway.

"Thanks for dinner. It was really nice seeing you, Carrie. I'll try to write more." And I ran for the house. In the morning, I flew back to California and didn't look back.

Back in California, disconnected memories related to the rape continued to haunt me, while my decision about the abortion spawned behavior rooted in guilt and anxiety. My husband's loyalty persevered through that difficult time, and he never pushed for answers to questions I am sure he had.

As the years passed, the dynamics of our liaison motivated me to strive for independence and control over his dominating behavior. I grew into a woman who learned to demand respect. After his death, I realized our difficulties had strengthened my character. I had become assertive and independent. I knew who I was and what I wanted.

Although I missed my husband terribly, his death reminded me that life surged ahead, with or without my participation. I recalled my mother's advice from her deathbed. Determined to experience life before it passed me by, I now headed home with trepidation, hoping this package called Judy was wrapped tightly enough.

Throughout the years I had pushed aside my desire to see Brad. I had left so much unsaid, clinging to so many regrets. Now it was time to tie up loose ends and uncover the shame and fear I had hidden when I ran away.

Voices of doubt hung in the air. I knew Brad had never married. Did he feel the same as I back then? Would he fall down on his knees and profess his love? Would he say he had always waited for the day I'd return? Or would he just laugh and say, "That was a long time ago. We were young and foolish."

I wanted to know. Didn't I? I needed to know. Time and two thousand miles would tell the story.

I could count on my fingers my visits to Springfield during the last forty years. When I did visit it was only to check on Dad. The computer age had left him in a cloud of microchip dust, and he refused, or was unable to, join the race of technology. My sister purchased and educated him on the use of a cell phone, but he refused to use the computer she installed. The technological monstrosity sat on his desk and became an expensive, electronic deck of solitaire cards.

When I flew into town, I was always in a rush, with work as an excuse to return to California. I restrained my brain and heart from venturing on any side trips.

But life's events and maturity had seasoned me. I planned to revisit what remained of my youth, the last physical vestiges: the grade school, high school, the house where I grew up, the park where I ice skated, and the drive-in theater where no one watched the love story but discovered a world of hot emotions of their own.

After my husband's death, I learned to live alone. As the months moved through their paces, they took me further from my grief and I embraced widowhood. I appreciated the freedom, but soon tired of watching TV alone, eating alone, sleeping alone. A year ago I couldn't imagine another man's touch, but now the possibility intrigued me, teased my sensibilities, and caused me to hope...for what? Another love? I believed at my age I would be trying to weave a rope of sand, but still, I was compelled to dig up and dust off desires buried forty years ago. My steadfast journey continued toward my past and my future, two thousand miles away.

Chapter Ten

Two thousand miles away, in Springfield, Brad sat under the porch light, his calloused farmer's hands cleaning his .38 revolver.

From the parlor, the television's glow beamed through the screen door while he heard notes from the theme song from *Cops*—"*What you gonna do when they come for you? Bad boys, bad boys...*"—infiltrating the evening's shadows. He thought how the room had not changed in sixty years. His mother's starched doilies still protected the Early American coffee table. A pinewood gun cabinet protected the shotgun he had used on his first hunting trip. He remembered shooting his first rabbit as a boy with that ten gauge while his grandfather, father, and uncles puffed up with pride and cheered, consuming too many cases of beer in celebration. Over sixty years of warm, wild, and drunken stories danced in Brad's mind. As he sat on the porch, he watched the windblown motions of the elms create silhouettes that stalked across the side of the barn. In the parlor, the two high school reunion tickets rested on the coffee table, causing other memories to speak loudly, drowning out the TV's tune. *After forty years, how could she still consume my thoughts?*

His mind drifted back. He was in English class that first day of sophomore year and studied Judy as she shuffled into the classroom, her arms loaded with books. It was as if she had locked and loaded a shotgun at his heart. He'd tried to dismiss her disarming presence with a puffed-up bravado as he straightened up from his slouched position. He felt a powerful spark when she looked at him and then took the desk next to his. The electric energy tingled again now as he reminisced. *Perhaps our fates had welded that day.*

He argued with himself. *Judy's a nice girl compared to the chicks I run with in my wild, alcoholic, and barroom fight-filled existence.* He wondered if back then his reservations had been born of respect or a fearful reverence. Every time he spotted her at the bowling alley or the Roxy Theater, their eyes met, Judy's questioning. But he read promise there, even though he always looked away.

He thought of the rare instances, weak moments, when his restraint waned, when he felt like a boy whistling in the dark. It was then he surrendered to Judy's unspoken, per-sistent pleas. He would park at the corner and she would sneak out of the house. They shared an evening snuggled in the backseat of his Chevy, talking until dawn.

"Mom thinks I'm at Jackie's." She giggled and pressed closer.

Now as he reminisced, he shifted his weight, propping his boots on the porch railing. His gun rested in his lap as he drifted back to that summer day at the Illinois State Fair. He stood with his buddies at the carnival entrance.Musical laughter over the jabber of the carnival's crowds had turned his head like a siren's call.

It sounded like an old love song. His heart pounded. Unable to fight the urge to rush to her, he approached with long strides. That was the day he bought the locket. He remembered how his pulse hammered when his hands lifted her hair—its scent he could still smell now—and secured the clasp. Now alone on the porch, he smiled warmly at the memory of his youth and how he had vowed, if only to himself, to love her.

He never spoke of his oath because he felt unworthy. He was born the son of a farmer, as his father had been before Him. Although he knew his family's values of pride and patriotism grew deep roots in their three hundred acres, he could never shake the feeling of being only a hayseed ploughboy without a row to hoe. He passed the long summers alongside his dad and uncles, from dawn to dusk performing the endless chores farming required. When nightfall forced the day's end, he showered his heritage down the drain and hit the door running. He climbed on his Triumph motorcycle, aimed it at a night of drinking and barroom fights, hoping the alcohol and fists would wash and pound away the fear of his destiny. He dreaded his future would be the same as his father's, and his father's father, who gave it their all just to keep it all together.

Brooding, Brad cleaned his gun. His dad and six uncles also loved to drink and fight, joining him on a regular basis. Swooping into the local bars every night, the clan drenched their dust-filled throats and sloshed their bib overalls with the golden liquid that drowned their life's struggles until dawn. Storming into a bar, they'd announce, "There are eight of us and we need eight barstools, and we don't much give a fuck which ones." They loved a battle and hoped no one would relinquish their seats, because then the fights began. Brad recalled bartenders who, intimidated by the family's drunken reputation, rarely refused service to his underage drinking When dawn broke on the untilled rows of corn,

Dad his uncles, and Brad, drunken and spent, would stagger to their homestead in time to fire up the tractor, nurse their hangovers until dusk, and then begin the brutal cycle all over again.

Brad knew his father expected no less from him, and the Barroom bravado became the only lifestyle he knew. He watched his dad and uncles come and go from jail as if there were a revolving door. Bribes and bail money were pressed into palms as handcuffs were removed. Brad's life-blood became saturated with adrenaline and alcohol and he became addicted to both. Brad, too, did his time in the jail's revolving door. Money, never an issue, flowed as his father supplied him with funds to keep his Triumph and '57 Chevy immaculate and running hot. His dad, who scolded him in public and in front of Brad's mother, privately patted him on the back. "Way to go, son. Did you kick some ass?"

Brad's high school attendance was contingent on how severe his hangovers were and how loudly his body ached from the nightly brawls.

Post-graduation life took a dangerous direction after his father's death. Brad's anger centered on the waste his family's drinking and fighting lifestyle had caused. And his involvement with Judy stirred even more emotions. He thought of a different kind of waste that encouraged him to nurse a broken and regretful heart. Regrets that he never made his move on Judy caused a burning in his gut that only alcohol cooled. He spent endless hours feeding his disappointments. When he learned Judy had married, his drinking escalated into blackouts, resulting in the loss of large blocks of time.

Chapter Eleven

Brad envisioned the bar—a shanty was all it really was—that leaned alongside the two-lane highway outside a small community whose commercial population consisted only of a gas station and a small market. If the bar sat aslant on a beach in Mexico, an observer would call it quaint and romantic, but on the outskirts of this one-gas-station village in Oklahoma, it was just a shack.

His last drunk. In an alcoholic blackout, he'd traveled hundreds of miles to Oklahoma, to a town he couldn't recall or never knew. Awareness that he wasn't in Illinois nagged at his drunken stupor when he pulled in front of the bar. It was Christmas day.

The warm December day intensified his thirst for a cold beer. Several pickups, a car, and a Harley were parked in front, waiting for their owners who were packed inside the hovel. For Christmas day, the place was busy. He backed into a parking space directly in front of the weatherworn structure, he stepped onto the boot-scuffed porch. A wooden screen door hung askew on its hinges. When he pulled the rusty handle, it creaked in protest as it scraped across the stoop's floor. The jukebox played a Willie Nelson tune and the notes rushed through the screen door, carried by cigarette smoke and loud voices laden with alcohol.

With his boots covered in the parking lot's dust, Brad stepped from the glaring sunlight into the darkened, musky interior. Inside the cramped space, he stopped as the screen door slammed behind him. He stepped sideways around a pool table, waiting for his eyes to adjust to the smoky dimness. A few more strides carried him past the pool table to the plywood bar. Several locals stood leaning against it in T-shirts and jeans or coveralls.

From experience, he read the tense body language. They were aware of his entrance even though no one turned in acknowledgment. Approaching the end of the bar, he rested an elbow on the plywood surface. Brad's imperceptive nod to the redneck beside him was returned in the same manner.

"Beer?" The bartender held a yellowed towel, wiping his hands as his biceps bulged from beneath his wife-beater t-shirt. His black eyes fixed on Brad's and, with a practiced sweep, scanned Brad's demeanor.

"Yeah." You take what they offer, he thought. When he stretched up and leaned sideways to reach into his front pocket for change, the guy next to him tensed in response and then relaxed. Brad threw the coins on the bar while he focused on the action at the pool table.

"Hey, Joe, you out already? What'd ya get? Time off for good behavior?" A man in coveralls prodded a biker with his words and looked to his buddies for encouragement.

"What's it to you, farmer boy? You got a problem?" Joe paused his pool shot, turned, and faced the man.

"Hey, no problem." The farmer held up his hands and backed away. "Just bein' friendly. I see they didn't steal your pleasant personality while you were in there. You're just as mean as ever." Farmer Boy took his place next to his two neighbors, each holding a beer in one hand while the other hand's thumb hooked on a coverall pocket.

"You bet I am. I am who I am." The grimace under his three-day beard was Joe's attempt at a smile. His biker pack of friends crouched in the opposite corner of the crowded bar, laughing loudly in Joe's support.

With a couple practiced swallows, Brad drained his second beer, pulled himself up, and headed for what he assumed was the bathroom. Inside the room he saw no toilet, no sink, and for a moment thought he was in a closet until he noticed an old fruit can nailed to the wall at groin level. At the bottom of the can was a hole plugged with rubber tubing that reached through another hole in the wall and outside. The urinal. He shrugged in acceptance as he stepped in front of the can.

He finished his business and headed back to the bar, accidentally bumping Joe's cue stick. Brad grabbed his third beer, but before the bottle dripped its icy slush onto the raw plywood, the big biker swung around.

"What the hell!" Joe cracked the pool stick onto the pool table, splintering it in half. He raised the half cue menacingly in the air. "You're gonna die, meathead!"

No stranger to a bar fight, Brad turned. "Bring it on, road rash!"

But Joe immediately upped the ante. He flung the broken stick, and as it cracked against the wall, the redneck reached under his stained denim shirt and yanked a .38 revolver from his scarred leather belt. The cue's shattering crash filled the filthy room, switching on an immediate silence as the barroom froze and held its breath. Then, as if triggered by a shot from a starter gun, a roar of obscenities exploded as the biker pack howled, rooting Joe on while the locals barked out their own opinions.

"Hey, Joe, kick the guy's ass!" The biker pack was keyed up but kept their corner position. "Santa Claus will bring you another beer if you do." The crowd yelled, charged with fervor.

"You better back off, Joe. You'll be back in the joint before the door can hit you in the ass." Words of wisdom from the farmers' corner.

"I'll kill you, shithead!" Joe disregarded the warning and moved toward Brad. Brad faced him and matched Joe's movement, by keeping his distance and back-stepping his way toward the door.

"Hey, Joe, you got him on the run now. Don't let him get away." The bikers and locals continued shouting obscenities. Scared, Brad raised both arms in an act of surrender, his beer still clutched in one hand and carefully backed into the screen door, pushing it open and out into the harsh glare of sunlight. Joe continued forward through the door, forcing Brad to back up against the tailgate of his truck.

They had only stood for a moment, face to face, when Joe's buddy came out the screen door, slamming it, and yelled at his friend, "Don't let the mother get away." In the second it took Joe to turn his head in acknowledgment, Brad reached into his truck bed and grabbed the pistol-grip, sawed-off shotgun he kept hidden under a towel. In one fluid movement, he swung the firearm down low to his side, crouched, and with both hands on the pistol grip, fired low.

The scene played out in slow motion, as Brad watched the biker's boot float through a dust cloud stirred by the biker who had fell to the ground, flopping and twisting like a chicken does when its head's been chopped off. When the dust cleared, Brad saw a boot resting in the Oklahoma soil several yards from the biker's body—with a bloody stump inside. Brad had blown Joe's leg off at the knee. In his alcoholic fog, Brad shuddered as he realized the result of his defensive reaction. *But I'm alive,* he thought.

The biker's buddy leaped off the shack's porch as he yelled for someone inside. Before Brad could assess the situation, Oklahoma backwoods justice played out in an unbelievable scenario. A man approached Brad before he could collect his thoughts, explaining Brad had just shot his son. The information caused Brad to slip his finger back onto the trigger as he stood tense and ready for the next confrontation, but the father's words took him aback.

"Thank you for not killing my son. Joe's on parole after doin' a nickel for pistol-whipping a guy almost to death. He's been nothin' but trouble since he got out. I don't know what to do with him. Really, man, thanks for not killin' him. Just get outta here. Get gone before I change my mind."

Brad stood in place, stunned. He saw the father wave back the biker pack. "It's all right, boys, let'm go." Joe's friends grumbled and looked at each other in disappointment. They had wanted to fight, but it was the dad's call.

Shocked but warily grateful, Brad scrambled into his truck just as the paramedics and sheriff arrived. He heard the biker's buddies explaining the justice of Oklahoma's backwoods, that Joe's shotgun had accidentally gone off and he'd shot himself in the leg. No one wanted the law involved. Their friend was alive, no fault, no foul. All heads were nodding in agreement to the story as Brad gunned the accelerator and disappeared into a cloud of Oklahoma dust.

Chapter Twelve

Brad's next conscious memory was watching his jailer slide the heavy barred doors shut. An agitating clang and a final leaden clank finalized his future for the next twenty-four hours. In the cell's corner a rank, rumpled figure slumped on the floor with folded arms, supported by knees drawn tightly to his chest. The drunk slept off what the cops had jailed him for. His reddened, whiskered face, almost obscured by greasy, stringy hair hanging in black cords, rested on gritty forearms. The gap between his pant legs and tattered tennis shoes exposed layers of clothing bulging out in varied colors and textures. Brad's urge to retch was not from alcohol consumption, but from the stench of his cellmate.

Where am I? How did I get here? Panic filled his brain as it struggled to fire on all cylinders while he processed his surroundings. *I must be in an Oklahoma jail cell.* The father must have lied to him and had him arrested...or maybe he'd imagined what the man said. Maybe it was all a bad dream. Fear and confusion caused sweat to bead his brow, replacing bewilderment and anger when he realized he did not know where he was or why he was there. Another cellmate sat on the only cot, watching Brad's every move.

"Where am I?" Brad met his stare. "Am I in Oklahoma?"

"Oklahoma? No, man! You're in the Sangamon County Jail. You're in Illinois. They brought you in last night. I heard the coppers say they followed you with lights flashing for five miles on the freeway 'til you finally pulled over and climbed out of your truck. You stumbled to the front, hung onto the grill, and proceeded to take a piss." His cellmate laughed, followed by a bout of hacking that racked his body. Weak and out of breath, he paused and then continued. "Man, you were out of it when they threw you in here last night. You're here for drunk driving." He coughed violently again and spat a green blob streaked with webs of red onto the floor.

Brad scanned his quarters and processed the old man's words. *How could I be back in Illinois and not remember anything?* It was almost sunrise, which meant possible bail and arraignment, and answers. By noon the guard returned. The clank and clanging of the heavy cell door reverberated inside Brad's pounding head as the guard waved his Billy club, directing Brad to step outside. "Put your hands behind your back." He applied cuffs that cut Brad's wrists and shackles that shrank his gait, causing him to shuffle alongside his jailer down the corridor and into a courtroom.

The guard lined him up with other prisoners who stood soberly awaiting the bailiff to call their cases. After forty-five minutes Brad's name was called and the charges read. "You are charged with drunk driving on Wabash Avenue. Sangamon County and the city of Springfield have filed these charges. How do you plead?" *What? Not armed assault? Sangamon County? How did I make it all the way back from Oklahoma?* The relief from hearing the charges instantly evaporated, replaced by a deep, unfamiliar terror he did not know how to handle. *How can I not remember traveling from Oklahoma to Illinois?*

"Guilty, Your Honor." He was always guilty when it involved alcohol.

"You will be released on your own recognizance and are to report to the High Roads Facility on Ninth Street. It is an alcoholic recovery program. You will also attend AA meetings daily for the next ninety days. You will be given a card from the court to be signed after every meeting as proof of your attendance. Do you understand, Mr. Jones?"

"Yes, Your Honor." Brad's hopes, which had soared when he'd heard the charges, now sank. He just wanted to do his time and get on with his miserable life. He had no use for some recovery program and he told the judge as much. "I don't need any recovery program. Just give me the time. I just want to do my time."

"Well, Mr. Jones, jail doesn't seem to be working for you, as indicated in your arrest records that could fill a wheelbarrow, so the court is going to try this avenue." The crack of the judge's gavel reverberated off the courtroom walls and echoed in Brad's aching head, sealing his fate.

Two hours later Brad was released. He blinked in the bright sunshine and hailed a cab to the impound yard and his truck. Thirty minutes later, he gulped down a warm beer from the ice chest in the truck's bed that he always kept stocked for emergencies. This was definitely an emergency.

He felt better the minute the warm brew flowed through his veins. In less than twenty minutes he gulped down two more. With his jittery nerves calmed, he fired up the engine and followed the directions to the High Roads Recovery Program, located in a strip mall a few miles from the courthouse. With a surly attitude and his court papers, Brad marched through the door, slapped the forms onto the counter, and challenged the man sitting behind it. "I'm here because the judge sent me."

The young man looked up. Thick black hair and a tanned, smooth complexion told of an indoor life of leisure. He studied Brad's challenging stance and leathery farmer's features. Defiantly, Brad met his stare. Who was this pipsqueak?

"Well, you can lose the attitude right now and we'll all get along a lot better." The pipsqueak had a smirk on his lips and his Adam's apple wiggled his tie. Brad hated him instantly.

"Look, I don't want to be here. If you don't like my attitude, you can send me back to jail. I asked the judge to just let me do my time and he wouldn't do it, so if you can, go ahead!" Brad yelled in frustration as his fist banged the counter.

"No, this is the right place for you. We're going to have a lot of fun." Now the man was definitely laughing. Brad knew he would lose it if he said anything more.

The little man scratched and scribbled as he shuffled the forms on his desk and handed Brad a stack of papers.

"Here is your class schedule. Mondays, Wednesdays, and Fridays at nine in the morning. The classes are three hours long. You must attend twenty-four classes. You will be given a sobriety test before each class. If you fail, you will be sent back to the courts for reevaluation. Understood?"

Brad nodded.

"Good. That will be five hundred fifty dollars. Check, cash, or card."

Still, Brad said nothing as he reached for his wallet. He slapped down his credit card and wondered how much more this was going to cut into his budget. He'd already spent a thousand dollars in court fees and fines, and two hundred and fifty dollars at the impound yard. In less than twenty minutes, his account was charged and he flew out the door, headed for his truck. He avoided the ice chest of warm beer, climbed in, gunned the accelerator, and sped out of the parking lot. Tomorrow was Friday, his first class. He headed for the Alano Club, listed in his paperwork as where the AA meetings took place. He figured he might as well check out the place.

He found the address easily, parked, and entered the small building. The interior reminded him of a dimly lit bar. He sized up the figures sitting at the counter.

One of the losers—you had to be a loser to be there—was built like Brad's dad's old barn, weathered but solid and strong. Brad watched the man's eyes register every movement in the room while appearing to focus on the rim of his coffee mug on the counter. The back of the shirt identified the stocky man as SPRINGFIELD POLICE DEPARTMENT DEA. His elbows supported his torso as it hovered over the coffee bar, and he laughed at a comment from the man on the barstool next to him. Thick fingers wrapped around the porcelain, covering the letters that spelled out BAD COP. Sandy hair curled onto his forehead, giving him a boyish appearance. But Brad noted the mature muscles that pulled his T-shirt taut against thick arms, and knew this man would be someone to reckon with in a bar fight. In the short time it took Brad to approach the coffee bar, he had sized up Bad Cop as one not to be messed with. The relaxed demeanor of the man disguised an attitude of a coiled rattlesnake. Brad could relate to this man. *Maybe he's here to keep these losers in line.*

A woman passed behind the two seated men, her eyes lowered as she scanned where their jeans met the barstool. *Just like a bar.* Brad threw his long leg over the tall barstool and sat down next to Bad Cop, with a cool bravado that masked the churning in his belly that he had not sedated with enough alcohol. He refrained from drinking more, sure they would do a sobriety check at his first AA meeting. After his eyes swept over the half-dozen people seated at the bar, he and Bad Cop's eyes met with a challenging stare and they came to an unspoken respect of one another.

"What's your name?"

"Brad."

"You got a court card?"

How did he know? "Yeah."

"The meeting starts in ten minutes. Down that hall." Bad Cop tipped his curly head to his left. "Afterwards, they'll sign it."

Brad nodded. A nice-looking redhead, in skin-tight jeans and a low-cut T-shirt, tittered and flirted with a suit at the end of the bar. *Just like a bar*, Brad thought again.

"What'll you have, coffee or Coke?" The bartender, a middle-aged balding sort, stood before Brad, wearing a tie and a nicely pressed baby-blue dress shirt covering the curve of his belly that bulged against a too-tight black leather belt. *Are all these people alcoholics? They didn't look it.*

"Coffee."

"You got it. There's donuts over there." He pointed to the end of the counter, but the suggestion made Brad's stomach lurch. The bartender set a mug in front of Brad with one hand, and the other poured the steaming brew to the rim. Irritated there was now no room for cream, Brad said nothing.

Several people sat at tables, talking quietly. When the bartender rang a bell, the room came alive with movement. Everyone rose and made their way down the hall.

"Meeting's starting. You can take your coffee with you. You'll be drinking a lot of the stuff if you stick around." Bad Cop rose, merged with the crowd, and Brad followed closely. The hall led to a large, stark room furnished only with long tables and chairs. A rickety podium occupied one corner. The noises of scraping and shuffling competed with the banter and laughter. The losers spread out to various tables and sat down. Most everyone clutched a coffee mug.

The meeting began with no apparent leader. Randomly, people spoke. "I'm Ted, and I'm an alcoholic. Today I have thirty days. I can't believe it. I did it one day at a time..." The stories told of the attendees' "drunk-a-logs," what it used to be like, what happened, and what it was like now. No way was Brad going to tell his sad stories, and anyway he wasn't like these people who got drunk because the dog died or the girlfriend left. He didn't need an excuse to drink. If he wanted a drink, by God he'd have a drink. He jumped up the second the meeting ended, got his card signed, and hit the door running. Now he could go to a bar, have a cold one, and figure out what to do next.

He floored the accelerator as he left the club's gravel parking lot, squealing rubber when his tires hit the asphalt. Two blocks down the road, an unexplained force caused him to make a U-turn and head back to the Alano Club. *Maybe I just won't drink today.* He pulled into the parking lot and parked by the back door. Inside, he ordered, "Give me another cup of that coffee." Brad spent the next thirty days attending meetings and classes, while his spare time was spent bullshitting at the coffee bar. Somehow he didn't drink.

Brad's relationship with Bad Cop—or Ken McCourt, as he had come to know him—strengthened into a bond over the next several months, and evolved into a lasting friendship that eventually inspired Brad to join the police force. His sobriety, built on a solid twelve-step program along with Ken's friendship, made it possible to enter the police academy. He thought about the moment at the academy when he realized it was the first time his life had a direction other than drowning the emptiness he felt. With a meaningful purpose in his life, he had decided at that moment to apply the same dedication to his studies and training as he had to his drinking, and thus exchanged one addiction for another. His ambition quickly moved him up the chain of command, gaining him respect and recognition.

His sponsor, Ken, constantly reminded him, "Never forget your last drunk." Brad knew he could never erase the nightmare of that Oklahoma bar and the last time he couldn't remember. What happened at that bar led to the end of an existence of staggering through an unending fog, unable to tell the highs from the lows. It was that final encounter, tragic as it was, that propelled him toward a new beginning, and brought him to this place on the porch and his position on the force. Life, with all its twists and turns, still intrigued him.

When Brad joined the force, he told no one his reason for becoming a cop or the events that had spurred him in that direction, only that the job provided good benefits and he liked carrying a gun.

He recalled being a rookie, on the force only a week. The call came in at five in the morning. An abandoned car had been found in the ditch out on Wabash Road by old man Crosby's cornfield. When Brad and his partner arrived, he discovered the car was Jackie's, the driver's door open, keys in the ignition, and headlights dimming from a dying battery.

Brad rode shotgun with Ken, his AA sponsor and lieutenant. They parked behind the vehicle as Brad scanned the area with a spotlight. Satisfied, they exited the police car with guns drawn, but shielded themselves behind their respective car doors.

"Springfield PD!" After no response, Ken and Brad nodded to each other and slowly approached the Buick, whose lights by coincidence chose to go out at that exact moment. The ominous blackout spooked Brad even more.

The scene's stillness seemed to saturate the area, hushing the rustle of the dried cornstalks in the bordering field. Taking positions on each side of the vehicle, the partners aimed their flashlights into the little red convertible. The beams danced inside the car's interior like flashes from a thunderstorm. Finally, assured there was no one, they relaxed only a notch, unable to shake the foreboding.

"Where's Jackie?" Brad asked, not expecting an answer.

Moving around the abandoned vehicle, their flashlights tracked the tire ruts and followed a path of trampled cornstalks leading into the faded yellow field.

"Let's call for backup." Ken wanted to do everything by the book. He and Brad concluded what lay hidden in the cornfield was no longer a threat to anyone.

Now, four decades with the department, and with as many years of sobriety, Brad had realized his goal of being Chief of Police. Brad tipped his chair onto its back legs, his feet crossed at the ankles and propped on the porch's railing. Sometimes those days felt like yesterday, but tonight the forty years were just that—forty years of regrets and unfulfilled dreams.

The night sneaked onto the porch. In the barnyard's shadows, a neighbor's dog howled while crickets sang background. Brad's heavy sigh startled him as it intruded on the night's soft melody. As he sat on the wraparound porch, he brought his attention back to the task of reassembling the revolver. He rose, shoving the cleaned, oiled weapon back into its holster, and headed inside, leaving the night's creatures to their elements. The eighty-year-old house creaked its own classic song as Brad entered. His body identified with the house's timeworn tune as he eased it into the leather recliner and clicked on the TV to watch the news.

The reunion tickets still rested lightly on the starched lace. They seemed to breathe in and out in the television's light as if whispering an omen. Or was it a premonition? Forty years. So much had happened. Life had happened.

It was hard to imagine how he had ever wanted to leave this place. At sixteen, he had not only been ashamed of his roots but also hated the life this place offered. Farm work was consuming from sunup to sundown, sometimes for naught when weather or insects wiped out a year's worth of labor in a day. He watched his dad and uncles work themselves into the grave to make this place stay alive. However, time, maturity, and, most importantly, sobriety tempered Brad's attitude and gave him an appreciation for farm life, the land, and his heritage. Now his love for police work took all of his time, forcing him to contract out most of the farm work.

He could hear the locusts outside as they chattered their clicking noises like an accomplished drummer's staccato with his sticks. The frogs croaked in the creek at the pasture's edge. The night was heavy with humidity, and the moon shone like a reading light, illuminating the drying yellowed grass in the meadow.

Forty years had passed, but it seemed like overnight. As Chief of Police, responsibilities occupied his time, leaving little left for self-pity. But every night for four decades, his mind closed out the day with thoughts of missed opportunities... and Judy.

Chapter Thirteen

As I continued east on I-40, the morning sun blinded me and I tipped my cowboy hat to block the rays the visor missed. This journey was historic and nostalgic in more ways than one. The sign advertising the Petrified Forest compelled me to take the next exit. I pulled up to the kiosk and bantered with the ranger, explaining Cowboy Jack had no money.

I felt the quiet like a warm coat on a winter day as I scanned the barren landscape. I imagined life millions of years ago. Entire trees lay by the roadside, frozen in an ancient time zone, the road desolate, cars passing only now and then. I followed the park map to the Agate House, a large, nine-hundred-year-old pueblo built from petrified wood. My second stop was at larger ruins built over two thousand years ago. The young history of the two pueblos mingled with the 225-million-year-old history of the now petrified Black Forest. A moaning vibrated in the winds throughout the quiet canyons as I stood at a viewpoint, absorbing the petrified presence, the only sound being the soft hum of an occasional vehicle passing slowly by before evaporating into the distance.

Before I headed back to the interstate, I pulled into one of the turnouts for a bathroom break. I parked behind a large motor home towing a little Suzuki. Although I had never worried before, this time I considered the fact I was out in the middle of nowhere. What if I turned off the engine and it wouldn't start back up? *I think I'll leave it running. It will only take me a minute to go to the bathroom.*

I had taken two steps toward my bathroom in the rear of my coach when BAM! My body slammed against the kitchen counter. What? I regained my balance and rushed to the front, only to discover the little Suzuki's rear end embedded in the grill of my Wizard of Winnebago. I jumped into the drivers' seat, shut off my engine, opened the door, and landed shakily on the pavement. A bearded man, in a Dodgers baseball cap, T-shirt, and jeans, barreled full steam around the corner of his rig.

"You just backed into my motor home!"

The man's eyes grew large, almost red, in anger at my words. I stretched up to my full height. The man towered in front of me, and I noticed a chain to his wallet dangled from under his biker jacket. He was clearly angry and took the stance of a person not to be messed with.

"You! You. You just ran into mine!" His fists remained close to his chest. *Would he hit a woman?*

My adrenaline erased my sanity. "No, you backed into mine!" I couldn't believe this man. I wasn't even in the driver's seat. How could I have run into him? The exchange escalated like two billy goats with horns locked in battle, the anger resounding across the Painted Desert.

"Lady, we can't back these things up!"

A tiny voice of reason whispered, *He's right. You know they can't back up when they are towing a car. It can cause damage to the transmission.* As the realization seized my sanity, I choked on the angry words spewing out of my mouth. I had not put the Wizard in Park. My attitude shifted gears. Overwhelmed with embarrassment and regret, I began to apologize.

"I'm so sorry. I'm so sorry. Oh, dear, I'm so, so sorry!" I thought I was going to cry.

The man's wife appeared. She was shaken, but not yelling.

I pled my case to her. "I'm sorry. I can't believe I did this."

"It was brand new." The man shook his head, examining the damage. He ran his fingers through his hair, massaged his neck, reining in his anger.

"Let me get my insurance information." We retreated to our motor home corners and began calling our respective insurance companies. After exchanging information and reviewing the damage, again I apologized profusely. By now the man, a little calmer, began either to tire of my contrition or he genuinely felt sorry for me.

"It's okay. That's what insurance is for." We shook hands, I squeezed in one last apology, we retreated to our rigs, fired up our engines, and pulled back onto the highway. It wasn't long before the little Suzuki's smashed rear end disappeared from sight.

Cowboy Jack sat quietly, undisturbed by the entire situation. Wouldn't he have been a little bit upset? I thought I heard him say, "These things happen."

What? That's it? That's all he has to say? Isn't he concerned about the damage? The insurance going up? Isn't he worried I might be losing it, doing such a stupid thing?

Sportster jumped onto my lap. Thank goodness he was unhurt. He snuggled, rubbing his head against my arm in a comforting gesture that I believed he knew I needed. He laid his head on the armrest, and before the first mile was purring in sleep. His tranquility soothed me.

As I drove and the day wore on, I wished there had been someone to talk to. But what was there to say, anyway? Try to get reassurance I wasn't really losing it?

The red ribbon of New Mexico's interstate stretched endlessly in front of the Wizard of Winnebago. It could not have been straighter or the direction more easterly, allowing my idle mind to dissect the "incident" over and over, examining every detail.

As the sun sank hundreds of miles behind me into the Pacific Ocean, I used up the time thinking. I imagined lovers on the beach holding each other. Loneliness and depression filled the motor home's interior. A forlorn wind whispered a rhythm through the open window. The tires wished, swished, wished, and swished in sync.

I passed Pecos National Park, which protected the ruins of yet another pueblo and a Spanish mission. My dark disposition dismissed the possibility of touring the Glorieta Battlefield and the ruts that still remained from the wagon trains. I continued on to Tucumcari and stopped at the Cactus RV Park, nestled behind an old motel lovingly restored to its grandeur of the Route 66 era.

The plump owners bumped against each other as they moved in unison and approached the counter from the recesses of the building. They introduced themselves as Stan and Mary, explaining Stan's parents had owned and operated the Cactus Motor Lodge, which was now a national landmark. My eyes scanned the interior. The walls, counters, even the ceiling of the registration office supported Route 66 memorabilia.

"It's wonderful how you've kept this piece of history. You've certainly enriched my trip."

When I parked and set up camp, I started coffee brewing. The java's aroma aroused my desperate need for caffeine. Stretched out in my recliner with my book and coffee, I exhaled a long deep sigh. I admired the last rays of sunset while Sportster studied a blue jay. What a day. Relieved it was almost behind me, I pushed thoughts of the earlier episode out of my mind.

I read a line or two from my book, only to find myself back at the turnout, trying to make sense of my scary lapse. The knot in my stomach tightened and I forced my attention back to my book. But as the evening ticked on, my mind was off and running. I pictured myself the old spinster with friends too kind to inform me of my condition. They nodded in sadness behind my back, knowing a "home" was in my future, while I laughed, scoffing at the latest mishap.

And then I heard a noise. A scratching. I felt the motor home rocking, swaying. Sportster was sleeping soundly. Didn't he hear it? Cowboy Jack sat awake, smiling out into the darkness, oblivious to the rattling noise and the swinging movement. I knew someone or something was trying to enter the motor home. The scratching became louder as the motor home rocked violently now. I screamed but there was no one to hear. I was in that haunting black hole again. The sickening spicy scent from my past and that disturbing tune filled the space. I screamed as I felt something touch my face.

A feather-light touch on my cheek snapped me back to reality. My eyes sprang open to see Sportster standing on my chest, his soft paw retracting from brushing my cheek. When my brain processed the last chords of my panicked yell for help, I realized I had been dreaming. My muscles slacked with relief. I looked around. Sportster sat on my lap, gazing at me intently. Now wide awake, I noticed the campground was quiet and streetlights flickered on in response to the dusk.

That night, I tossed and turned in a restless sleep until the promise of daylight peered over the horizon and backlit the adobe motel. The red and yellow neon sign still flickered on and off. Another day. I put the accident and the nightmare away in a box and crammed it into a corner of my mind.

I lay under the warm covers considering the fact there was no one in my life. And what would I do if there were? Perhaps solitude was best. I wouldn't be embarrassed by my nightmares, and who would care anyway? I was no spring chicken. This trip was foolish. What was I chasing after anyway? A forty-year-old dream that had never been able to blossom? I felt like a silly old woman.

I shook off my doubts, dressed, and decided on a walk down historic Route 66. It was a beautiful day and a walk would feel good. And later, I would splurge on an early dinner. I passed a Whiting Bros. gas station; the Odeon Theater, an art-deco building; and browsed through several shops, all with equal amounts of Route 66 history. Back at my campsite, I spent a leisurely day reading.

Tucumcari boasted of vintage neon signs that lit Main Street at night. When the New Mexico sky turned slate gray, I took one more stroll up Route 66, marveling at the array of fluorescent primary colors. They blinked and flashed like the Las Vegas Strip, announcing vacancies and good food. My mind saw Dad's Jeep creeping along Main Street and I remembered his impatience as he observed the fifteen-miles-per-hour speed limit, anxious to get through downtown and back to the open road.

That night I thought of my childhood. I saw my mother's laughing face, round and rosy from heat as she slid a cherry pie from the oven. My father's Anglo-Saxon features framed by a full head of hair once Irish red, now bleached by his years. Scrapbook memories of our home's grassy backyard flanked by cornfields filled my head. I drifted off to sleep and woke refreshed. Maybe going home wasn't such a bad idea.

Chapter Fourteen

Standing on the porch, Brad inhaled the wet scents from the previous night's rainstorm while the sunrise restored the daylight. He watched the winds push the dark clouds to the south. There in the distance, the thunderous anger of the lightning storm flooded the distant fields. The electricity made him feel alive. He took another deep breath of the morning.

In the kitchen, Brad reviewed the daily reports spread out on the counter. He began to see a pattern emerging. The Computer Forensics Unit, the Auto Theft Task Force, and the Division of Drug and Crime Control provided information generated from Missouri, Mississippi, and as far as Louisiana.

During a raid in Missouri, sixteen stolen trucks and trailers were recovered from a trucking company. Two of the trucks had been heisted from the Springfield area.

The operation of the Road Hogs Auto Body Sales, a chop shop set up by the Feds to infiltrate a well-known motorcycle gang, culminated in the arrest and conviction of six of its members. Forensic analysis of the data recovered from the computers of these various stings continued. Weeks of man hours would be spent deciphering the mass amount of information stored in each computer. The amount of intelligence involved with police work today amazed Brad.

The investigation revealed a congested highway of drugs and stolen cars along the Mississippi River, originating in New Orleans and reaching as far as Chicago. When the theory first emerged one sleepless night, Brad scoffed at his own imagination of transporting drugs up the river. Although drug task units used most of their resources for the suppression of organized crime and the crackdown on cocaine, Brad had a personal vendetta and searched for data on the less common seizures of the date-rape drug GHB, or Rohypnol, commonly known as roofies on the streets.

Throughout his career, a particular drug ring had endured, led by a kingpin known only as Pit Bull who eluded Brad's highly trained DEA units. The intelligence gathered over the years sketched an ominous picture. Pit Bull dealt date-rape drugs, known as Mickey Finns in as early as the sixties. When his known associates were arrested, they rarely talked, and the ones who tried to make a deal were "extinguished" before ever making it to trial.

Brad recalled a five-year-old case involving a female suspect who agreed to turn state's evidence. She disappeared within hours after her release. Six months later, by the railroad tracks near an abandoned shack, her skeletal remains were unearthed by a hunting dog. Alongside her badly beaten body was her eight-year-old son, who had been gunned down next to her. Evidence like this proved Pit Bull was a cold, calculating monster, and the reason he survived over four decades. Brad hated the results of Pit Bull's reign of terror.

He had experienced the far-reaching effects of the date-rape drug at the age of sixteen. The victim was his own teen angel, Judy. The drug, then known as a Mickey Finn, had the same disarming effect as the roofies of today. In the fifties and sixties, rape was overshadowed by guilt, shame, and misdirected responsibility, and thus rarely reported. And true to the statistics, he and Judy had kept their secret. Judy's rape became the underlying motivation that had driven him to join the police force because he, too, was filled with guilt and shame. For forty years he nursed the "should haves" and the "what ifs." If he had followed his feelings back then, if he had done his own investigation, he should have done something...but instead he had drunk away his feelings.

From the kitchen window, Brad watched the storm clouds part, allowing sunbeams to radiate onto the fields, creating a scene for a religious pamphlet. He took a swallow of his now-cold coffee and tossed the remainder down the drain. The chance to make everything right was almost here, he thought, as he calculated how close he was to wrapping up the longest and most intensive investigation of his career.

On a personal level, he had already decided not to make the same mistakes twice. Life was short and too many years wasted. Time had made him wiser. There would be no more missed opportunities. He did not intend to waste another minute. He felt his pulse skip as he again thought of the two reunion tickets lying on the coffee table.

Setting the mug's black, bold letters, BAD COP, facing him, Brad poured another cup of his dark, aromatic, special blend. His AA sponsor, Ken, had presented him with the cup for his first AA birthday. Brad studied the sweetener dissolving in the hot liquid and added a generous amount of cream until the drink resembled silky beige. His eyes scanned the counter for stray crumbs.

In the living room, he pressed the TV's remote. The news anchor's voice burst into the room, accompanied by a downtown scene.

"We have just been informed a female was discovered at the Deere Stop Motel. Uncorroborated witnesses reveal the girl to be eighteen and, although badly beaten, still alive. More news at ten..."

The news anchor, Steve Rumsey, didn't hide his grim expression. Brad knew Steve had a daughter the same age. Brad had graduated from college with Steve's dad.

The cell phone's urgent ring interrupted. The ringtone matched the theme song from *Cops* so Brad knew it was dispatch.

"Chief Jones here." He stood taller, his jaw twitching as he listened to his detective's voice on the other end.

"We have another victim. A motel maid at the Deere Stop discovered the girl barely alive. She matches the description of a missing teen. I'm at St. Johns Hospital with her. We're waiting for her parents to come down and give permission for the exam. If you hurry you can talk to her before they get here."

"I'm on the way." He grabbed his holstered firearm from the table and picked up his keys, leather jacket, and helmet. Outside he fired up his vintage Triumph and kicked it into third gear before he reached the parkway.

Brad's detective, Ken, met him outside the emergency room. Ken's crisp uniform rustled in the hospital's quiet halls as he approached Brad. In hushed tones, he filled Brad in on the sparse details.

"Her name's Lacey. Her parents reported her missing early this morning when they realized she'd sneaked out last night and never returned home."

They approached the nurses' station.

Brad leaned over the counter. "We just need a few minutes with her if we could." The nurse on duty looked down the hall to a doctor quietly conversing with a couple.

"That's the girl's parents. Just a few minutes." She hurried them into the room, unnoticed. The nurse had worked a lot with Brad and Ken and respected their calm, reassuring demeanor when interviewing a victim.

"Hi, Lacey, I'm Chief Jones and this is Detective McCourt." The girl moved her head slightly toward the sound of Brad's voice. Her swollen right eye allowed only a slit for vision and a patch covered her left. The monitor's beeps spiked in frequency. Brad kept his voice low and calm. "We're sorry for what you've been through. The doctors say you are going to be fine. We saw your folks. They're right outside. As soon as they finish talking to the doctor, they'll be right in."

"I don't want to see them!" She began crying uncontrollably. "I can't tell them what happened. They told me not to go out."

"They're worried about you, Lacey, and relieved you're safe. You don't have to worry; they're not angry. Can you tell us what happened?"

"I don't know. I was at the mall trying to hook up with my friends when this guy I'd met before told me my friends were in the parking garage."

"What's his name?" Ken stood back, notebook in hand.

"I didn't know his name. I'd just met him last week. He'd been hanging out with us at the food court."

"So what happened next?"

"He told me to follow him and he'd take me to where they were. When we got out to the parking garage, he saw some friends. He told me to chill while he stopped at their van to talk. I had a Coke while I waited. I think they put something in it, because I started feeling funny after that."

"How many were there?"

"I think five."

"What did they look like? Do you remember what they were wearing?"

"I don't know. I hardly remember anything after that. I remember we were all in the van and..." She covered her eyes; her shoulders shook.

"It's okay. You take it easy and we'll talk more later. The doctors just want to check you over and then you can go home with your folks. Everything's going to be okay."

The door swung open and the room flooded first with the rushing movements of her mother. Behind her, Lacey's father stepped no further than the threshold. His eyes, flaring like a firestorm, swept the room and zeroed in on his daughter's battered form.

"Lacey, honey! Oh, honey, are you okay? Everything's going to be okay." The mother pushed past Brad and Ken and started to gather her daughter in her arms but held back, afraid her touch would cause more pain for her baby. Instead, she hovered over Lacey. "Don't cry, honey." The father stood by watching, then turned his attention to Brad and Ken, his expression full of angry questions.

Brad extended his hand. "I'm Chief Jones, and this is Detective McCourt. You see to your family. We'll wait outside."

In the hall, Ken said, "As you see, we only got a vague description of the boys and the van. We're counting on the security cameras to fill in the blanks. That's the sixth victim in the same amount of months in this county alone." Ken's wrinkled brow added more age to his appearance. He had more years invested in the investigation than Brad.

"We'll get them." Brad's jaw muscles flexed. "We're close. The FBI sent McNalley up from St. Louis to assist. Remember him? He worked on that case out by the railroad tracks with the woman and her son. The Feds know Pit Bull's in this area, probably right under our noses, and they're sure the creep's connected with the carjacking ring. They've impounded several cars with false compartments installed like they used to do to run moonshine in the thirties."

Ken added, "Reports suggest the drugs are moved on barges up the Mississippi from New Orleans. McNalley believes our boy Pit Bull takes his share at Browning and floats it up the Sangamon to our lovely city for distribution."

Brad nodded. "They know that's how he did it twenty years ago, and the lock and dam system still makes it possible. When the drugs arrive here, that's where the chopped hot rods come in to play. The cars distribute the product to Decatur and all the college towns as far as Chicago.

"Did you know that Abraham Lincoln navigated a flatboat from New Orleans all the way to Springfield? Look it up." Brad zipped up his leather jacket. "I told you my theory wasn't so farfetched."

Ken nodded with a grim smile. "I know you like your history, Chief." He slipped his notepad into his jacket. "I'll stay and talk to the dad. Are you heading back to the station to see what Forensics has?"

"Yeah. We'll catch up later."

At the station, Brad ran the video from the shopping mall's surveillance cameras for the third time. Three males, hunched facing each other between a white panel truck parked between a black Dodge pickup and a Honda Civic. Their movements portrayed casual conversation and playful punching as they consumed beer and seemed to be waiting. With no audio, Brad's mind filled in the clanking echoes as the youths tossed the aluminum cans to the garage floor.

A male leading a female meeting Lacey's description appeared at the edge of the screen, and met nods of recognition from the huddle as they approached. Lacey appeared ill at ease as her eyes darted around the garage's area. She took a Coke offered by one of the boys.

Fifteen minutes passed. One of the males exchanged the girl's Coke for another. The group's movements became more animated, and Brad sensed their anticipation as Lacey supported herself against the vehicle, clearly unsteady. They herded her toward the side, out of view of the camera's eye. The five figures disappeared and a moment later the vehicle pulled away, leaving the camera's sight.

The video hissed as Brad stared at the grease-stained empty scene. One of the males looked familiar. Exhaling a tired, heavy breath, he pushed away from the table. The day was gone. Framed by his office window, the Capitol building glittered, its dome outlined in lights. Before he headed home with the stack of forensic reports, he poked his head into the CSI detective's office.

"Got anything yet?"

"We've run the plates and we've got an ID on the owner of the van, Chief. His name is Timmie Thompson. He was picked up a couple of years ago for rape and selling but walked."

"Good work." Brad picked up the detective's write-up. The photo of Timmie Thompson matched one of the perps in the video, but more intriguing, Timmie Thompson was the figure in George's photo from the car show. As Brad processed the new information, his brain linked the feeling of familiarity to the arrest two years ago. Timmie was a mid-level drug dealer charged with trafficking and rape, but a high-powered Chicago attorney had gotten him off on a technicality with time served and probation.

"It looks like our boy will be making reservations with us again. Let's make sure he gets an extended vacation sponsored by SPD this time. Put out an APB out on him."

It had been a long day. Brad hit the kill switch as the Triumph coasted into the barn, and as he dismounted, thought he never used to ache like this. His practiced gaze scanned the unused stalls looking for Charlie, his old dog, who, even though hard of hearing and arthritic, loyally greeted him every night with exuberance. Brad made his way outside with long strides, removing his helmet along the way.

Bright lights exploded behind his cold blue eyes. He felt the blow to his helmet-free head, and with the sharp reflexes of a man half his age, Brad swung his leg out and around in a sweeping slice, and brought the hooded intruder to his knees, onto the barn floor. But as fast as the black form went down, it rose from the straw.

Muscular arms lassoed Brad from behind. Pinned and unable to counter, he watched the dark bulk grow back to its full size. Fists of bricks delivered a pounding force to Brad's stomach and groin, and if not constrained, Brad would have collapsed.

"You should've backed off. You woulda lived longer." Blackness replaced the white lightning in his vision, and the restraining arms retracted. Mercifully, Brad slumped to the straw-covered ground. Muskiness filled his nostrils.

Appearing like a scud missile, Charlie charged onto the scene, tailed by the dog's young golden retriever girl-friend, Bridgette. She rocketed past him, airborne, and sank her teeth into the outstretched hand that held a gun to the back of Brad's head. The connection and force of Bridgette's eighty pounds swung the dark form around and onto the ground. With precision teamwork, Charlie's jaws locked on the man's throat. The gun skidded into an empty stall, as the man's scream became a gurgle.

An accomplice stood temporarily hypnotized by the change of events, but pulling himself from his trance, he grabbed a gun from his belt. Bridgette's focus whipped around to the glint in the dim light. Again she charged, clamping onto his hand before it cleared his belt. The pistol dropped into the dirt and the man scrambled to stand his ground.

With Bridgette clamped on one arm, the man grabbed his buddy's leg with his other arm and, yelling at the dogs, began to drag the lifeless body toward the door. Charlie, still clamped to the other man's neck, shook the figure like a dead rabbit. Bridgette, sensing victory and the man's retreat, released her grip, giving up the fight. She turned to focus her attention on Brad, with worried whines and warm licks to his face. Stunned, Brad could only watch the staggering accomplice reach his truck with the limp body of his buddy in tow. Charlie, satisfied with his job, relinquished his hold and, responding to Bridgette's bark, abandoned the mutilated attackers. He bounded back into the barn to check on his lifelong friend.

Lying in the darkness, Brad heard a diesel motor fire up. Years of barroom fights with his dad and uncles had trained him well as he overcame the desire to surrender to oblivion. As Charlie and Bridgette sat, intently observing his movements, he reached up and wrapped his arms around both dogs.

"Charlie, you old dog, you picked yourself a good woman. She's a keeper." He buried his face deep in their fur, thanking the universe for these two loyal friends. They squirmed in delight and covered his face with slobbering kisses. He gathered up his beaten body and, using his last reserve of energy, he stood up. Excruciating pain and light flashes competed with darkness as the two energies fought for dominance inside his head, but he refused to surrender. He punched in numbers on his cell phone as he began searching the scene.

"Brad here. Get CSI over to my place. Now!" He slammed the flip phone shut and his body jerked from a stabbing jolt of pain when his hand rubbed the bulge on his head. The long day had just become longer.

Chapter Fifteen

"Back it right in here, Cal." The smudge from the semi's smokestack spewed into the early morning's clean air. The transmission squealed when the bearded trucker with the Chicago Bears cap stripped the gears, and shoved the diesel in reverse. Six wheels crept slowly backward, bringing the transport within inches of the body shop's only empty bay. The din of screeching metal and rat-a-tat of air guns forced the workers inside to shout to one another.

Pit Bull waited for Cal to kill the engine. "How many have you got?"

"Only two, boss. The other two got held up on the barge at the locks in Granite City. We got word the Feds were sniffin' around so we held 'em back. I'll have 'em here next week."

"Goddamn Feds. I had it that the river was clear. You can bet I'll have a word or two with that Feeb. He better get his story straight or he's gonna lose his side job. Get these unloaded. I got two for you."

When the trucker yanked the semi's roll-up door, it reeled overhead with a loud clatter, competing with the racket inside. In less than twenty minutes, two cars backed down out of the trailer and sandwiched into the bay, while two others crawled up the ramp. Cal pulled at the roll-up door, slammed it down, and locked it.

In his office, Pit Bull filed the trucker's paperwork that listed two vehicles in need of repair. The semi would transport the two redesigned vehicles with new VINs to the abandoned barn on old man Crosby's farm. There, two drivers would drive them to Chicago for distribution. Pit Bull unlocked the safe. Filling the opening, a framed photo of him and his mother at the state fair smiled up at him. He gingerly set the photo to one side and removed two brown paper bundles, stuffing the packets into an envelope. He handed it to the driver who stood in the doorway.

"Good job. Timmie'll be waiting for you at Crosby's barn." Pit Bull scratched the head of his dog, which stood alert by his side with an intense, unwavering stare focused on the truck driver. One wrong move and the dog's jaws would be locked on Cal's greasy throat.

After the driver left, Pit Bull reviewed the week's figures. The Honda Civic and the Escalade Cal just hauled to Crosby's barn would bring over eighty thousand dollars in Chicago, while the Camry and Dodge that just arrived would be chopped and parted out for an equal take. The car business was good, but drugs were a close second. *The car business has been the most profitable, but I love the drugs and what they could do for a fella*. He laughed. The drugs were a personal venture.

He considered how sophisticated the date-rape drugs had become since the Mickey Finns of the fifties and sixties. In the beginning, he and his buddy scraped together twelve hundred dollars to set up a front. In high school, they got their business off the ground selling to friends, the kids at the skating rink, and the cruisers at the Top's Big Boy parking lot. He remembered how his buddy had become careless with the deliveries and lost some of the product, forcing Pit Bull to "let him go." Other more experienced dealers reassured him a ten-percent loss was to be expected. "Not in mine," he told them. He had big dreams back then.

He laced his fingers together behind his head and leaned back in his chair. He recalled how badly he wanted to leave home as a teenager and take his mom with him. He was going to buy her a big house, everything, so she would leave his dad. He knew he could love her enough so she wouldn't want the cheating, beating, no-good son of a bitch. But that never happened. No matter how badly Dad beat her, even when the abuse was dealt to Pit Bull, his mom always made excuses for the sorry son of a bitch. No matter how long the lowlife stayed gone, she always took him back. Pit Bull squeezed his eyes shut; his mouth turned down. The thought of his dad, the sweetest of the sweet talkers, put a vise grip on his stomach. The drama that played out at home when he came home from school played out in his head. There was a fifty-percent chance he would walk in on the fighting, screaming, and crying. He hated the exhibitions but the action excited him. He studied his dad as he wielded his power, forcing his mom to surrender her will.

Business boomed as he transported one to two million in product and cash without losing a nickel bag. The high stress of the business led to his love for the roofies. He smiled. A bitch on roofies made his blood pound. He laughed, thinking of the first time he spiked a Coke. He had great memories of that night with Judy. His loins throbbed as he craved a repeat performance.

After he had his way with her that night, he stood outside in the shadows and watched Judy fumble with the swinging glass door. He recalled how the music and voices bottled within the building's walls spilled out into the cold air as she struggled to pull the door open. The loud discord was smothered when the door swung shut and pushed her inside. The scene through the glass showed Judy's friend, Jackie, glide, spin, and come to a stop by her side. Their backs to him, the girls talked. He compared the two. The rush he felt from what he had done to Judy was like starring in his own porn film. He wondered if he could lure Judy back outside again but decided he best not push his luck. But watching Judy's girlfriend, Jackie, taller, blonde hair hanging loose down her back, caused his mind and blood to race as he imagined the fantasies she could fulfill.

He had never done anything like that before Judy. Oh, sure, he'd had girls before, but this had been the ultimate pleasure. He hated sweet-talking a cunt into submission. Bitches were so predictable. Again, he thought of his mother.

But this, what he had done to Judy, stirred him with an addicting ecstasy. It would be difficult to wait for another opportunity. That night, as he hid in the shadows, he made the decision that his second time with Judy, there would be no holding back.

He had wondered what the girls talked about, worried the drug might not have performed as the dealer promised, that Judy might have been remembering. Nervousness nagged him to leave, but he forced himself to stay and read the girls' body language. His concerns decreased when Jackie skated off, waving in a relaxed fashion. The bitches were clueless. If they knew the scheme he plotted, they would be running for their mommas.

The first time was said to be the best, but if he ever got the chance with Judy again, even after all these years, he vowed he would do it better and longer. Her friend Jackie had been another ecstasy he would never forget. Doing Judy's friend until there had been nothing left of her had been a first as well. He chuckled. There wouldn't be any chance for do-overs with her.

He should have grabbed Judy when she was in town for her mom's funeral. Over the years other girls had kept him sated, but maybe your first time is the best because he never stopped wanting Judy. His spirits lifted as he remembered the reunion. My second chance will be coming to the reunion.

He pushed his chair from his desk. His dog, Magnum, jumped to its feet. The mastiff carried a bodybuilder's stature but moved with agility. Pit Bull reached down, pulled the dog's boxy head to his face, and kissed its forehead. The dog's rear end swayed back and forth in pleasure.

"I got you a breakfast burrito." He reached into the McDonald's bag and unwrapped the still-warm sandwich while Magnum watched intently. Pinching off a hunk, Pit bull held it before the dog as it obediently sat upon its haunches, paws crossed, waving in the air like a poodle begging for a bonbon. The bone-crushing jaws barely opened as the dog's lips gently took the morsel from Pit Bull's fingers. He laughed out loud. "Magnum, you act like one of those frou-frou dogs. What am I gonna do with you?" He bent down and wrapped his thick arms around the dog's neck as the dog chewed playfully on his ear. Pit Bull dismissed the canine's advances, stood up, and stepped toward his office door. The mastiff moved quickly, blocked his advance, and again took its begging position on its haunches. A sharp kick sent the hundred-pound dog floundering and yelping in pain. "It's not cute anymore." Pit Bull exited the room. The dog gathered its balance, glared only a second with its tail high, hair on end, watching his master's back, then tucked his tail between his legs and scrambled to catch up.

The next day Pit Bull sat in a corner booth. The Sand Bar, nearly empty of biker patrons, served only two lone fishermen who nursed their icy drafts after their hot, humid stint on the river. Pit Bull sipped imported beer kept in reserve for his pleasure. The coolness slid smoothly down his parched throat.

He too had spent the afternoon fishing on the Sangamon River. Earlier Timmie had arrived in the bass boat from up river. The boy fronted as a fishing buddy, his job maneuvering the boat through shallow waters and baiting hooks. At midday, they nosed toward a secluded crook in the river. Timmie cranked the outboard down to a sputtering, easing it into the stagnant cove. As they passed, dragonflies and a cloud of mosquitoes rose from the mirrored surface, stirring the humid air. Timmie killed the motor, allowing the reclusive atmosphere to pervade.

"Let's see if everything's here." Pit Bull handed over his state-of-the-art fly rod, the reel copied from Formula One race-car braking systems. He reached under the bench seat, released a hidden latch, and exposed a hidden compartment to the dappled sunlight.

Fifty brick-sized paper packages filled the space under the seat. The boat's design gave the illusion of sitting high in the water, disguising its heavy load of drugs. Pit Bull inventoried the shipment. "Looks like everything's here. You did good, Timmie." Lowering the seat, he fastened the latch.

"Thanks, boss."

The drug lord watched his runner take a deep breath and pull up his sweatshirt to wipe the sweat beading on his forehead. Pit Bull liked to see him sweat.

"Let's go. Stop at the Sand Bar."

With a fast yank to the pulley, Timmie commanded the engine back to life. A flock of crows clamored from the cypress, the thunderous sound of their wings matching the roar of horsepower. Timmie twisted his wrist, gave full throttle, and, in spite of its heavy load, the boat raised its nose to the sky, did a water wheelie, and Pit Bull leaned back as the boat surged down the river and cut a path around the bend. When they reached the Sand Bar, Timmie waited in the boat while the drug lord cooled off inside.

In the booth, Pit Bull savored the cool draft while his mind labored over the girl in the hospital. Out on the river, he had warned his runner. "Dammit, Timmie, you gotta be more careful. You've used up your get-out-of-jail-free tickets from me."

"Don't worry, boss," Timmie had assured him. "She was out of it. You woulda wanted some of that. She was ripe for it. It's too bad I had to share with the others."

"My sources say there's video from the parking garage. When will you young punks learn to be more careful?" It angered him that the kid could be so casual. *We'll see how casual he is when I don't come to his rescue.*

Pit Bull thought the runner should know better, but Timmie was young and his hormones had taken control. Hell, Pit Bull understood. His own urges still demanded release on a regular basis. When he was Timmie's age, nothing got in his way, but he was always careful. Timmie couldn't afford any more mistakes. Twice the kid squeezed through the system, arrested once for drug charges and another for rape. Both times an expert lawyer and a little witness persuasion from Pit Bull's boys got Timmie off. *I can't afford any more of Timmie's mistakes.*

Pit Bull tossed back his fourth ale, gathered up his Gore-Tex vest, and made his way back outside to the dock where Timmie waited. When Pit Bull climbed back into the unpretentious boat, Timmie again gave a forceful yank. The boat surged from the dock, leaving a deep channel of displaced water.

They steered the boat up to a weathered dock hidden by cattails and poison ivy, and disappeared into a large boathouse. Minutes later, they reappeared, loaded with coolers, tackle boxes, two catfish, and three bluegill all caught with night crawlers. As they ambled up an obscured path to their vehicles, they laughed about a raccoon they'd seen upriver that had seemed to wave as they passed. At their vehicles, Timmie raised his hand in a high five. "Later." Pit Bull shifted his belongings and returned the salute.

"You better hope later. You better hope the Chief got the message I delivered in his barn. And you better hope that cunt don't remember anything. I'm not your mama. I didn't take you to raise."

"It'll be fine. Like I said, the bitch was out of it. And Brad's probably smellin' manure and lookin' for a light at the pearly gates."

Timmie laughed too easily, Pit Bull thought. He watched the kid climb into his white van and waited until it reached the road. Only then did he turn, throw his gear into the truck's bed, and climb in. His men hadn't reported in after delivering "the message." His eye twitched as he felt a haunting feeling, like when the sky changes from gray to black and becomes as still as death. Before a tornado.

Every time he headed down the long drive leading to his bungalow, he felt powerful and safe. He had made it through another day. The excitement, intrigue, and challenge of his lifestyle were invigorating but as he aged, it took its toll. At this secluded place, he could unwind. The wide, screened porch of his cottage faced the river. Sunsets often painted the water with a fiery glow.

He dropped his gear next to the chaise longue on the porch and stepped into the kitchen. He noticed his wife's eyes darted up without her head turning. She hunched over, focusing on the tomato she sliced. A surge of power quickened his heartbeat every time his wife shrank when he entered a room. "What's for dinner?" She fussed nervously, head down, concentrating on her chore.

"Did you catch anything?" He saw her eyes jerk from her chopping board to catch his movement.

"Yeah, but I gave them to Timmie. His mom wanted them for dinner tonight."

"Oh, well, I can take some catfish from the freezer. We'll have that and a salad."

"A salad! You know I don't like rabbit food! I need something more than that. You never want to put in any effort. Just slap something together. I'm sick of your shit." He paced the small kitchen, enjoying her fear. Aroused, he watched her hunker over the sink. In one stride, he grabbed her arm. She dropped the knife and turned.

"I can fix something else. What would you like?" She begged now. He loved it.

"Why don't you do something with your hair?" He twisted some of her locks in his fingers as she reached up to push his hand away. "Don't push me away!" His pulse raced. He shoved her up against the sink. He felt her body tremble and she began to cry.

Expertly he changed gears. "Oh, I'm sorry, honey, but you always piss me off. When are you ever gonna learn how to treat a man? I just had a bad day."

She turned back and stayed huddled over the counter, crying quietly. Hadn't he told her tears enraged him more? He moved in close, smelling his own beer breath as he blew it hot on her neck. He wrapped sweaty arms around her. She stiffly turned back into him. He knew she wouldn't refuse him. He led her outside to the chaise longue because he liked the risk of being seen. He pulled her housedress up and took her quickly and roughly. As he pounded away unmercifully, he said, "I'm your bad boy, aren't I?"

She answered predictably. "Yes. What are you going to do to me, bad boy? Give it to me, bad boy." She squeezed her eyes shut. He knew she did it to block out the pain he inflicted and that excited him more. When he was done, he laughed, got up, and with everything exposed, walked into the house. In thirty minutes he was showered, doused with Old Spice, and sat in front of the TV watching the news while she rattled around in the kitchen making dinner.

On the other side of town, Timmie greeted his mom with a kiss and a hug as he entered the kitchen. Showing his catch, he watched her face light up.

"Oh, wonderful! You are such a good boy. I'll clean these and get them fried up. We'll have them with some cornbread and home fries. Oh, it'll be so good!" Timmie loved his mother and would do anything for her. Long ago he gave up bringing home girls. But its okay, he reasoned. *Mom always sees the girls for the whores they are and reminds me they would only be in the way.*

"They would never love you or take care of you like I do. And besides, I need you. Since your father left, you're all I have."

They sat down to the meal laid out on his grandmother's starched-lace tablecloth over a mahogany dining table. Vintage yellow napkins edged with satin ribbon lay neatly beside crystal goblets of ice water. Sweat droplets squiggled down their stems. A silver serving fork lay next to the platter of fish. Dinner was always proper and pompous.

A crashing explosion of bodies in blue burst through the front door. Timmie jumped up, sending the high-backed chair hurtling into the yellow-rose wallpaper. He was reaching into his boot for his gun as the room filled with a mob of uniforms. Eight cops, guns drawn, stood frozen, encircling the dining room table. "*FREEZE*" Timmie, accustomed to the procedure, canceled his reach into his boot and dropped spread-eagled to the parquet oak floor.

His mother, in contrast, rose from her chair in one graceful movement and said, "Hear, hear, gentlemen! What's the fuss? You've frightened Timmie. There's nothing to be alarmed about. Why don't you sit down and have some dinner?" Confusion flicked across a couple of the rookies' faces, but the veteran officers remained tense and alert while one held his shotgun high and kicked Timmie in the ribs.

"Put your hands behind your back and spread 'em wider!" Timmie knew the drill. He spread his legs wide and clasped his hands behind his back. With one hand, the cop expertly snapped on the cuffs. He grabbed the perp's arms and yanked him onto his feet. Another officer holstered his weapon and began to pat Timmie down, retrieving an automatic from his boot and marijuana from his pockets.

The remaining cops watched in amazement. Timmie's mother busily set more places at the table. She placed each silver spoon—soup and teaspoon both—upon a napkin, oblivious to her son's predicament. "Everything'll be ready in a minute, boys. You just have a seat." Everyone exchanged questioning looks.

"It's okay, Mom. They don't have time to stay for dinner. We're going to go out for a while. I'll be back later."

"You're not going to be back for a long time if we have anything to do with it. This time you're going down," Ken McCourt said. He was Brad's top detective. "The girl in the hospital didn't remember anything, but the cameras in the garage took a pretty picture. We'll send one to your mom."

Timmie lunged at Ken even though cuffed, and another cop punched him in the gut. The drug runner doubled over but didn't collapse.

"Boys! Boys! Let's not fight!" His mother wrung her hands together.

"Let's go." The same cop jerked Timmie's arm, spinning him around toward the front door. "You have the right to remain silent..."

Two officers shoved him into the backseat of Ken's squad car, one of four units. With lights flashing, the vehicles reached the end of the drive as three unmarked cars pulled in. Car doors sprang open and plainclothes detectives spilled out, swarming the premises.

Chapter Sixteen

As I left Tucumcari, the sun crawled over the horizon and chased last night's blackness away, filling the sky's dome with brilliant blue. A contented expression on Cowboy Jack's fabric face proved he enjoyed the scenery. Sportster, who never had issues slept at his station on the dash. I settled into the doldrums of the day, sipped coffee, and thought of the road behind me and the road ahead.

There were still moments when the memory of my late husband burned raw. Our song, or the scent of him...where it came from after two years, I didn't know. The ache fluttered in my heart, not all-consuming as it had been, but a twinge of sweet memories and yearnings for the comfort of our long friendship. How could I ever expect to find anything like that again? We could say nothing for hours on a trip like this, and that said everything.

Endless miles of landscape passed my window and I came upon the Texas state line. A rugged Texas Ranger smiled as I pulled up to the kiosk. "Where ya headed, ma'am?" His deep brown eyes focused on Cowboy Jack.

"I'm headed for a high school reunion in Springfield, Illinois. He's my date." I tipped my head to Cowboy Jack. "But he doesn't have any papers."

The ranger's eyes twinkled as he laughed. "Well, ma'am, then we're gonna have ta haul him in." Still laughing, he stepped back and motioned for me to drive through. "Have a great time at your reunion." His eyes fixed on me and then Cowboy Jack. "Y'all drive safely now." He touched the brim of his Stetson as I entered Texas.

And what if I met someone like that ranger? I dismissed the question as quickly as it had arisen, realizing the man was in his thirties or forties. As I recalled the reflection in the mirror from this morning, that age bracket passed me by twenty years ago. My jawline sagged and my neck stretched like a turtle's, as it reached into my blouse's dipping neckline that was designed to imply robust cleavage. The Texas Ranger type would never be putting his boots under my bed.

And what if I aroused the fancy of someone my age? Then what? Someone my age could have health issues. Did I want to take on the role of nurse again? I couldn't imagine caring about someone enough to do that. And there were compromises in a relationship. Was I willing to make them? Did I want to cook for him? Do his laundry? Did we watch his shows or mine? If he didn't like traveling...I won't give this up. Would he be a cat lover? Love me, love my Sportster. And would I have to put my husband's memory away in a box? I didn't think I could do that. I wouldn't do that. I'd hidden too many feelings in the past. There wouldn't be any more secrets, no holding back.

As the miles added up on the odometer, so did the reasons for remaining alone. I sighed in resignation and returned my attention to the road and Route 66.

I was approaching Groom, Texas. The landscape leveled out from gentle rolling hills into flatlands. I spotted the Leaning Water Tower, built intentionally with a tilt to attract attention to the Britten Truck Stop that now was only an outline in the sand. A skeleton of a sign stood with only a few of its neon letters that survived the Texas wind and weather. The bones of the advertisement reminded me of Pat Sajak's TV game show, *Wheel of Fortune*. I picked a vowel and one consonant and guessed "restaurant."

In McLean, Texas, I pulled in to a restored Phillips 66 gas station to relieve and stretch my tired muscles. I had read that the Phillips Company had tested its new grade of gasoline in 1927 on Route 66. The test cars sped along at sixty-six miles per hour, so they named the fuel Phillips 66. After a brief respite, refreshed and wide awake, I settled back into the saddle for more of the Texas Panhandle.

Other remains of Route 66 strained to survive along the roadside. The Rattlesnakes sign from the Mother Road's heyday had not given up its attempt to lure travelers into shops that were now only dust in the wind.

In contrast, when I arrived in Shamrock, the Tower Conoco gas station and the U-Drop Inn Restaurant, once the "swankiest of the swank eating places" on Rte. 66, were now a historical landmark and the inspiration for Ramone's body shop in Disney's movie, *Cars*. I cruised on down "life's highway" and crossed the state line into Oklahoma without incident or a state ranger.

The next hundred miles ticked and clicked with the rhythm of the asphalt cracks and the dishes' rattle in the cabinets while my country music played softly. I recalled when I left for California and how I resented the decision I had been forced to make. My motivation to leave had not been born from the natural flow of life, but compelled by the ugliness of my tragedy, an event that could not be revealed in the age of innocence I lived. Women stayed home, men were men and did manly things, and if a woman's character was compromised, it was usually her fault.

As the Oklahoma wheat fields waved me by, I questioned: So, what am I looking for? I felt the loss while I reviewed my memories. My parents were gone. My husband was gone.

Could I capture what I lost? They say you can't go home again. I was not that sixteen-year-old girl. Time and life's experiences had matured me. Maybe?

Although I suffered nightmares and anxiety at unexplainable moments, I felt this old book called me, with all its dog-eared corners, tears, and broken spine, would not surrender or turn tail in defeat, if put to the test. I hoped I was someone not to be crossed. Sighing, I decided I was tired of examining and laboring over the past and the future. I was missing Oklahoma as it scrolled past my windshield.

A sign announced a KOA campground when I approached El Reno, Oklahoma. It had been yet another long day and I was ready to call an end to this day's journey. The campground's inviting billboard advertised its restaurant featuring buffalo burgers. Before heading to the campground, I stopped for gas and my body protested as I climbed out of the motor home. I had sat too long. A long walk would stretch my tired, travel-sore muscles when I got settled. For now I purchased hot coffee to spike my energy.

Efficient and full of information about the area, the young girl at the registration desk mentioned Fort Reno as a "must-see," and pointed out that Tahlequah, Oklahoma, to the east was the capital of the Cherokee Nation. "And if you are up for a walk, there's the Cherokee Trading Post just down the street. Don't forget to see our hundred-and-fifty-foot mural depicting the Trail of Tears. It's amazing and was painted by a local Cherokee artist."

"A walk's just what I had in mind. I've been driving all day."

"We also have paddleboats on the pond. That's always fun in the evening as it cools down. Oh yes, don't forget to check out the buffalo in the pasture. You know, in the day, thousands of buffalo roamed this area? El Reno was not only on Route 66, but the Chisholm Trail crossed here as well. Here's a couple of brochures on the history and landmarks in the area."

I watched as she circled my campsite space on the map and quickly marked the route from the office to my spot. She gathered up the brochures, the map, and my receipt, and handed them over with a welcoming smile. "Have a great stay with us."

At my site, Sportster woke from his long day's nap, ready to blaze his own trail of discovery in "the wild." I set him outside to start his adventure while I performed the ritual of plugging in and hooking up. In less than thirty minutes, I had fresh coffee brewed and was stretched out wearily in my recliner. I sighed, listening to giggles, shouts, and playful splashes from the children in the paddleboats. The aroma of burgers barbecuing rumbled my stomach. Stiffly, I pulled myself out of my lounge chair and gathered up Sportster, who was not eager to detour from his trailblazing. I set him safely inside and began my walk, my aching body crying its own petty tears in protest.

The Cherokee Trading Post and Restaurant occupied an entire block. The inventory included everything from moccasins to raccoon hats and home décor to Western saddles. I drooled over the Black Hills Gold jewelry, but resisted temptation and headed for the fort.

The Fort Reno museum housed albums of German POW letters and was crowded with images and artifacts, the most inspiring a painting of a horse named Black Jack. The oil, titled *The Riderless Horse*, was by the famed artist Frederic Remington. In history, a riderless horse represented the warrior who would ride no more. This particular horse, Black Jack, named by General Pershing, served in his army. The steed had ridden in the funerals of Hoover, John F. Kennedy, and Lyndon Johnson, and was buried at Fort Meyers, adjacent to the Arlington National Cemetery in Virginia. Black Jack lies in state with full military honors, only one of two military horses to ever be given that honor. I made a must-see note to visit the horse's gravesite in Arlington. I left the museum in a humble mood, ready to view the Trail of Tears mural.

Oklahoma's past claimed its own sadness, the Trail of Tears. In 1838, over fifteen thousand Indians had been forced at gunpoint to relocate from Georgia, Tennessee, and other southern territories to the Indian Territory of Oklahoma. On the march, eight thousand died from starvation, exposure, and disease. It was here at El Reno that the legendary death march ended for the Cherokee—if they had not succumbed along the two-thousand-mile torturous trek. The mural depicted the Cherokee crossing a river, some on hands and knees, while the military, mounted on proud steeds, overlooked them on the bank. An Indian chief stood just as proudly on the opposite bank. A particular section of the mural touched me. It portrayed an Indian standing, his back to me, arms raised, chanting to the heavens where an eagle soared.

After dinner, I strolled along the path to my site and reviewed the day's images: *The Riderless Horse*, the Trail of Tears, Route 66, my parents, and my late husband. There is a season for everything. And I recalled a Lakota warrior's words when asked, "Where are your lands?" The Indian had answered, "My lands are where my dead lie buried."

Chapter Seventeen

Thursday afternoon, I pulled into Mr. Lincoln's campground. I made it! Over two thousand miles. Stressing over whether to do this or not was now moot. I had arrived. Too late to turn back.

Setting the parking brake, I patted Sportster's head and climbed out of the cab, slow with weariness. Humidity drenched my T-shirt before I reached the office door. With quickened steps, I escaped the heat's fingers tightening around my chest and entered the ice-cold environment inside.

The woman behind the counter glanced up when she heard the musical tinkle of bells hanging from the door's push bar. Her entire aura lit up with a homegrown Midwestern smile that spread across her round face framed by gray curls. I heard angels singing and harps strumming but assumed it was my imagination.

"Good afternoon." The woman's voice was accompanied by a heaven-like melody floating from a back room marked PRIVATE.

"Good afternoon." I made a feeble attempt to match her welcoming smile, but here, so close to my past, my familiar sense of foreboding became stronger. My skin prickled, and as I took a deep breath, an involuntary shiver grabbed me. My dark mood, like a specter, took its stand to compete with this woman's angelic quality. "Hello, I have reservations."

"Are you Judy?"

"Yes."

Her finger traced a line in her reservation book. "Oh, there you are." She looked up. "What brings you to Springfield?"

"My fortieth high school reunion."

"At Springfield High?"

"Yes. The Class of '65."

"Oh, I'm going to that reunion, too!" I didn't know how she could have lit up any more brightly, but she did. "What was your maiden name? Mine was Coburn. Now it's Alice Deerbourn. "

"Mine was Dietz. Judy Dietz."

She studied me. "I don't remember that name. What clubs did you belong to?"

"None, really. I wasn't much of a joiner." I began to feel inadequate.

She noticed my discomfort and glanced down at her book again to check my reservation information. "Wow, you've come from California? How was the trip? You came all that way by yourself?" She gazed out the window then back at me with a questioning look.

"Oh, he isn't real, but he's a good traveling partner. That's Cowboy Jack." I laughed at her surprise. She approached the window for a closer look.

"Well, I'll be! Don't that just beat all? I can't wait to tell Bob. He'll get a kick out of that."

Recognition clicked in when I heard her husband's name. "Bob Deerbourn?"

"Yes. Did you know him?"

"I think so. Didn't he go to Lanphier High?"

"Yes! Yes, he did!" She was delighted that we had finally made a connection. Bob Deerbourn had been Brad's best friend, even though they attended different schools. Their parents ran neighboring farms, and the two boys shared a love for fast, hot cars, much like their women. But observing Alice, Bob must have sown his wild oats, curbed his hormones, and settled down.

"Well, it's nice meeting you, Alice. It's nice to know Bob picked himself a very nice bride. I knew his best friend, Brad Jones."

"Actually I picked him, truth be told, and made it clear I knew what was best for him." She laughed at her own joke and her entire body jiggled. "We'll be celebrating our fortieth anniversary next year. I can't wait to tell him about you. Are you going to look up Brad before the reunion? Bob and Brad both work for the city, you know? Brad's with the Springfield Police Department. He's Chief of Police, and my Bob is our district attorney."

"I know. It's so hard to believe. They were both so wild in high school. And yes, I plan on calling Brad as soon as I get settled. He's the one who invited me to the reunion."

"You know," she lowered her voice, leaning in closer, pausing for effect. The music hung in the air. "He never married. He ran wild for a year or so longer after Bob and I hitched up. I always felt something happened to him back then. My guess? Somebody broke his heart." She paused, looked carefully at me. When I didn't respond, she took a breath and continued, "But then he had it rough with his dad and all. His dad died a year or so after he graduated and his mom a few years after. Brad still oversees the farm but he's so busy being the chief and all. Oh, listen to me, rambling on." She smoothed her blouse with her hands and pushed up her sleeves. "Let me get you checked in. I'm sure you're tuckered and can't wait to stretch out and rest a bit, but we're all going to have to get together for dinner."

"That sounds like a plan. I promised Brad I would call when I got in. We'll definitely get together." We finished our paperwork. I couldn't wait to get settled. I looked forward to a week or more of not driving.

Bidding Alice good-bye, I stepped out into the sweltering air. Sportster watched my approach while Cowboy Jack surveyed his surroundings. The RV Park was situated on the Sangamon River. The registration office, a cabin, was also Alice and Bob's living quarters, and looked out upon a small dock with two aluminum fishing boats tied to weather-worn posts whitewashed by bird droppings. The scene was a Midwestern version of a California coastal campground. Pigeons replaced seagulls.

The sun, low on the horizon, sent rays skipping over the water, leaving a pattern of golden ripples on the blue-green surface. The light illuminated silver dragonfly wings as the gossamer insects darted along the river's edge. The elm and maple trees' green hues were sprinkled with yellows and crimsons, evidence they were preparing for the cold winter months. Shouldering cane fishing poles, a father and his two sons paraded from the dock. The tall-est boy, about ten, walked ahead but backward to face his father, proudly holding up a string of catfish. Eagerness was in his step as his excited words carried in the breeze. "Can I gut these and clean 'em, Dad?" The magical atmosphere of the place contrasted with my doomsday mood.

The Wizard of Winnebago roared to life and I crept down the paved road until I reached my site and pulled through. Forty-five minutes later I was set up, had called the car rental company, and was relaxing in my chair while Sportster inves-tigated his new surroundings. Sipping on a Pepsi, I held my cell phone, took a long deep breath, and tried to find my vanished courage. It was showdown. I looked at my palm holding the cell phone. It sweated, but not from the sum-mer's humidity. I asked myself one last time: Why did you come here?

Two thousand miles had allowed me time to worry and twist my eagerness and hope into dread and fear. My fingers hovered over the dial.

My mind leaped back into my childhood bedroom, where I wrestled with the decision to run away from the rape, the abortion, and Brad. Behind my bedroom's closed door, I had concluded I was used-up, damaged material.

On this journey, in the confines of my Winnebago woman cave, I convinced myself forty years had taken its own indiscriminate toll, leaving me used up and damaged. I was fifty-seven and on the downhill side of love and romance.

I wanted to cry, I wanted to give up. *But you've come so far.* I sat up straight and inhaled deeply. I was not going to turn tail and run again. I steeled myself, promising I would not be disappointed. I would not expect more than two friends catching up on old times. I wanted nothing more. Right?

I tapped in the numbers. He answered on the first ring. I asked, "May I speak to Brad Jones?"

"Hello, Judy." I sucked in air. How did he know it was me? "You've made it safe and sound? How was your trip?"

My mind went blank. His words came in a rush. Was he just being nice? Was he in a hurry, trying to brush me off?

He was still talking. "Did you run into any problems?" I exhaled so hard I was sure he heard.

"The trip went well except for a few incidents. I'll have to tell you all about it. I'm staying at the Lincoln RV Park and I've met Bob's wife, Alice. And now I have gotten the whole scoop on you, Brad." I struggled to make my voice sound lighthearted but instead it squeaked.

"We have a lot of years to catch up on. What about dinner?"

Still tongue-tied, I was slow to respond. I took a breath to answer.

"How about Saturday night?" Was he nervous? He talked so fast. Maybe he rethought his intentions and regretted inviting me. He probably wanted to get this over with.

"That sounds great. Alice and Bob said they'd like to get together, too. They suggested the Pizza Machine Company." *He'll be more comfortable if he doesn't have to be alone with me.*

"I'll pick you up at five?"

"Sure. I'll tell Alice." I flipped my phone close, staring at it as if it were an alien substance.

I sat a long time, afraid to move, afraid to alter the moment. *I'm happy, right? Should I dare be excited?* Dinner with Brad. I continued to wrestle with the loose ends in my mind. The longer I twisted and turned the threads, the more entangled my thoughts became.

Brad had never married. He was Chief of Police and sober. Alice beamed when she talked about Bob and Brad. They both scaled the ladder of success and maturity and were respected community members. My life was not insignificant, but Brad's status intimidated me. Surely there were women in his life. He certainly had his pick in high school. I refused to question Alice because I didn't want to appear interested. Because I wasn't. Was I? Hadn't I gone over this issue for two thousand miles? For forty years?

Over the years, I softened the difficult times with my memories of Brad and me at the state fair or snuggled by the lake in his '57 Chevy. No one stirred emotions within me as he did. I loved my late husband but it had not been young and innocent love. In the light of maturity, I reasoned my feelings for Brad were only quivers left from a lingering high school crush, an infatuation, a romance only for the young.

Pulling myself from my musings, I walked to the dock and watched the river's flow. A red leaf floated past on a lonely journey, its life nearly over.

I checked my watch. They were ten minutes late delivering the rental car. I heard the screech before I saw the outboard. With its rear buried in the water, its nose pointed skyward, the vessel sped past. I jumped back to avoid the river's spray from the silver bullet as it just missed drenching me. The boater's large frame was hunched over, filling the hull, and appeared not to have a neck. A purple cap perched on top of the thick head. I watched the boat navigate a wide sweeping arc and disappear into the reeds and shrubs.

Chapter Eighteen

Brad sat on the porch, feet on the railing, and performed the ritual of servicing his weapon. His fingers worked the cleaning rod back and forth into the barrel as his mind rewound the day's events. His thoughts wandered to Judy. They had talked only briefly when he called months ago to invite her to the reunion. His pulse quickened, anticipating her arrival. He was wondering how she'd fared over the years when his cell's vibrating buzz brought him back to the present. Her name appeared on the caller ID as if his thoughts caused her to materialize.

"Hi, Judy. You've made it. How was your trip? Did you run into any problems?" Slow down, he thought, there's plenty of time to catch up. He asked her to dinner and before she answered, he blundered on, "How about Saturday night?" He couldn't stop gushing. He hoped it didn't show in his voice. When the short conversation was over, Brad laid the phone down and stared at it.

He checked his watch. It was going to be another late night by the time he finished all the reports he brought home. He traced over the events of the day.

Brad and Ken entered the interrogation room. Both men, intimidating in size, read Timmie's fear when he twisted his body, refusing to look at the officers. Ken slammed the report onto the table, causing the perp to jump.

The hours dragged. Unending questions pounded at the drug runner's bravado and he began to fade. He swore, "We just drove around and dropped the girl back at the mall. We ain't done nothing wrong."

Ken paced the room. "The girl's been tested and we're just waiting the results. We all know what they'll show, don't we?" Again, the drug runner squirmed. His metal chair scraped the floor. "You know your buddies are telling an entirely different story? They're telling us your slogan is, 'I drug 'em, you plug 'em.' What a piece of work you are, Timmie. Maybe you should go into advertising."

"They're just makin' up shit. They wanna save their own asses." He acted surly but sweat wiggled down his temple.

"They're saving their own asses, all right." Ken leaned down, his face inches from Timmie's. "We've offered them a sweet deal and they're taking it. You want to get in on it? You take us to Pit Bull, and you only have to do a nickel with good behavior. Otherwise you're going away for a long, long time. It'll break your mother's heart."

Timmie lunged at Ken. His chair hung in the air behind him, linked to his cuffs. It dug into his wrists. The FBI man, McNalley, hung back in the corner, listening to Brad and Ken work the interrogation. Brad had allowed him to sit in but insisted it was SPD's case.

"Do you want to tell us about your trips out of town? It seems you've been wearing the asphalt out between here, New Orleans, Chicago, and all points in between."

"I got a big family."

"Where's all the money coming from? You don't make all that money rubbing wax on fenders at the body shop."

"I want to talk to my attorney."

"It seems he's not calling you back, doesn't it? Looks like Pit Bull's leaving you out to dry this time. I guess you screwed up once too often and he's taken you off the payroll." Ken's voice taunted, pushed, as Brad stepped up and lowered his voice to a softer, good-cop attitude.

"Look, we've got you in the crosshairs. You better take the deal. Your mom's going to need you. How's she going make it with you doing twenty-five to life?"

Timmie folded. He slumped over the table ringed with coffee stains. His shoulders shook as he sobbed. They had him. With no one to take care of his mom, Timmie knew they'd put her in the looney bin. And the kid knew Pit Bull had already signed his death warrant. There were no easy outs for the perp. Between sobs, he said, "What do you want to know?"

"It's not what we want to know, it's what we want you to do." Ken and Brad nodded at each other. "You're going to take us to Pit Bull." They studied Timmie, his head down on the table. They read each other's thoughts: "Dead man walking."

The drug runner's fear was justified. Brad threw him into a private cell with a round-the-clock guard. The perp could lead him to Pit Bull and he wasn't taking any chances. Back in his office, Brad paced as he studied reports.

The evidence recovered from the raid at Timmie's house included receipts and cell phone statements indicating regular trips and calls to Brownsville, Peoria, St. Louis, even New Orleans, and Chicago. Timmie was a busy man. Bank records showed unexplained deposits CSI was examining along with computer and other records. As Brad expected, the perp's career in crime reached out further than rape.

Brad's secretary entered quietly with a thick pile of folders. Her black skirt stopped just above her knees and was as snug as her blonde hair, which was tied firmly by a black bow at the base of her neck. Flawless skin free of laugh lines and age marks proved time had been kind. Her rimless glasses were invisible.

"Here are the prelims from CSI, Chief. I knew you'd want them right away. The lab reports on the DNA and the computer forensics are going to be a couple more weeks." He took the folders and, as his hand brushed hers, a comfortable smile traced her lips. He returned her gesture with a dutiful flicker of his own. "Thank you, Darlene. Let me know as soon as the other reports come in."

"Yes, Chief. And I just wanted to remind you of the governor's award dinner." Her fingers squeezed the pen she held. Brad knew she and everyone else expected him to be her escort.

"I didn't forget. What time should I pick you up?" He tried for a more gracious response and used his charming grin. He hated the obligations that went with the job.

"I'm sure seven would be acceptable. Don't forget, sir, it's black tie." She exhaled. His reassuring charisma released her uncertainty and she turned to leave.

"Thanks again, Darlene. I don't know what I'd do without you." She beamed with warmth at his kind words and, hugging herself, she returned to her desk, her heels clicking sharply.

Brad returned to examining the reports before her perfume followed her out the door. After forty years, he was going to close this case. Friday afternoon would be the showdown. Timmie and his public defender had accepted the deal. Pit Bull would be behind bars before the week's end.

Friday afternoon, the full force of the Springfield Police Department attended the squad meeting.

"So, is everyone clear about their position? I want this to happen." Brad was keyed up, every muscle taut. He had gone over every detail in the operation, covered every possible situation that could go wrong. Today Pit Bull was going down, his identity would be revealed, and justice would be done. Brad's eyes aimed at each officer, each detective, in the room.

His stare focused on Ken, who would be in the surveillance van monitoring and directing the entire undertaking. Ken looked ready. John, working undercover, would monitor the action in the bar. He, too, was tense with anticipation. McNalley, the FBI agent, stood quietly at the edge of the room. Clean-shaven, his poker face was like a mask with no features. Brad noticed none of his officers conversed with McNalley, but they were usually distant with the FBI. The Feeb would be posing as the bartender. Brad would be staked half a block away in an unmarked sedan ready to roll. The eyes of his men looked to him for leadership. The old-timers were pumped, supporting him with a do-or-die respect. The rookies hung back with a fearful reserve, but Brad knew they all read their chief correctly: primed and ready. And he was.

After examining the final SWAT member in the room, he said, "Okay, let's do this." He slapped his gloves to his thigh and donned his Stetson. The room came alive with scraping chair legs, loud talk, and back-pounding as the team gathered gear and moved toward the door. Brad stood aside as each exited, grasping a hand, shaking it firmly, and administering a solid slap on the shoulder.

"Watch your back," he said to the rookie who just started last week. "Hey, John, careful out there. Ken, see you tomorrow at the park? Got that old bucket of bolts ready for the show?" Ken nodded with a smile. Brad prayed all would go off without a hitch today, and tomorrow everyone would be alive to fulfill their plans.

By two thirty everything was staged. Timmie's nerves triggered a tic at the corner of his mouth as the tech wired him for sound. The drug runner put the word out he wanted a meet up with Pit Bull. The procedure was to wait at the bar, sit at the third stool from the back door, and read the menu—a signal for the messenger to deliver the instructions from Pit Bull.

Brad parked in an unmarked car while Ken, staked out with the special investigative team, waited in the cable service truck in front of the bar. Brad's breath came tight and quick as he checked his watch, willing the operation to run as planned. If it did, this forty-year-old drug investigation would be wrapped up, and he hoped it would give him personal closure. He admitted to no one how much it meant to put an end to Pit Bull. He wanted the kingpin from that day at age seventeen, when he sat in the doctor's office and watched Judy, innocent and scared. That day changed both of their lives. Who knows how it all would have unfolded if Pit Bull had not existed?

Timmie swung his short leg over the barstool and the FBI agent/bartender slid a napkin onto the counter.

"What'll it be?"

"Bud with a chaser. And have another lined up." Timmie figured the cops were footing the tab and he needed the fix desperately. No one crossed Pit Bull and lived to tell about it, but he had no choice. If he didn't snitch, he'd be facing twenty-five to life on the rape and battery charge of the bitch from the mall, and he knew he wouldn't survive going back to the joint. His small stature was no defense against the burly cons he'd have to play bitch to. He had to do this. He reached for the menu. As he opened it, a napkin fell out. The words THE SAND BAR were inked raggedly on the backside of the linen that had been tucked inside the menu. There would be no courier this time.

The Sand Bar was a dive and a favorite watering hole for bikers because it offered seclusion and the river provided a quick escape route if needed. Although the meeting place was never the same, he and Pit Bull had used the Sand Bar as a meet up many times. The ruse was to discuss a ripe deal on roofies. Pit Bull's greed and love for the drug guaranteed a meeting.

Timmie's hand shook as he slid the message under a fresh napkin, chugalugged the beer, then, anxious to finish the deal, jumped down from the stool, and hit the back door running. The bartender palmed the napkin, checked it quickly. No one heard his words, "Sand Bar," voiced into his earpiece. Outside, the drug runner yanked open the door to his van and hoisted himself up into the van. His body twisted, collapsed, and he laid his head to rest on the van's seat as the crack of a rifle reverberated off the buildings.

The pop from the rifle, followed by Timmie's contortion, spurred the surveillance team to burst forward like marathon runners reacting to the starter's gun. They scrambled over each other to reach the informant, but the small red pool soaking the van's seat signified the end of Timmie's short-lived informant career. His eyes were glazed open in a look of surprise. Inside, the bartender had already bagged the napkin, sending it on its way to the lab.

"It's the Sand Bar! Move!" The black and whites squealed as they scrambled to turn around and fly across town. Brad, with a three-minute lead, was the first to arrive.

At the Sand Bar, Pit Bull waited in the dark corner booth. He observed a biker snap his cell shut and nod. Pit Bull returned the gesture. The drug lord's lighter lit up a twitch of a grin as he took a long hit on the joint. He slid out of the bench seat, and his black boots clomped across the bar's warped floor that was singed with charred worms from cigarette butts. As he moved to the screened door, the barroom's life froze as if in video pause until he stepped out into the sunlight. When the screen door slammed shut, he heard the barroom patrons resume breathing.

Pit Bull strolled down to the river as if taking a walk in the park. At the dock, he climbed into a small aluminum boat and, with one powerful yank, commanded the engine to life. The Evinrude's high pitch resounded down the river, and the boat lurched as it sped away in chase of its own echo.

Before Pit Bull vanished around the bend, he heard a wail of sirens above the boat's screech. The boater noticed one squad car arrive, followed minutes later by five black and whites slamming to a stop in front of the bar, their lights flashing. The doors swung open, spilling out ten armed uniforms pumped full of adrenaline. He wondered if that first car sighted him and his purple hat as he vanished around the bend.

Chapter Nineteen

Friday morning, I gazed out the bedroom window and viewed the river's routine. Dragonflies darted in the daybreak. Last night's breeze had lain down and now warm sunlight refueled the wind. The air wafted up and gently rustled fall's pallet that was spread across the ground. Splotches of gold, green, and ginger scampered to the muddy banks and floated downstream on their last adventure of the season. Dirty cotton-ball clouds cast dark blemishes onto the river's moving current. Their shadows dabbed at the flickering light show from sunfish, like ballerinas, splashing, and performing grand-jetés as they lunged for dragonflies.

The clouds promised a rainy day and motivated me to dress and visit Dad before the storm began. Crawling out of bed, I made a quick call to my cousin John, leaving a message. I patted Sportster's head, ignored his attempt to make me feel guilty with his stare, and walked out the door.

As I drove across town, I passed the McDonald's where Jackie and I had eaten French fries that cost a dime, and Top's Big Boy drive-in restaurant, where we always ordered cheeseburgers from a car hop. I recalled Friday nights and friends cruising in their hot rods. They entered the Top's parking lot on South Grand Avenue, rumbled through, surveying who was hanging out, and exited on Fifth. The stream of teens then circled the block and proceeded again—in on South Grand, through the lot, and out on Fifth, over and over. Gas was cheap back then.

I passed another memory, the Den Chili Parlor, no larger than a catering wagon. Mom and Dad would send my sister and me bouncing inside. We'd watch the man ladle the best chili ever into a quart-sized paper cylinder. He'd slip the container into a brown paper bag and top it with a small sack of oyster crackers. In my mind, I smelled the aroma that spiked our appetites and filled the DeSoto on the drive home. Those were the days. Life was simple and food was just beginning to be fast.

At the house, I pulled into the cement drive with a strip of grass running down the middle. The bushes surrounding the front porch looked thirsty and overgrown. White paint blistered in the places the shrubs didn't protect. I eased down the full length of the drive and parked in front of the garage. In the backyard, dandelions waved their powder puffs above the browned-out yard. Across its expanse, autumn had sprinkled dirty, mustard-colored leaves from the bared elm. In the summer, the majestic tree shaded the glider swing that swayed with the help of the breeze. Now it waited for winter, stripped of its cushions.

I sat in the car for a moment and let my childhood scroll across my mind: lying in the grass on a warm summer day; picking out animals in the billowy clouds; collecting four, five, and even six leaf clovers; and scaling the red-dotted cherry tree. An empty nest now wedged in a fork of its naked limbs.

My tennis shoes crunched across the pebbled walkway that led to the back porch. I tapped on the screen door.

"Dad! Hey, Dad, it's me." Quiet. I pulled on the screen's handle. Its creak carried me back to summer nights when my sister and I sneaked back into the house with salt shakers in hand, after poaching tomatoes from our neighbors' gardens. Our eight-year-old giggles echoed in my mind as I remembered how the screen door complained, almost blowing our cover, as we scrambled into the mudroom. One night, concentrating on my stealth, I lost my footing, falling down the basement steps. I burst into screams of surprise and laughter, muffled by warning shushes from my sister. I made a mental note to ask if Dad had been aware of our escapades on those summer nights.

"Dad?" I made my way into the kitchen. My eyes went to the yellowed chip in the fifties plastic, green-marbled tile decorating the breakfast nook's wall. The dent, no larger than a pea, was forged from a fork flung in anger by my mother.

I stuck my head through the small pass-through window at the end of the kitchen and peered into the living room. Dad sat dozing in his chair, while the stereo cabinet hissed and clicked from a needle scraping an old seventy-eight record spinning on the round table. I smiled and entered the living room. Lifting the stereo's lid and the needle off the disc, I shut off the record player.

Dad's chalky hair, still full and thick, strayed across his forehead and covered an eyebrow. The newspaper had slipped from his lap and lay scattered on the carpet. As I took in the scene, it startled me. When had he grown so old?

"Dad?" I touched his shoulder, trying not to startle him. He opened his eyes slowly and looked up.

"Hello, Pumpkin. I must have dozed off." His smile renewed his face from the old one that had been sleeping, and hearing my nickname erased the years. "Did you just get in?"

"I got here yesterday. How are you?"

"Oh, I'm doing all right for an old man." He chuckled as he pushed back the lazy lock from his brow. Amazed at his limberness, I watched as he stooped down and picked up the strewn sheets of newspaper. "Let me fix you a cup of coffee. I just have to heat it up in the microwave." I followed him as he grabbed his cane and slowly made his way to the kitchen.

We sat at the table and caught up with family news. "Don't you get lonely, Dad? Mom's been gone almost forty years. I'd thought some woman would have snatched you up by now."

"I get along fine. But you remember the Pratts down the street? A few years ago I dated Helen after her husband passed. We kept company for a while, you know, dinner and bingo, that kind of thing. She began pressuring me to get married, but I just couldn't see it. I've never mentioned it 'cause it didn't mean anything. I still love your mom, I guess. Anyway, I'm all right. John comes once a week and checks on me. I can still drive. How about you? Anybody knocking on your door?"

"Oh, Dad. It hasn't been that long."

"Have you looked up Brad?" How did he know about me and Brad?

"What about Brad?" I feigned innocence as I twisted my napkin.

"Did you think you had the wool pulled over my and your mom's eyes? We knew Cupid was playing his love song for the two of you. It was just that we were concerned since he was living on the wild side. But look at him now. What happened between you two, anyway?"

"Oh, I guess when I went off to California, we just drifted apart. You know long-distance relationships usually don't work out."

"Are you going to see him? You know he never married?"

"Yes, Dad, I know. And yes, he's my date for the reunion."

"Well, hot diggity! It's about time, since you never made it to the prom. I never understood why you didn't go."

"It was a long time ago, Dad. It's not important any-more." I fussed with wiping an imaginary coffee spill on the table. "Have you ever thought about coming to California? At least for the winter? You could stay with me. Sandy would love to have you, too. We both worry about you."

"How about you coming here? There're dogs to groom here, too, you know. You wouldn't have to work that hard with my Social Security and retirement, and the house is paid off. You could do a grooming and dog training here. Why not? I'm too old for a change but you, you're still young. I sure have missed you, honey. You don't visit often and when you do, you're a whirlwind, here and gone, before I can even take a breath."

"Well, I don't see that happening, Dad. I have a business and house back home, and friends, and Sandy, too."

"Sandy has a husband. Why don't you think about it? I'm not getting any younger, you know." He threw the guilt card on the table. "Meanwhile, why don't you bring your RV over here? I have a thirty-amp plug from when your mom and I had our fifth wheel. There's even a sewer hookup. I really would like to spend more time with you."

"I could do that, Dad. I'm paid through Monday. I could move then." We chatted about Mom, and he admitted he knew about our tomato poaching. By noon the conversation had turned to food. "Get your shoes on, Dad, and we'll go get some chili. I can't go home without having Den's chili. We can get back here before it rains. What's left over you can have tomorrow."

The rest of the afternoon passed with us sitting in the breakfast nook, eating chili and watching a light rain drip off the sparse leaves that still clung to the elm. I headed back to the campground just as thunderclouds became serious in their intent. Streaked with jagged spikes of elec-tricity, they dumped a torrential flood onto the road. I hur-ried into my rig, clutching my small bowl of chili Dad insisted I take. Drenched, I quickly stripped and changed into sweats, ready to hunker down for the rest of the afternoon.

I spent the remainder of the day at the computer answering e-mails and paying bills. Like cloggers on the roof, the raindrops danced while Sportster curled in front of the electric space heater. Hours passed unnoticed until darkness interrupted and forced me to turn on the desk light and pull the curtains.

I settled back in front of my computer with a fresh cup of coffee just as Sportster jerked his head up in alert. He heard something outside. The solid pounding on the door made me jump as the cat sprung up on all fours, hair spiked from his neck to the tip of his tail. Reacting to his alarm and spooked from the storm and unpleasant memories, I stepped into the bedroom and retrieved my .38. With my arm folded, gun pointing up, I pressed my back up against the wall by the door. Leaning forward, I switched the porch light on with my free hand. I pulled the door's shade back only a crack. As the pounding began again, I asked, "Who is it?" The light flooded the outside, revealing a policeman. Still unsure, I held my breath and waited for an answer.

"It's me, John." I exhaled. The sound of his voice wiped away my tension. I dropped my arm, pointing the weapon to the floor, and flung open the door. John bounded into the motor home. My heart swelled with love as I looked him over. He never changed. Still lean, towering above me, the only one in my life who never let me push him away. He was smiling until his eyes surveyed my stance.

"Well, this is a nice welcome." His eyes focused on my gun. "Were you expecting someone else?" His expression turned to concern.

"No, not really. I guess I just got spooked." I stepped back into the bedroom and replaced the gun, embarrassed by my reaction.

"You've been spooked for forty years. You ever going to tell me about it?" I guess John was ready to tie up loose ends, too. "I've missed you, Judy. Everybody has." He leaned over and enclosed me in a long hug. His uniform smelled of rain and dry cleaning, mixed with the scent of the same hair gel he used forty years ago. A tear ran down my face and joined a rain blot on his blue uniform. The lone teardrop pulled a plug on a bucket of dammed-up emotions, and I lost control. A deluge of despair soaked his shoulder as I sobbed in the safety of his arms.

"Hey, it's okay." He squeezed me more tightly, rubbing and patting my back.

"I don't know what's wrong with me. What's wrong with me? I can't stop crying." Alarmed and embarrassed, I pulled out of his embrace and grabbed a tissue. I blew my nose. "It's just being in this town, the memories, seeing Dad, and you...and talking to Brad." I gulped between sobs. John listened and waited.

"I've been spooked for forty years. You should know what happened back then." I felt relieved, making the decision to finally disclose my secrets. "I should have told you way back then."

"It's okay, Judy. I know what happened. Brad told me."

"He did? You knew? He wasn't supposed to tell...anyone." I caught my breath. "How long have you known?"

"Since we joined the force. You get pretty close when you're partners. It was when we found Jackie. He broke down. He told me what happened to you. He said he knew it was all connected and swore out there in Crosby's cornfield he would avenge your rape and Jackie's murder. He scared me because I knew if he ever discovered who it was, the man's life wouldn't be worth zilch. To this day, I worry about what Brad will do."

"I always knew Brad felt he should have done more. But there was really nothing more he could have done. He did so much. I would not have made it without his help."

My sobs subsided to sniffles and I dabbed my nose. No more secrets. "Wow. Sorry about the outburst, but I do feel better. I don't know what came over me."

"It's always better when everything's on the table. Now how about a real hug?"

I laughed, leaned in, absorbing his tenderness. "So how're Kate and the kids? I can't wait to see them. You want coffee?"

"Everyone's great. I'll talk to Kate and we'll have you over for dinner. I've been doing double shifts at work. We're getting close to one of the biggest takedowns in the department. In fact, we think the guy's responsible for Jackie's death along with six other women. They call him Pit Bull. He's been dealing date-rape drugs for four decades."

I was reminded my rapist had never been caught. The brief relief sank, and I stretched the imaginary yellow tape back around me.

"Well, listen, I just got off a double shift. I gotta get some sleep. Kate will give you a call."

After John left, I double-locked the door, turned off the porch light, and laid the gun within easy reach.

Chapter Twenty

Brad drove his turquoise, '57 Chevy onto the grassy area and scanned the crowd that milled around. Bob, already parked, polished the hood of his '56 torch red T-Bird. He pointed to the space next to him. The Chevy eased into the spot with a low rumble and choked out its last breath when Brad cut the engine. With the motor shut off, the early morning hush settled back into Washington Park. Car enthusiasts ambled past, coffee in one hand, many with a cigarette in the other, unable to give up their '50s addiction. Gray beards and white hair were the rule while cowboy hats and baseball caps covered the absence of the latter.

Brad climbed out and approached Bob with a high five while his left hand applied a warm, firm grip to Bob's shoulder. They turned in unison, faced their cars, and admired the toys they had tinkered with since high school. The T-Bird had belonged to Bob's dad, while the '57 Chevy was Brad's first car and clocked more memories than miles.

The two friends ogled their prized possessions in silence until their attention was diverted by the rumble of a deep purple, '49 Mercury with dark tinted windows. It crept slowly across the grass and came to a stop, growling as it idled in front of them. With the driver hidden inside, the illusion to the observer was a ghost driver. They knew George, their high school buddy, sat in the driver's seat.

George owned a large, auto-body repair business. When business was slow, he tweaked and modified his Merc until it was one of the hottest cars in the county. He owned ten vintage cars, all in cherry condition. Today it was the Mercury's turn to show off. Bob directed George to park his purple beast in the grassy area next to Brad. The thirty coats of purple lacquer flashed like a panther's, so black as to be iridescent. The vehicle crept into the space. The dark devil coughed and threatened to die if the ultimate was not demanded of its powers. George killed the beast's struggle, and it reluctantly surrendered to the morning's stillness with one last growl.

The chrome handle on the driver's door grabbed and flashed the sun's rays. The morning light that filtered through the trees' thin umbrella of fall leaves reflected off the myriad of chrome arriving in the park. The Merc's door opened slowly. George unfolded his bulky frame from the interior, and black alligator boots crushed onto the grass. His purple cap cleared the door's frame. Straightening, he smoothed his shirt of wrinkles and greeted his buddies.

"Hey." George slid over the short distance to his buddies with ease in spite of his intimidating size.

"How's it going?" Bob asked. Brad looked past George and focused on a business card lying in the crushed grass. Brad stepped over and picked it up.

"Jim McNalley, special agent?" Brad read aloud. "Who you runnin' with now, George, the FBI?"

Brad caught the flick of anger on George's face. "I did some bodywork for the guy. Seems his wife didn't look as she was backing out at the Burger Barn. He was ready to kill her." George reached for the card.

Brad released the card, but his cop alarm went off. The agent was out of Chicago, here on assignment—without his wife.

The morning hours rolled by with talk of fuel injectors, four-barrel carbs, and Power Glides, while the Beach Boys giddy-upped, giddy-upped through the park's loudspeakers with the rock 'n' roll beat of "My 409." Brad's AA sponsor and chief detective, Ken, stopped by to offer his condolences for the previous day's failed sting operation, as well as his regrets for not bringing his Model A.

George interrupted. "My buddy Tom has his Corvette for sale." He pulled a photo from his wallet. The muscle car was a canary yellow in prime condition, but Brad focused on the figure standing next to it.

"Is that your buddy?"

George leaned in to study the glossy. "I don't know who that is. It must be a friend of Tom's."

"Nice car. I'll spread the word." Brad handed the photo back to George. If the man in the photo was a buddy of Tom's, Tom no longer had a buddy, Brad thought. Timmie was the man in the photo and Timmie was dead.

"So I heard there was a shooting downtown." It was a question more than a statement from George.

"Yeah, the vic had drug connections and matched a description for a rape that happened last week." Bob chewed on a toothpick, his cigarette substitute since he quit smoking.

"Did you get the shooter?"

Brad interrupted before Bob could respond. "We've got some leads." He gave Bob a hard look, warning him to drop the subject. Ken took a couple steps back. The last few years, Brad had felt uneasy with George's friendship. The FBI agent's business card and Timmie's photo had Brad's jaw muscles unconsciously flexing. Even George's purple hat bothered him.

The chief looked forward to this day. He could unwind from the disappointment of yesterday, lean back in his

lounge chair, and enjoy the outdoors, listening to the attendees' oohs and aahs as they walked by. Instead, he sat in
the lawn chair only for short periods before rising to polish
and fuss with his car as he anticipated his date with Judy.

At noon, Alice and Carrie showed up with a picnic basket and an ice chest full of cold beer and Coke. The four
men shifted gears to mumbling family talk between mouth-
fuls of Carrie's hero sandwiches and potato salad.

"So, Brad, did you know Judy arrived yesterday?" Alice
handed Brad a Coke.

"Yes. She called. Did she mention going to dinner tonight?
I told her I'd pick her up at five."

Alice glanced over at Bob. "Oh, yes, I almost forgot. Is
that okay with you, honey?"

"Sure. I'll be back from Sue's by then." He looked at Brad.
"I'm helping Sue and Paul put together a new barbecue."
Brad and Bob had already discussed the underlying reason
for Bob's visit with his son-in-law. The kid had done a lot of
computer research for the DA's office and they hoped he
could dissect Timmie's data.

"Our daughter married a nice guy, but he's not handy.
He can track a trail of money from the shipyards in California
to a Home Depot in Timbuktu with his computer, but when
it comes to tools, he's totally inept." Alice beamed with
affection for her son-in-law.

Carrie glanced at George and looked away as she
made a complaint about the heat. She began stuffing the
dishes and leftovers into the picnic basket and gave Alice
a quick look. "I really should be going."

"Me, too. I have a lot to get done before we go out
tonight." Alice crammed the trash into a bag and stood up.
"Okay, Bob, I'll see you after you get done with the kids."

After the women headed home, afternoon shadows
moved into the park, dulling the show cars' luster. One by
one, the hot rods sprang to life and made their way home
to tidy garages, until another day of boasting and blue ribbons, flavored with rib-poking jokes and male camaraderie.

As Brad pulled away, he said, "See you tonight at five?"

"See ya then." Bob waved his best-of-show ribbon with a wide grin, loving his last chance to flaunt his victory over Brad and George.

Brad's gaze turned to George. "Are you and Carrie coming to dinner?" Carrie had been Judy's best friend in high school.

"I'll check with Carrie. Maybe we'll see you there." George didn't have the same enthusiasm as Bob. Maybe it's Carrie who's reluctant, Brad thought. She and Judy were never close after Carrie hooked up with George.

"Whatever." Brad floored the accelerator. When his tires hit the asphalt, they squealed in delight, leaving blue, rubber-smelling smoke swirling in his wake.

Chapter Twenty-One

I spent my Saturday catching up, fiddling, cleaning, and doing computer work. After so many days on the road, I had shoved my everyday chores to the wayside. When everything was in order, I dashed to the store. Knowing Brad didn't drink, I settled on an exotic coffee blend, along with cheese and crackers. Back at the campground, I stopped at the office and bought a paper. It would be fun to check out the town's news.

I set the bag of groceries on the counter, laying the paper on the table. My eyes fell to the print. I stopped, petrified. A beautiful blonde smiled back, posing proudly for the camera with her arm around the Chief of Police. My Brad.

My legs folded and my knees creaked as I sank into the dinette's seat. I picked up the paper.

Our Chief Receives the Governor's Award

The governor commended 28 Illinois law enforcement officers, 5 who were under Chief Jones's command. They were awarded the Law Enforcement Medal of Honor last night during a ceremony at the Executive Mansion in Springfield.

"It is both a privilege and honor to recognize the men and women of law enforcement who have gone above and beyond the call of duty to safeguard the lives of our citizens," said the governor. "And it is a special honor to give this award to our own Chief Jones for his outstanding leadership..."

Her name was Darlene. Her embrace proudly announced possession as Brad stood tall and taut, portraying a man of reserve and confidence. A ghost of a smile—or was it a grimace?—lined his mouth. I hoped the latter. What was I saying? *You knew he would have someone.* After all these years? It was obvious they were an item. But what if it was an obligatory function? *You know, those things make it almost mandatory to have an escort.*

I wanted to throw up. My mood plunged. Sportster slept soundly in the overhead cabinet and Cowboy Jack's head was slumped on his chest in slumber. Sitting at the table, I stared out the window. Melted ice cream leaked out of a rip in the grocery sack. My gaze fixed on the river.

Who was I kidding? I came all this way with dreams and hopes. A redbird hung sideways on a barren branch outside my window and then darted from limb to limb. Crisp autumn air drifted in from the open window, causing me to shiver. I inhaled deeply, a chill filled me, and my limbs ached in stiffness.

My watch read four. How long had I been sitting there? *Suck it up, Judy.* Sitting up straight, I made a conscious decision to stop nursing my depression. *You can't lose what you never had.* I put away the groceries, throwing the ice cream out. Mechanically, I went to the closet.

Earlier I had straightened, stashed, and dusted my small space in preparation for Brad's visit. Over and over, my mind inventoried the narrow selection of attire crammed in my tiny closet. I decided on my usual—a cowboy hat, nice blouse, and jeans. My best jeans. Only one dress hung in my closet. It was like new, but an old staple that could be dressed up or down for any occasion—funeral, wedding, or in this case, high school prom.

Now I wished for something more fashionable. Darlene had worn a low-cut, peach chiffon evening gown that feathered the floor with its scalloped hem. She wore a corsage. Good grief! It wasn't a prom, just an awards dinner. Was she going to be at the prom?

Brad was on time. The '57 Chevy, Brad's pride and joy, made its way into the RV park at a slow, chugalug pace, staying abreast with the river's lazy gurgling.

First the thud of the Chevy's door, and then his boots crunching on gravel. My heart could not have beaten any faster. I stopped breathing, then gulped a deep breath and opened the door.

Brad stood by the motor home's passenger door, smiling at Cowboy Jack.

"Hi." The greeting rushed out as I exhaled.

With his attention on Cowboy Jack, he said, "I thought to myself when I saw him, 'She didn't tell me she was involved with someone.'" And you didn't either, I thought.

"Meet Cowboy Jack. He's my perfect man. He never argues, always goes along with the program, and never gets hungry."

His deep laughter made me want to swoon like a girl, in spite of Darlene.

"That's a good idea. He'll have to meet Officer Joe. He's a dummy we place in a squad car at intersections to deter speeders and people running stop signs. He and Joe would have a lot to talk about."

Brad finally looked up. He stood still; only his eyes moved. I felt their heat wash over me, scanning slowly, and then lock onto mine.

"Hi, Judy." Just two words, slow, soft but deliberate. I felt the familiar current surge between us, amped by forty years of unspoken words. In spite of Darlene.

"Well, come on in." I remembered to breathe.

He stepped up into the motor home, moving with the same careful, precise confidence I remembered. In spite of Darlene, my heartbeat raced. *I'm too old for this.*

As we stood in the small interior facing each other, I experienced what a deer must feel when it freezes, lit up in a set of headlights. Brad leaned close, and his fingers brushed my chin. Again I thought of Darlene. Pulling away, I stuttered, "You haven't met Sportster yet." *How lame! That's what you have to say? He was about to kiss you!* Wasn't he?

Sportster sat poised, studying our encounter. Feeling stupid and embarrassed, I reached over and patted his head, hoping to distract the feline's stare.

Brad's eyes moved from me to Sportster. It seemed every muscle was bridled as he straightened. Then he smiled and patted the cat's head. The smile was bigger than the one in the photo. The feline, happy with his successful interruption, chirped and pushed his head into Brad's hand, his eyes closed in bliss.

"Now we're both in heaven," Brad whispered to the cat, and then looked at me. "Are you ready?"

I stammered, startled, but then realized what he meant.

"To go for pizza." Amused, his finger moved from the cat and tapped my nose. He knew what I'd thought.

"Uh, yes. Yes, all ready," I answered too quickly. My face burned with embarrassment. Distracted, I searched for my purse.

"Let's go then, before..." He paused, I was sure for effect. "Before we're late."

I chattered nonstop on the way to the pizza place. "I'm so proud of you, Brad. Police Chief! That's really something! How did you swing that? All the trouble you got into in high school?"

"Let's just say certain events made me do a hundred-eighty-degree turnaround. I'll tell you about it someday. I really think I'm Chief only because no one else wanted the job."

Alice and Bob pulled in behind us at the restaurant. Inside, the four of us scooted into a spacious booth in case George and Carrie showed. I noticed diners walking past our table, all nodding with brief gestures or words of respectful recognition. Brad acknowledged everyone's attention with his own humble nod. Menus in hand, we batted toppings and crust choices back and forth until we agreed upon a thick crust pumped with cheese and smothered with everything. The waitress tucked her pad into her pocket and was beginning to move away when Carrie and George came through the door.

I didn't see Carrie at first because George's bulk dwarfed her as she followed behind. When they reached our table, Carrie took a small step from behind him but clung to his side. Brad touched the server's elbow. "Make that two of those." She nodded and headed for the kitchen. George grabbed her arm.

"Hey, how you doing Lisa? How's your car running?" George's hand lingered on her arm, his thumb rubbing her skin. She yanked her arm out of his grasp and I twitched, feeling her disgust.

She stepped back. "Did you and Carrie need something to drink?"

"Yeah. A beer for me and a Coke for Carrie." George slipped into the booth, pressing next to me. I was creeped out by the scene with Lisa, and sweat beaded my brow. I smelled the river. George slid into the booth and I pushed away from him, leaning my back into Brad. George wore a purple hat and a jacket with a red stripe on the sleeve.

I wondered if George was the man in the boat yesterday. My chest began to tighten and I feared a panic attack in front of everyone. I gathered every ounce of concentration and forced my mind to go to my quiet place. Brad noticed my unease and frowned. He pulled me closer, calming me like a good bourbon.

"So, Judy, have you gotten to see much of Springfield since you arrived? Have you seen the new mall?" Alice glanced at me and then Carrie. "Us girls will have to get together and go shopping before you leave. How about it, Carrie?"

Carrie's eyes darted like a cornered animal. "Sure, that would be fun." I could hardly hear her answer.

"I hate to be a downer, but are you planning to visit Jackie's folks?" Alice asked.

"I do. I feel bad I never made it to the funeral. I just got busy at college."

"Oh, that's okay." It was Carrie's tiny voice. "It was probably best. It was so sad. The entire senior class showed up for her funeral." Her voice had tears in it and she twisted her fingers into knots.

"We just formed a team to work on cold cases," Bob said. "We're hooked up to the national database and hope to do DNA testing to clear up a lot of them. If the guy was ever arrested, we'll find him."

"Maybe they'll finally get the guy," I said. No one wanted him caught more than me. I changed the subject.

"How about lunch tomorrow?" I said, determined to change the mood.

"Oh, I can't go tomorrow. Bob and I are going to a barbecue and birthday party for his nephews. We won't be home 'til late. In fact, I need someone to run the registration desk while we're gone. Usually Greta does but she's busy."

"I could watch the desk. I'm not doing anything," I said. "I've been in enough campgrounds, I should know how."

"Oh, that would be great. I didn't know what we were gonna do." Alice glowed when pleased and I could almost hear her harp music. "But we won't be back 'til late. You'll be there all alone. Is that okay?"

"Sure, after all, I drove all the way from California alone. And Cowboy Jack's amiable, and Sportster's not a demanding cat, so they won't care." I relaxed. We were off ugly subjects and I could do something nice for Alice.

"Monday or Tuesday, we could do lunch and shopping after Bob leaves for work. How about it, Carrie?"

Carrie's eyes darted to George, who nodded without saying a word.

"Yes, I can go." Her words shivered.

"Great! So what time do you want me over at the office, Alice?"

"Five's good."

"I'll be there."

After more light conversation and arguing over the last piece of pizza, Brad was the first to make the move to pay the bill. Was he eager to move the evening along?

Chapter Twenty-Two

Brad kept his focus on the road during the drive back to the campground.

"Carrie sure seemed timid, as if she were afraid of her own shadow." I tried to fill the quiet.

"I think George might shove her around, though she's never said anything," Brad said.

"I know in high school she never talked to Jackie and me about her dad beating on her mom and her, but we all knew he did."

"If I ever got a shred of evidence about him hitting her, I would see to it George would never touch a woman again. I like Carrie, always have, but if she doesn't ask for help there isn't much I can do. Abusers usually have their victims so frightened with some twisted sense of need that they won't leave even when they have a chance." Brad's fingers squeezed the wheel.

"Abused children often marry abusers. Some women are brave enough to leave, but I don't think Carrie ever will." I felt bad for my friend. I thought of a movie called *Independence Day* that starred David Keith and Kathy Quinlan, but it was Diane Wiest's part that I remembered so well. The theme of the movie was, "In a small town, it is hard to have a big dream," but it was the undercurrent of the movie that moved me. Wiest's role was an abused, depressed wife trapped in her marriage as the town looked the other way. In the final scene, her husband comes into the kitchen and complains about the strong smell of gas. She is leaning against the counter, silent, as she stares at him and calmly brings her lighter to her cigarette. His brow peaks in alarm and his eyes go wide as he computes her intentions. And then BOOM! That was her way of leaving, but at least she took the creep out with her.

I noticed Brad's mind had drifted into his own world. Was he thinking of the night to come? I was too nervous to follow his thoughts.

"Do George and Carrie live across the river from Alice and Bob's campground?"

"Yes, they do. Why?"

"Oh, I think I saw him Thursday. He had his boat so cranked up, only the prop touched the water. I don't know how fast he was going, but fast. I recognized his purple hat and red stripe on the jacket he wore tonight. He made a wide arc and disappeared into the bushes and cattails along the bank across the way. I couldn't see the dock. I thought it odd, as if someone were chasing him."

"What time was that?" He was back to the real world, every muscle taut, waiting for my answer.

"It was 3:10. I had just looked at my watch because I was waiting for the rental car to be delivered." Brad's knuckles turned white on the steering wheel again. When he glanced at me, I was startled by the light that sparked in his eyes like a flash from a gun.

Back at my motor home, we sat side by side at the breakfast nook with the sun sinking into the river. I shoved Darlene to the side and soaked up the ambience. The evening passed pleasantly as we caught up. He shared the events of his past that brought him to join the force.

"As I sat in that jail cell thinking I was in Oklahoma, I can't tell you how scared I was. Dad wasn't around anymore to fix things and I knew I was going away for a long time. The worst were the parts I couldn't remember anything."

"I know what you mean. All these years, you would think I could remember what happened that night at the rink, but I can't. I still have nightmares." His arm pulled me closer and I felt safer than I had in a long time. Safe and warm.

We shared everything from my late husband's passing to a discourse about Brad's old farm dog, Charlie. Retired from raiding the chicken coop, Brad's loyal companion now spent afternoons soaking up warm rays on the porch until the sun went down.

"I thought old Charlie, who's neutered, by the way, had hung up his carousing habits. But a month ago, he came across the yard escorting a pretty little golden retriever gal, who followed him with a labored gait, into the barn. He shared his food and water and then a couple of weeks later, I found her curled up on the bunk in the tack room, nursing four puppies. I'll have to show them to you. They are the cutest little pups."

"Maybe Charlie takes after his dad, rescuing females in distress."

"Maybe so."

We sipped coffee and crunched on crackers and cheese, talking into the night like an old married couple. Sportster made an effort to sniff every inch of the real live man in his presence. He rubbed and purred his approval and began training Brad in Cat 101: How to Turn on the Faucet for a Drink. Brad was a quick study and took his new duty seriously. Cowboy Jack stared stoically out the windshield, refusing to join in.

The moon rose, lighting up the night and casting shadows as hours floated by. Brad suggested we stretch our legs and walk off the pizza. We stepped out into the white lunar glow; the air had cooled to a musky dampness. We strolled to the riverbank and stood on the dock. The moon's reflection cast a scalloped white path from shore to shore while frogs and crickets conducted a rhythmic symphony. The world was at peace and, if I believed in such things, it was a time for love. But I didn't. *You had your time with Brad*, I warned my heart. *He has his life now, complete with Darlene.*

And then he leaned over and kissed me.

The kiss was not like a teen testing the waters. It was not one of inexperience or shyness. It was not to be taken lightly. It was a serious kiss, full of maturity and self-confidence. Red-hot fear raced through me, competing with the heat of passion running its own race.

My world spun in confusion. Hadn't I already reasoned this out? I spent two thousand miles doing it. Now was not the time for doubts, but I couldn't stand steady. My legs weakened and I leaned into it. I was sixteen again, full of doubts, full of hope. And full of passion. Was it love? I was old enough to know the answer to that question, wasn't I? How could it be love? We knew each other only for a brief period forty years ago, just two teens experimenting in the dark. Now I had come full circle. All the years, all my experiences faded. There was only this moment, and I knew. Just like the sixteen-year-old girl, I cared about Brad, and just like then, I knew I would care forever, that I had never stopped.

"I'm sorry, Judy."

The words interrupted my mental turmoil. I knew the apology was for the lost forty years, the forty years he had been wracked with guilt. He always thought he should have done more.

"No, I'm sorry. There was nothing more you could have done. I should never have left."

We sat down on the river's edge, absorbed in the moment, both knowing nothing more needed to be said. There was no urgency, just a feeling of completeness, of coming home.

The birds outside composed a musical chorus, adding to an already blissful morning. Brad had taken his leave when the damp chill on the dock promised daylight. After he left, I floated into bed and slept soundly until daybreak. Remembering the night, I stretched in bed, long and lazy like a cat. Sportster, already up, was deciding which of the chorus members might be the tastiest. His tail twitched and his little chin quivered as he chirped his own bird calls. I found Cowboy Jack slumped over in his seat, his hat askew. He must have had his own party while I was out for pizza.

I stretched again, reluctant to put away last night's memories.

Chapter Twenty-Three

Brad was up at daybreak; a farmer's habit was hard to break. An hour later, he sat at his desk at the station, a Police Chief's habit, also hard to break. Sundays were his favorite day to work; he did his best thinking with no interruptions. He pored over the reports, and the facts bothered him. Who tipped off Pit Bull? Timmie's assassination definitely proved a leak. How else did Pit Bull escape the Sand Bar so quickly? The chief recalled the purple hat and the boat racing around the bend.

Brad's thoughts jumped to last night. His heart lurched. He quickly jerked his attention back to the case and recalled Judy's question about George. The timeline fit the puzzle. He began shuffling the pieces.

George had McNalley's business card. How did he know an FBI agent? And the picture of Timmie next to George's buddy—he must have known Timmie, but he didn't admit it. And he was too interested in the shooting.

Brad had had suspicions for a long time, but they were never strong enough to make them official. He questioned how George afforded more than a mere body shop business could provide. Sure, his business put out quality work, but to afford the alligator boots, the high-end fishing equipment, and all those vintage cars? The more Brad moved the puzzle pieces around, the more uneasy he became.

George had always been sinister, but Brad had discounted his suspicions. *I considered him a friend*. His attitude toward women was dominating and he liked his porn. It was not like he ever came out and admitted a lack of principles; he knew better with Brad. But did he fit the profile of a rapist and a drug runner? *What if George is Pit Bull, all these years?*

As his thoughts took form, Brad began scribbling orders for Monday. His adrenaline raced, but not from thoughts of Judy. This time it was like a bloodhound picking up the scent of the fox. He would investigate George quietly. Where was he at the time of the shooting? What were his whereabouts in connection with Timmie's receipts from Brownsville, Peoria, New Orleans? What was the connection between George and Timmie? And maybe Brad would make an off-the-record investigation of George's boat dock. During this quiet investigation, Brad would also order John to acquire DNA samples. As Brad's brain computed the possibilities, his anger started to swell. Instinct told him he was on the right path. He just had to find the missing pieces. His instinct was rarely wrong.

Considering this new direction, he realized the strong possibility that, for forty years, George had not only run a very successful drug trafficking operation right under Brad's nose, but also he was responsible for the rapes and deaths of many women.

Another hour passed in the stale air of the station. Only Brad's chest moved in and out. He pushed up his glasses, agitated that age required them. The lenses hid his intense focus as he examined the reports. Except for the papers' flutter, only the occasional moan of the police station's old pine floor disturbed the silence.

The preliminary reports revealed multiple charge receipts from an account in Timmie's name, for meals and gas at various locks and dams stretching from New Orleans to St. Louis. The title for a bass boat and a lease agreement for Crosby's farm both had George's signature.

The tick-tock, tick-tock of the station's old clock timed the pace of Brad's reactions to the information. His responses heated, building like the station's old boiler room furnace. The chief looked up, counting his decorations on the walls. All this—the plaques, the awards, the degrees—meant nothing compared to what he was about to accomplish. In his mind, the case was solved. With solid evidence, justice would be dealt. Pit Bull, who he now believed was George, was going down. But what would happen in court? The kingpin would have excellent attorneys.

Brad wanted Pit Bull dead. He wasn't going to let the system manipulate the law and free him on a technicality. As the thought of Pit Bull's death festered, it didn't frighten him, which in itself frightened him. Brad wanted justice for Judy and for himself. He couldn't rein in his thoughts as they wove a hangman's noose.

The scene unfolded. His Magnum aimed at the thick-necked scumbag. George, being the coward Brad knew him to be, would cry and beg for his life. Brad would laugh maniacally, knowing no other woman would suffer from the kingpin's terrors. And then he would pull the trigger. Brad's body jerked, a reflexive action to the imagined gun's explosion, forcing him back to reality and the stillness and reverence of his office.

Chapter Twenty-Four

After a leisurely cup of coffee and honey on toast, I dressed for our day of sightseeing. Brad turned into the park with the top down on his Chevy, the sun was warm, and the autumn air crisp. I grabbed my camera, crammed on my everyday cowboy hat, and stepped outside. As the car neared, I saw a boy in his teens in the passenger seat. Blonde hair tried to escape from under a blue baseball cap. His ears peaked from the locks when the wind whipped the curls into his eyes as it did now. Freckles crowded his cheeks and forehead. The teenager's knees neared his chest because long legs bent sharply to fit into the low passenger seat.

"Hello." I greeted the two. "How did I get so lucky as to have two handsome escorts today?" The boy said nothing, but his cheeks reddened.

"This is Roy. He's on furlough for the day. I thought we could go out to the river and go walnut hunting. He says he's never done that before. Can you believe it? Missing out on such an adventure? Say hello to Judy, Roy."

"Hello. Nice to meet you, ma'am." His eyes met mine for only a second. He switched his focus back to the piece of rope in his lap.

"Nice meeting you, too, Roy. What do you have there?" I pointed to the rope tangled in his fingers.

"I made it." It was, upon closer examination, several lengths of rope a couple feet long, braided and tied tightly at each end with colorful dyed strands of the same twine.

I took the curious item that he offered. "That's a tug-o'-war toy for the puppies," Brad explained. "I figured after we collected the walnuts, we could go back to the house and barbecue burgers for lunch. Roy's been helping me socialize and train Charlie's puppies. What do you say, Judy?"

"I can't think of anything more fun. Scoot over, Roy." I opened the door and plopped down next to him. Brad and I exchanged a quick look.

Brad pulled over and parked in a clearing by the river. Gunnysacks in hand, we tromped down a dirt road lined with alder and buckeye trees. Raspberry bushes crept over fallen trees and attempted to choke off an adornment of purple violets as they competed for space on the forest floor. Yellow and crimson leaves spiraled down through filtered sunlight. Landing on the water, the fall foliage set sail around the bend to unknown destinations.

We educated Roy on how to recognize a black walnut tree, and also the poisonous leaves of ivy and oak. He was a quick study and before long, I could tell he forgot whatever past had brought him to this point in his life. He became just a boy exploring the woods, marveling at squirrels' chatter. A couple hours later, we slung our sacks full of walnuts into the trunk and headed back to Brad's.

On the drive home, we expanded Roy's education, explaining what would become of our bounty. "I have a place behind the barn where I spread the walnuts out so the sun can dry the green hulls that surround them," Brad said. "After they dry, a small tap with a hammer will pop off the green hull that turns black when it's dried. What's left is the nut. Always wear gloves when you're removing the hulls because the walnut oil will stain your fingers black for months."

"I remember snowbound winter days when my sister and I suffered cabin fever," I said. "We would go down into the basement, sit cross-legged on the floor with a hammer, and crack walnuts. That was long before television and video games."

Roy looked up at me, his face full of wonder. "Why didn't you watch TV?"

I laughed. "There was no TV."

"You couldn't afford one?"

"No. People didn't have television sets." His eyes grew big, but he said nothing and returned to fiddling with his rope. I was sure the concept baffled him.

We cruised through Washington Park, passed Lincoln's home, and the town square. We stopped at each location and bounced out. Roy snapped pictures of Brad and me, then I returned the favor, capturing Brad and Roy. Finally, we commandeered a passerby for a group picture. Back at the farm, before Brad had the car in Park, Roy bounded out and was halfway to the barn.

"Just say hello and then come help with lunch." Brad's voice boomed with authority as Roy disappeared into the barn's shadowed interior.

"Yes, sir."

"He must be really attached to the puppies."

"He is. I'm amazed. He's a totally different boy when he's with the dogs. He has a way with them." I watched Brad's chest puff up with pride.

"So how'd you get involved with Roy?"

"His mom's a crackhead and she's not sure who his dad is. She just turns a trick for whoever will get her a hit. Roy is Jackie's grandnephew. He's been in and out of juvie for possession but at sixteen, he got mixed up in an armed robbery at the 7-Eleven. His public defender couldn't prevent the judge from charging him as an adult, so he's doing seven to ten in the county. I guess I have a soft spot for kids when life is stacked against them. And it's a way of doing something for Jackie."

"I can tell he respects and admires you. You're doing a good thing."

Brad shrugged off the compliment. "Let's go see the puppies."

We entered the darkened barn to find Roy lying on his back, giggling in boyish glee as four puppies climbed upon his chest, slobbering kisses across his face, and then sliding and toppling onto the straw floor. Roy held his rope toy in the air as the puppies grabbed hold with tiny jaws, huffing and puffing their practice growls. Each baby growl released large belly laughs from Roy.

I knelt down and scooped up an adorable, golden fur ball with white paws. Its ears were tipped in black to match its wet nose. "He has Charlie's ears," Brad explained. "Usually Charlie ambles out here and stands by like a proud papa. He can't be the sire because I had him fixed a long time ago, but he thinks he is." Brad scratched the puppy's ears as it squirmed to be free.

"Like I said before, Charlie is like his daddy, likes to help women in distress." I smothered the puppy with kisses and inhaled its puppy breath.

Again, Brad ignored my comment. "Check on their food and water, Roy, then come in and help with lunch."

"Yes, sir."

Brad showed Roy how to light the coals on the barbecue and allowed the boy to tend the burgers. Inside, I tossed up a salad with fresh vegetables from Brad's garden. Where did this man find the time? We ate on the porch and Roy inhaled his burger with the ravenous appetite of a teen.

I turned to Roy. "You know, I've trained dogs for obedience and protection work."

Roy paused from devouring his burger. "Could you teach me?"

"I'd love to, but I have to go back to California soon. But maybe next Sunday I could give you some pointers." I looked over at Brad.

"The reunion wraps up on Saturday night. We could do this again Sunday," Brad said.

As the afternoon shadows lengthened, the puppies tired of their tug of war games. Brad had to take Roy back and I needed to return home to oversee the campground office for Bob and Alice, and Brad had an early flight to New Orleans on business.

At my rig, Brad jumped out of the car and came around to open my door.

I turned to Roy. "It was so nice to meet you, Roy. I'm looking forward to Sunday." I held out my hand. He hesitated, but after a nod of encouragement from Brad, he beamed and shook my hand. Brad walked me to the door, leaned down and kissed me lightly, both of us aware of the young impressionable mind observing our actions.

"I'll call you when I get back from New Orleans." His eyes clouded from the kiss and his shortened breathing matched mine. He stepped back, holding me at arm's distance, took one long look, turned, and walked in fast strides back to the car. I watched Roy study every movement of his idol, the Chief of Police.

I hurried inside, stuffed a book, an apple, and some crackers into my bag for a snack, expecting an uneventful evening. I entered the registration office promptly at five, as Bob and Alice emerged from the private door of their living quarters.

"All set? Do you have any questions? Probably nothing will happen, but there's my phone number, so call if you have a problem." Alice was dressed in a fashionable pants suit and Bob in jeans and a sweater. He placed his hand on her back as he opened the door.

"I'm sure I'll be fine. What could possibly go wrong?" We all laughed. "You guys have a good time."

"Thanks for doing this, Judy. We won't be too late."

When their taillights disappeared onto the highway, I putted around the office, straightening brochures in the display racks. I found a feather duster and whisked at the inventory of groceries and RV products stocked on the shelves. Later, I took a break, slicing my apple with a steak knife I found under the counter, and munched idly. My mind brought up the day's events, and the memories swept over me like a warm blanket.

Brad and I had not discussed the future, but I felt permanence, a security, a "come home" feeling whenever I was with him. I wanted to believe he felt the same, but I had to consider the facts: it's been forty years, there's Darlene, I have a life in California, Brad has a career here. And then there's Darlene. *Why does life have to be so complicated?* And yet I wanted the day's sweet, simple events to erase the facts. I sighed, forcing myself to face reality. Age, time, and circumstances extinguished the folly of an old woman's high school dreams.

I glanced up from my musing when I noticed high-beam headlights in the darkness, creeping like animal eyes past the park's entrance, and crawling toward the registration office. Their glare penetrated the glass and cast ghostly shadows. So engrossed in my brooding, I had forgotten to turn on a light. I flipped on a switch. It didn't erase the ominous atmosphere that had crept into the area.

The headlights died in front of the office and the car door thudded in the dark. I wondered if it went unheard by the campground residents curled up in their rigs. The warm, golden incandescence inside their rigs cast beacons into the night. I saw a figure emerge from the dark metal shadow and step under the porch light. I recognized George—his shape, size, and movement. My reaction confused me as blood pulsed in my neck, my fingertips tingled, and my legs drained of any sensation. When the bell on the door jangled, I drew a deep breath and forced myself to stand tall.

"Hi, Judy."

"George."

He took a step back, feigning hurt by my cold reception. "I remembered you were working here tonight and thought I would come by to keep you company." His eyes narrowed as he grinned. "You don't have to play hard to get." He moved closer to the registration desk. My hands rested on the counter, grateful for the barrier.

"I'm fine. I don't need company." I hated my voice as it took a higher pitch. My skin crawled as if spiders scampered up my arms and pant legs. I flicked invisible creatures off my upper arm just as George pushed past the swinging gate. It creaked and he slunk around behind the counter.

"Everyone needs a little company now and then." His voice, a sneer, caused my stomach to hurl. I steeled myself as I realized in two more strides we would be face to face. Again my reaction confused me as I took a step closer to him. But my new position hid the movement of my hand as it palmed the knife lying on the shelf under the counter with my apple.

Before I calculated the seriousness of my situation, George had pushed me toward the darkness of the back office. His hand hit the light switch and he thrust me into the dimly lit room.

"I've been looking forward to tonight, Judy. When I heard Brad was leaving town, I figured we can keep each other company all night long, just like I did with your friend Jackie. Did you know that? We did it all night long, too, until she couldn't do it anymore." He was up against me. The river-beer smell soaked with Old Spice made my head spin. I tried to back away.

"What's the matter? Don't you want it again?" His laughter caused prickling chills up my spine like a needle screeching across a vinyl record. "I still remember how good it was." His thick arms reached behind me, grabbing my buttocks, and yanked me closer. "Oh, I'm sorry. I know you didn't get to enjoy it like I did. But I'm giving you a second chance tonight. You'll never forget tonight." He restrained me in a crushing embrace that made it difficult to breathe. I babbled like an old helpless woman as he threw me to the floor and crushed his body on top of mine.

In slow motion, my brain processed the few minutes that passed from the swinging gate to the office floor. The timeline fizzed along like a short fuse on a stick of dynamite. When George grabbed me, the spark reached its target and a flashing explosion of memories erupted, springing open the barricaded door of my mind. Forty-year-old details imploded. From a bumbling senior, I mushroomed into the sixteen-year-old teen, restrained in the back of a Ford Mercury with dark tinted windows. With the mental door blown open, I saw everything clearly. This time I was not drugged. My ears stung from a shrill shriek that filled the room. The piercing wail originated from my own lungs, where it festered, trapped for forty years. My arm thrust up and over my attacker's body. With four decades of bottled vengeance, I sank the steak knife deep into his back. I heard it rip into his flesh and crunch past bone. His body jerked as the serrated blade embedded in his flesh and the handle broke off in my grasp. His body went still.

For a moment. "You bitch! You stuck me!" His hand released my wrist and was rising to strike me across the face when the office lit up. Moving shadows and lights stormed into the room. George's hand froze in midair. He scrambled to his feet. Gathering up his jacket, he shrugged into it, the knife blade still penetrating his back. He kicked me sharply in the ribs. "Get up and shut up." Then he yanked me up and shoved me into the reception area.

The bell on the door tinkled and Alice and Bob entered.

"Isn't that George's car outside?" Bob's gaze landed on George. "Hello, George. I didn't expect to see you here." I hung back, watching Bob scan the room. I didn't know what to do. What had just happened? I couldn't believe what had just happened. The DA's eyes darted back and forth between George and me.

"I was driving by, saw the light on, and thought I'd keep Judy company 'til you guys got back. Right, Judy?"

My mind was in the back room. Heat surged through my veins from the disappointment of not killing him. My reason vanished. I planned vengeance as I stood there. And yet, what would happen if I said something? I had just stabbed a man. George was a respected member of the community, a businessman, for God's sake. I was like a stranger in town. Who was going to believe me? *Maybe I should wait.* I needed to talk to someone.

I nodded. My hands shook. I tucked them close to my body, folding my arms tightly against my chest. I still clutched the knife handle in my fist. If they noticed, they said nothing.

"Well, I'd better get going." George turned his back to Bob and Alice, and with a look that sent invisible fingers of fear tightening around my throat, he said, "It's been fun, Judy. I'll catch you later."

I said nothing, only nodded. My whole body shook but no one seemed to notice. The door slammed in his retreat and my eyes glanced to the floor. A drop of blood stained the threshold. "Well, I'd better be going, too." I watched the Mercury's taillights pass through the campground's gate and disappear into the night.

"Are you okay, Judy?" Bob's arm was around Alice. Because of my guilt and confusion, the question felt like a cross-examination.

"I'm fine. It's been a long day. I'll talk to you guys tomorrow."

Bob's eyes burned into mine, but Alice broke the spell. Pulling away from him, she embraced me. "Thank you so much, Judy. We sure appreciate everything."

"It was my pleasure." I dismissed her and hustled out the door into the darkness. When I reached my motor home, I slammed the door, locked both locks, and dug out my .38. I laid it within easy reach.

I collapsed onto the couch. Relief and triumph, then guilt and fear washed over me, sweeping away any confidence I gained from my new discovery. The ghostly shadow in my nightmares had a name. The scenes from my past were no longer clouded images. I had not turned tail and run. I had fought back. My hand touched my chest as I reached for the long-lost locket. For now I was keeping quiet about what happened to me. I had to sort this out. Brad would know what to do. Revenge would have its day.

I glanced around the motor home's interior. Cowboy Jack sat still in his seat. *"George probably didn't mean any harm. He probably just likes you. Did you say something to lead him on?"*

WHAT? That lousy, no-good doll couldn't have said that! I yanked open the kitchen drawer and rattled through the contents for my carving knife like a mad woman. The urge to stab the doll until his stuffing filled the air and floated down the river was overwhelming. *What is wrong with me?* I couldn't believe the rage running through my veins. For the doll?

Sucking in a deep breath, I exhaled, and then I laughed. I couldn't stop. The comic relief sent tears streaming down my face. Sportster leapt onto the counter from his safe place and laid his paw gently on my arm. I scooped him up and squeezed him as I buried my face in his fur. I was dizzy, lightheaded. I felt free. Was I? I knew there would be no more nightmares. But had I created a new threat? George wanted to kill me. I saw it in his face. But was he going to report me? I did stab him.

When I crawled into bed, I lay awake while scenes of revenge played in my mind. Who would have their revenge, me or George? I laid my fingers on the cold steel of the gun.

Chapter Twenty-Five

Brad was packing his carry-on while gulping his third cup of coffee when his cell rang the Beach Boys' tune, "My 409."

"Hi, Bob. What's up?" He looked at his watch; Bob couldn't have gotten the evidence reports yet. It was seven in the morning.

"Judy had a visitor last night."

"She did? Who?" Brad held his breath.

"It was George. Do they have something going on? Why would he be coming by without Carrie? He said he just came by to keep Judy company. She didn't discount it. They acted as if they got their hands caught in the cookie jar. That's not good, Brad. This case is stacking up against George. What has Judy got in common with him? I'm worried. I just thought I'd give you a heads-up. I know how you feel about her."

Brad's grip on the phone tightened in his sweaty palm. An invisible fist sucker-punched his gut. He stared out across the fields. He attempted to process the information but it became tangled in his mind. "Yeah, sure, thanks, Bob."

What could she be doing with George? *She tenses up when he's around. I'm sure she can't stand him. I wonder if he has something on her. Have I misjudged her?*

"I'll be on the alert." *What else can I say?* "I've sent you a pile of evidence reports. You're right. It's not looking good for George. Review them and when I get back from New Orleans, we'll have a powwow."

"Okay. I'll watch for them. Meanwhile, watch your back, buddy. Ya hear?"

"I'm good. Got it covered." He hung up, wishing he felt as confident as he hoped he sounded. Darlene invaded his mind and he attempted to explain to his heart. Darlene and he had a comfortable, no-nonsense relationship. Why not just keep it status quo? No complications. Even if he was right about Judy and she hated George, she had a life in California. She hadn't indicated she wanted to make any changes. Let her be. He imagined his heart scoffing, "Are you crazy, man?"

He rinsed his dirty cup, placed it in the sink, and hunched the strap of his carry-on over his shoulder. He went outside and the screen door banged shut as Darlene pulled up in her Sebring convertible, tooting her horn. She wore a colorful scarf over her tight hairdo. He tried to remember— had he ever seen her hair down? He threw his bag into the backseat and folded his big frame into the passenger seat. He would rather drive but she never offered the wheel. No sooner had he slammed the door, she stomped the gas, throwing dirt and gravel onto the porch steps. She barreled down the long drive, creating a tunnel of dust in her wake. Darlene, always staid and tightly strung, became possessed by a competitive racing fever when she got behind the wheel. Her driving, which Brad normally tolerated, irritated him today.

"Slow it down a little, will you, Darlene?" He didn't try to hide his impatience.

"What's the matter, Hon? Have a late night? Kind of cranky, aren't you?" Her attitude, usually constrained and respectful, was uncharacteristically bold and taunting.

"I just don't want an accident on the way to the airport. Rein it in. Or you can pull over and I'll drive."

He saw her bottom lip protrude and her eyes narrow, but she said nothing. She had worked for him long enough to know he wasn't a man to be pushed. She eased off the pedal. They finished the route in silence. When she pulled up to the drop-off area, Brad jumped out of the car and grabbed his bag from the back.

"I'll let you know the return flight number and time." He disappeared into the terminal, but not before he heard her mutter, "Yeah, sure," and then lay rubber as she peeled away, cranking the radio up to a thundering boom-box level.

When I woke in the morning, my mind was clear. I dressed carefully as I thought of the day I planned. I wanted to visit Jackie's parents. Until last night, I had picked at threads of doubt as to how my friend died, but now the proof was sewn tight. I knew it futile to reveal what I knew. It was so long ago, but it helped me come to terms with Jackie's death.

I punched in Carrie's number on my phone, hoping George didn't answer. When she answered, I asked, "I was wondering if we could go to lunch at the Cozy Dog?" To her, I would tell the truth. All of it. She deserved to know. If the facts I unveiled were unbearable, at least they would force her to make a decision about her life—stay or go. I hoped my friend had the courage to do the latter.

"Sure. Is noon good?"

I felt guilty knowing I was going to cause an upheaval in her life. "I'll meet you there. See you."

Jackie's house still looked the same, a sprawling brick ranch style with a matching brick driveway. The maple trees in full, fall splendor had grown massive. Before I reached for the bell, the door opened and Jackie's mom burst across the threshold with open arms. "Judy! It has been so long! It is so good to see you. Come in, come in." She herded me inside. She still carried her small frame with a certain dignity. Her hair, now salt and pepper, was shorter. Jackie's parents lived modestly, never buying the new model car, as was the trend in the sixties. They kept the old one. Their only extravagance had been for their daughter when they purchased the little red convertible. Jackie's mother always projected elegance no matter what time of day. I had never seen her in a housedress or curlers. Always matching earrings and a necklace.

"Tom! Judy's here. Come in and say hello." Jackie's mom ushered me through the living room, past the bookcase that still displayed her daughter's pictures and skating trophies. In the kitchen, she said, "Sit down. Would you like some coffee? I just made it."

"Yes, but I can't stay long. I wanted to see you guys and thought we could go to dinner before I go back to California."

I sat down just as Tom ambled into the room. I rose and he wrapped me in his big bear hug. He had been like a second dad to me. Sealed tight in his arms, I regretted my flight from this town and these people forty years ago. We sat chatting about news around town and I gave them a brief synopsis of my life. "Yesterday Brad and I went walnut hunting with Roy."

Kathy's forehead creased. "We tried so hard to give our support to Roy when he was growing up. But his mom refused our help, calling us "interfering do-gooders.""

"He seems like he's on the right track, and if Brad has his way, the boy will come out of all this as a man with values and self-confidence . You should see him working with

Brad's puppies. I'm going to give him some tips on dog training next Sunday.

"Do you still do the training and grooming?" Tom had been the inspiration for me to become a groomer and a trainer. My sister and I had hung out at his kennels for hours after school, helping with the feeding and cleaning.

"No. We just have Jenny here." A gray, muzzled golden retriever lay sprawled in her cushy bed in the corner. "She's getting old like the rest of us, and I'm not as agile as I used to be. Mom wants me to rip out the kennels in the garage so she can make it into a studio for her art." He smiled warmly at Kathy.

"You always were an accomplished artist, Kathy. And Tom, if it hadn't been for you...well, I just want to say thanks." Tom blushed as I continued. "You and Tom should come out to Brad's on Sunday. We're barbecuing burgers. We can catch up and you can see Roy, too."

Kathy glanced up at Tom. "We'll think about it," Tom said. I knew he didn't want Kathy to get her hopes up about Roy.

I checked my watch, not wanting to miss my lunch with Carrie. "I'd better be going. I promise not to be a stranger. Too much time has been wasted."

"Oh, we aren't going to let you get away from us again. Anyway, we've been thinking about a trip to California. We'll come out and drag you back here if we have to."

We laughed. I soaked up their hugs that seemed to smother everything bad in the world. As I climbed into the rental car, I looked to the heavens. "They are doing fine, Jackie. Don't you worry about your folks."

I drove slowly, weaving my way through town toward the Cozy Dog restaurant, a Route 66 icon. I pulled in and parked. I sat still, gathering up my determination. I didn't doubt my intentions and felt this was an unpleasant but necessary conclusion to the events of the past. As I pulled open the door, ignoring the cardboard cutouts of the cuddling Cozy Dogs, I heard Carrie behind me. "Hi, Judy."

Turning, I smiled as we hugged. I cherished the moment, knowing everything would change between us after this lunch. I wanted so much to reconnect with her after all these years, but was sure this lunch would end any hope of that. "Let's grab that table in the corner."

We sat down and examined the simple menu. "This place brings back memories, huh?" I said.

"We spent a lot of hours here. All we talked about were boys and then clothes. And when we covered those subjects, we talked about clothes and then boys. There wasn't anything else." She giggled at the memory like she was sixteen again. The waitress chewed gum as she took our order and could have been the grand-daughter of our server from the sixties. When she left, I breathed, in gathering my courage. "I wanted to have this time together to tell you what I should have told you long ago..." I let out the breath I had been holding. "Why I shut you and Jackie out of my life and left town with hardly a good-bye."

"That's okay. I was guilty, too. Once I got with George, I did the same. We just got busy with our lives."

"No, it's not all right. I should have told you and Jackie. You guys were my best friends. We were the Threesome."

Carrie seemed nervous. She stirred her Coke with her straw, making the ice tinkle. She wouldn't look up.

I dove in. "I was raped one night in the skating rink park-ing lot." Carrie still didn't meet my eyes. "Someone put a Mickey Finn in my Coke. I could never remember the details or who did it. I couldn't tell anyone what happened. I was so ashamed."

"Oh, Judy, you don't have to talk about this. It's okay. It doesn't matter now. That was a long time ago. You couldn't help it."

Did she know? "I got pregnant from the rape. I had an abortion, Carrie."

Carrie looked up and stared at me now, her eyes wide. "Oh, Judy, I didn't know." *But she knew about the rape?*

"I'm so sorry. You should have told us. We would have been there for you."

"I was so ashamed back then. I couldn't tell anyone. Brad arranged the abortion."

"And you don't know who raped you?" *Didn't I already tell her that?*

"I didn't know then, but I do now." I studied her reaction. Her eyes darted around the restaurant. She continued to stir her Coke with fervor.

The waitress interrupted, serving two plastic baskets, each with a corndog, heaped with crispy golden fries, and a small cup of potato salad. "There you go. Will there be anything else?"

"No," we both answered in unison.

Carrie stared at me until the waitress was out of earshot. "I know who did it, too," she said. I noticed she couldn't say his name. Would it make it too real?

"You knew?" People at the table turned their heads at my raised voice.

"I didn't know then. It was much later. Maybe a year later. After you'd gone." Her words were choppy and rushed. "George told me one night when he was trying to taunt me. He's always tried to make me feel, well, like I'm no good. By then you had gone to California so I didn't see any reason to bring it up. I figured it was best to let it lie." Her body slumped. She hung her head like an inflatable doll that had lost its air. I couldn't believe it, but I felt sorry for her. "But I didn't know he drugged you," she continued. "And I didn't know about the abortion." She looked at me, hoping for some absolution.

"That's not all. He raped and killed Jackie."

Carrie's eyes locked onto mine. Did she know that, too? I hoped she didn't.

"How can you say such a thing?" She began to cry. People stared, but we were caught in a space of time that excluded everyone but the two of us...and George. "How can you say such a thing?" she repeated.

She didn't know.

"He told me, Carrie."

"Why would he tell you such a thing?" she pleaded. "Why would he say that?"

"Last night, I was watching the registration office for Bob and Alice, and George came by to see me." My voice was steady, calm, as I destroyed the wall of denial Carrie had built over the years. "It was not a nicey-nicey social call, Carrie. He forced me into the back office and tried to rape me. Again! When he threw me to the floor, it brought back everything from that night in the skating rink parking lot. I remembered everything, but I wouldn't have had to remember, because he told me he was the one. He bragged about it, and bragged about Jackie, too. How he tortured her all night long. He bragged about it, Carrie!"

Her head hung and her tears fell on the tabletop. Her small body shuddered.

"I swear I didn't know, Judy. I swear." She grabbed my hand and clutched it. I placed my other on top of hers and rubbed it gently.

"You needed to know. Now you do. There's no way I can prove any of this but you need to know." Carrie's mouth puckered. She looked green, as if she were going to be sick.

"I have to go. I have to go." She gathered up her purse, sending her untouched Coke shattering to the floor. The two baskets of Cozy Dogs sat untouched.

"Don't go." I grabbed her arm, but she yanked it away and ran out the door, colliding with a couple of teens entering.

"Get out of my way!" She shoved them aside and I saw the red flutter of her skirt move across the parking lot and the flower from her hair drop to the asphalt. She was gone.

I felt drained. I gathered up the bill and laid a twenty with it by the register.

Chapter Twenty-Six

Brad found his buddy at the end booth, nursing a Coke. He picked up the drink and sniffed the contents, surprised his friend wasn't already glassy-eyed. "You quit, too?" He set the drink down, slapped Dave's shoulder as he slipped into the seat.

"Hey, doc's orders. He said the X-rays showed my liver with its meaty little hands raised in surrender. It can't take anymore. Gail's happy about my clean living. How you doing, old buddy?"

After photo sessions with the New Orleans police chief and mayor, a long day of speeches, lunch, and happy hour, Brad had headed back to his hotel. After shedding his formal attire for jeans and a T-shirt, he'd called his old friend and colleague, Dave.

"How about dinner at the Kingpin?"

"Well, son of a bitch!" his buddy answered. "Look what the Mississippi's coughed up. Sure enough, buddy."

Dave worked undercover, living on the edge of the law. When Brad met him, they were both young and wild with no ties to the force or a woman. They watched each other's back in the bars and fronted each other's tab when the other was short on funds. Now Dave made his home in the Big Easy with his longtime, live-in girlfriend, Gail. Dave's undercover years on the force strained the couple's relationship as they wrestled with the stress of his underbelly acquaintances. Somehow they remained together in a love-hate passion, never marrying and never having children.

Brad liked Gail, a down-to-earth gal who was all shapely legs and long, flaming hair that always looked tousled. She kept Dave grounded, kept him from burying himself too deeply when he tried to right the injustices of the job that kept him awake, and there were many. Brad got to know Gail ten years ago when he stood by her side as they nursed Dave back to life after a shootout during a sting operation. Brad learned then their love ran deep even when they acted like two Louisiana tomcats on the back fence.

"Just trying to get by." Brad motioned to the waitress.

"I've read about you down here. You're getting to be someone to reckon with. The word on the street is don't do business in your town unless they're feelin' real lucky. How's the big investigation going?" Dave threw back his Coke and motioned the waitress for another.

"That's why I wanted to touch base with you. What's the latest?" Brad slipped a five on the table when the server approached and pointed to Dave's Coke. "I'll have the same."

"Well, the word about Pit Bull's main man, Timmie, going down has made even the lobsters squeeze their claws shut. I couldn't poke a penny joint up my informants' tight asses. They're terrified, thinkin' they might be next, and their dicks have shrunk so far out of sight a kilo of Viagra couldn't get 'em up."

"That's not good." Brad smiled at his buddy's metaphors.

"But I got this buddy in Vice—Charlie. You know him?"

"Charlie the Tuna? Yeah. I did a stakeout with him back in the day when he was out of St. Louis. They called him that because he looked like a fish. His eyes bugged out, and he worked his big lips like a catfish trying to grasp air every time the sergeant dressed him down, and that was pretty often."

"Well, Charlie told this loser informant on the docks that the whisper on the river was there was a dime on the guy's head because back in February, he ratted to the Feds. Charlie promised the rat he could fix his prob and make the dime go away. My buddy Charlie told him he would trade his wise for a free ticket out of town."

"You guys have no mercy. Like that's going to happen. I'm listening."

"Seems the loser informant got a photo op with the main man you guys call Pit Bull. How he did that, I didn't ask, and he didn't tell. He and the drug lord grabbed a woman jogging the boardwalk and the two shared drugs and her un-consenting company. Seemed Pit Bull and the loser both liked their women drugged and easy. They spent the night with the broad and left her for dead, floatin' in the Mississippi."

"Why'd he admit to murder?"

"Oh, she didn't die. She was made up of some strong stuff. She was able to swim, or maybe float, to shore with a broken arm and her leg dangling. A fisherman found her unconscious. The photos show her jaw broken and eyes swelled shut. I don't even want to describe her baby maker, but the doc says she won't be having any more kids. She's a wife and a mother of two."

Dave chugalugged his Coke like he used to do his beer. "So, with the perp believing first, his playmate would ID him, and second, that there was a dime on his head, well, you can bet he started singing. He knew his life ain't worth shit anyway with Pit Bull putting the finger on him.

"'Course he doesn't know the mother of two can't remember anything. Charlie tells him the drugs must have been watered cause she's real busy weaving a pair of hangmen's nooses with his and Pit Bull's names on 'em." Dave reached into his bomber jacket, pulled out a manila envelope, and slapped it on the table. "Merry Christmas, buddy."

Brad bent the clasp and slid out the photos. The first was an eight-by-ten of the woman jogger. His stomach churned as his mind flew back to Jackie's crime scene. From the jogger's appearance, she was lucky to be alive. Others in Pit Bull's stable hadn't been so fortunate.

The second glossy was a Latino, dark, shoulder-length hair with a small dagger tattoo on his neck. The man's expression was one of surprise, his eyes wide open, and brows almost to his hairline. A bullet hole adorned the center of the man's forehead, explaining his expression. Either he had known his demise or the force of the bullet entering his skull caused the mask of tragedy.

"That's the loser. You're right, he wasn't able to pick up his ticket out of town."

Brad began to slide the woman and her loser attacker back into the package when a small Polaroid snapshot dropped onto the table. Picking it up, he stiffened at the faces staring back at him. The faces in the photo smiled at him. He cleared his throat and swallowed, trying to contain the eruption of emotion welling up inside his gut. Brad picked it up and studied the glossy. Nothing else existed, not the tinkle of beer glasses, the crowing of voices talking smack at the bar, or the glimmering jukebox as it scratched out another forty-five from the fifties. Bar patrons, his buddy, and the outside world evaporated into the blue smoke-filled room.

The photo, old and yellowed, was creased, its edges cracked and broken. One smiling face was a younger George sitting in a restaurant booth. Next to him sat Judy, who matched George's youthful smile. Brad's stare bore into the sepia print. He thanked the gods of destiny he sat at a bar in New Orleans, eight hundred miles from home... and from Judy. All these years, he held her on a pedestal.

He loved her from afar. He could handle her being with any-one, anyone except George—except Pit Bull. *How could she?*

"Where did you get this?" He had to restrain the urge to rip the happy faces to shreds. *How could she?*

"The loser slipped it from Pit Bull's scrapbook. Evidently the slime cherishes his keepsake moments, and likes to save them for posterity. Charlie said the scrapbook spanned decades. Do you know the girl?"

Brad ignored the question. "How's the chain of evidence? Is it clean?" Brad knew if there were one kink in the link, Pit Bull's lawyers would make sure he walked.

"That's the hitch, buddy. Our Bindi-bearing perp is too dead to finger the guy. So all the snap proves is a happy couple having a happy meal together. Do you know the girl?" Dave didn't let Brad's slight go unnoticed.

"She looks like someone I knew in school. " Brad kept his voice steady. "Well, at least we have an ID on Pit Bull. Thanks, Dave." He couldn't wait to get out of the bar, away from his friend's inquiring mind, and back to Springfield. "It's been great seeing you. Say hi to Gail. And really, thanks." They stood and embraced, pounding each other's back. "I'll let you know how it turns out."

"Oh, I'll hear about it. You watch your back, buddy. You're pitchin' in the big leagues now."

In an hour, Brad was packed and on a red eye back to Springfield.

"Would you like a drink, sir?" The stewardess smiled down. Her tightly wrapped hair and skirt reminded him of Darlene. His stomach twisted tighter in anger. *H.A.L.T. Don't let yourself get too hungry, too angry, too lonely, or too tired.* The voice of his AA sponsor and friend, Ken, penetrated his tortured musings. He was all those things. The jet engine's vibrating roar filled the cabin as if it too wanted to explode.

Brad was starving for justice, but the hunger was based on his love for Judy. Now he doubted everything he worked for. The decades he spent seeking justice for his teen angel—maybe he was the fool. Maybe she was no different than the rest of the women he had known. But none of those women settled comfortably in his mind and heart as Judy did. He remembered how well the alcohol had soothed him after she had moved to California.

He yearned to rid himself of the doubts. His anger flared, flushing his face. She should have told him she had something going with George. Unable to conceive of any other explanation, the photo he now studied was tainted green by his jealously.

"Sir? Would you like a drink?" He had forgotten she stood there, still looking like Darlene. He wondered if she ever let her hair down. Since his dad died, he had never had such an urge to cry.

Don't get too tired. Oh, God, he was tired. The forty-year vendetta was too big to carry, too heavy to drag. He wanted to drop it, bury it in Crosby's field along with all the unanswered questions. *But how can I quit? And yet how can I go on?* Without loving Judy, what was the point?

He stared at her smiling face; he knew his love wouldn't die. *There's no fool like an old fool.* He would see this miserable saga to its end. Now, more than ever, he wanted Pit Bull dead. And Judy would return to her life and he to Darlene.

When the plane touched down, he breathed in and again tried to bind up his emotions. He had a job to do. He hailed a taxi, not wanting to disturb Darlene. In the taxi he called his deputy chief, Ken.

"Ritchter here." The voice, heavy with sleep, reassured Brad. Ken always had a way of sorting out Brad's stinking thinking.

"Hey, how about meeting me at Abe's for breakfast?"

"It's four in the morning!" Ken paused and then Brad heard him sigh. "I'm putting on my jeans. I'll be there in twenty."

The café was empty of customers and Ken found Brad in the last booth, staring out the black window that revealed the streetlights not yet snuffed out by daybreak. He said nothing as he sank into the booth across from his friend.

Brad reached in his jacket and threw the worn Polaroid onto the table.

"What's this? You got the hots for George now? Am I the last to know? How long you been carrying around his picture in your wallet?" Ken was always good at taunting his friend when he needed to get something off his mind.

"Look who he's with." Brad's voice cracked.

"Yeah, so?"

"What's she doing with him?" Brad wanted to cry. The woman had reduced him to a heartsick old fool. His heart felt like it was made of paper and Judy was tearing it apart. He was panicked at losing the one decent thing he had found in his life. "What's she doing with him?"

"Looks like they're having dinner." Ken looked Brad in the eye and smiled.

"Yeah, I know they're having dinner! What's she doing with him?!" Brad saw the waitress look up from behind the counter. She had known the chief for a long time but never saw him out of control. She dropped her gaze and briskly wiped down the counter.

"Why don't you ask her?"

"Why don't you ask her? Why don't you ask her?!" He stuttered when he was out of control. "Well, aren't you a bundle of wisdom?" He hated it when Ken used common sense. When his mind became poisoned with emotion, it begged for alcohol to perform a cover-up. That's when his AA sponsor put on his detective gloves, taped off the area, and dusted for the underlying evidence of Brad's insanity. "Yeah. Why don't you ask her?" Ken prodded.

"You don't understand. It's not just this old picture. Bob told me George paid her a visit Sunday night. I want to know what that was about. But the closing argument is— and I have it from a strong source—George is Pit Bull."

"That's what we thought all along. Maybe when forensics gets done we'll be able to prove it. But you still have to talk to Judy. There could be a logical explanation. You're letting your heart cloud your judgment."

Brad leaned back in the booth, his adrenaline drained. His siege with jealousy and insanity curtailed. Resigned, he said, "You're right. I'll ask her."

"Good. Now let's have breakfast." Ken signaled for the waitress.

Brad went over the strategy with Ken for finalizing the investigation and set the meeting for the task force. Two hours later, stomachs sloshing with coffee, biscuits, and sausage gravy, they trod out of the café just as the sun melted the night's chill.

Chapter Twenty-Seven

Leaving the Cozy Dog, Carrie drove blindly through the streets, wiping her tears with the back of her hand. Her thoughts jumped around as if they examined hot coals. *I should have gone to Judy and told her I knew way back then. But if George had found out, he would have killed me. How could he have done what he did to Jackie? I know he did. Judy doesn't lie; she has no reason to lie. He's capable. He's all but told me.* When he beat me so badly, I had to go to the hospital. "You better tell the doctors a believable story, Carrie, or I can make it even worse for you. You have such a pretty face. That's why I never touch your face. But if you cross me, I'll see to it no one will be able to stand looking at you. You'll wish you were dead."

But don't I love him? All these years I've spent with him? But no children, except the miscarriage. He killed my baby, sure as he took a knife to it and stabbed it dead. The night he beat me for burning his steak. God, I know what Judy has lived with all these years. The pain from the loss of a child never goes away. She pounded her fist on the steering wheel.

No, I don't love him. I hate him to my core. If I had feelings, they died with my baby. I probably never did love him. He was a way out, the exit door from my miserable home life and Dad's beatings. I'm tired of running from the truth and not being strong enough to go on. Judy's something else. After all these years, she's come back to face her ghosts. I always wanted to be like Judy.

Carrie pulled up alongside George's Mercury and, drained, dragged her body into the house.

"Where have you been? Out fucking around?" George sat at the kitchen table, a six-pack in front of him. Two empties were lined up next to the cold one he clutched with fat fingers. Without answering, Carrie set her keys on the counter and proceeded to the pantry to start dinner. "Hey, bitch, I asked you a question. You too good for me after running with your hoity-toity friend, Judy? I shoulda killed that slut when I had the chance." He jumped up from the table and grabbed Carrie's arm to yank her around. She swung around to face him, her hand raised, clutching a butcher knife. She met his glare with a fierceness that stopped his advance. With his hands raised, he said, "Whoa! What's got into you? I haven't seen this side of you. You want a little S&M?" Her fierceness became replaced by confusion when she didn't get the reaction she wanted. George snatched the knife from her hand and, in one swift movement, wrapped his arm around her neck and grazed her cheek with the blade. "How do you want it? Slow and easy or hard and fast?" Carrie stood frozen. He tightened his chokehold. "I said, how do you want it, Carrie?"

"Whatever you want." Inside her, something died.

"That's what I like to hear. Just 'cause your friend Judy got to stick me, I don't want you thinkin' I'm fair game. Now I'm gonna remind you who's in charge here."

He threw her onto the cold tile. With one hand, he unbuttoned his jeans and jerked them down. Carrie's head hit the unforgiving tile. Her eyes glazed and she went to another place.

The hours passed as he continued to force her back with new tortures to her body. When he tired, her limp form lay still. "You won't be trying to stick me again now, will ya?" He laughed, climbed up off the floor, and buttoned his jeans. At the table, he grabbed his beer. "Goddamn it, my beer's warm. How about getting me a cold one?" His boot poked her lifeless body. "Did you get too much of my good thing? Okay, cunt, I'll get my own beer." He stepped over her and, with his foot, shoved her body away in order to open the refrigerator door. He took his special draft and retired to his recliner, just in time to catch his favorite show, *Cops*.

Chapter Twenty-Eight

Tuesday morning I rose early and dressed carefully. I had made a decision during the night to continue with my confrontations and pay a visit to Darlene. As I parked in front of police headquarters, the architecture reminded me of a condo in LA. I entered the foyer, passed through the metal detector with no hitch, and found the building's directory. I traced my finger over the words POLICE CHIEF BRAD JONES. My courage wavered as my hand lingered, but I took a deep breath and headed for the elevator.

The elevator doors opened to a lush carpeted area imitating a lavish living room, with plush couches and chairs positioned to face a large mahogany desk behind which Darlene sat. She looked small and unintimidating until I approached. She wore a champagne silk blouse that shimmered, and a bright yellow scarf around her neck. Her hair, drawn tightly at the nape of her neck, was secured with a gold clip. Adorning her temple was a flower made of ribbon matching the scarf and her blouse. Stopping in front of her desk, I felt frumpy and inadequate. Although I knew she had seen me step off the elevator, she looked up now as if startled by my interruption.

"May I help you?"

"Yes. I'm here to see the Chief." I figured I'd play the innocent visitor.

She played the game. "Do you have an appointment?"

"I'm sorry, no, but I'm sure he will see me." *Am I? Here's where the rubber meets the road.*

"What was your name? *I'll bet she knows who I am.*

"Judy Howard." The only sign of recognition was a minute pause as she struggled with how to play her next move. Would she play the gracious secretary and, with surprise, welcome me to Springfield? Or would she stick with the proper professional act and play it through?

Her upper lip twitched. She took the gracious route. "Judy, it is so nice to meet you. I'm Darlene, Brad's personal secretary." I guessed her voice was an octave higher than normal and she paused to emphasize the word "personal."

Now it was my turn to score. "It is nice to meet you." I reached over the rich, red grain of the desk and offered my hand. She had to stand up to acknowledge my gesture and in doing so, bumped a neat stack of folders to the floor. "Oh, dear, let me help you." I knelt down, suppressing a grin as she hustled to gather up her mess.

She stood up, shuffling her forms back into order, and said, "He's in meetings all day." *Score one for Darlene.*

"Oh, that's okay, I just thought I might catch him in. He told me he'd call me tonight." *Now who's up close and personal with the Chief, huh?* Darlene's lip contorted into a sneer, just as the elevator doors opened with a low rumble. Our heads turned in unison to see Brad stride unawares into our catfight.

I saw his surprise as he recognized me, but his reaction seemed guarded. "Hello, Judy. What brings you here?"

Stopping in front of me, he stared, ignoring Darlene. Was I being examined? I felt as if his gaze went right through me.

"I, uh...I just thought you might be in. I wanted to say hi." How lame, but I couldn't say, "I wanted to meet my competition."

"Well, I'd love to talk. In fact, I need to talk to you, but unfortunately I have meetings lined up all day. How about tonight?"

"Oh, that won't work, sir. You and I have that appearance at the Women's League tonight. It's a charity dinner." Darlene smiled.

"Cancel it and send a check with my condolences." Brad turned his back on Darlene and ushered me to the elevator. "So, tonight? Dinner? I'll pick you up at seven." The elevator door opened and the pressure of his hand on my back encouraged me to step in.

"Seven's good."

What just happened? I tried to evaluate our encounter during the ride down. Was there something wrong? It felt like it. Something had changed. Did he not want me meeting Darlene? Was he ashamed of me? Maybe he was just preoccupied with work. Well, it looked like Darlene and I parted with the catfight score tied, along with the knot in my stomach.

Brad glanced at Darlene as he headed into his office. Her lower lip protruded in a stubborn pout and she stiffened as he strode pass. He felt her stare bore into his back. "Bring me everything on the Pit Bull case. Everything. And hold my calls. In fact, take the rest of the day off. I won't be needing you." The sight of Darlene angered him. How could he have tolerated her company all these years? She was pompous and played her cards with a sinister agenda. He really didn't know anything about her, though they spent many evenings together at different events and were even engaged for a short time.

He quickly backed out of the commitment and canceled the engagement when he began to see a side of her that made him uncomfortable. She liked to talk dirty, really dirty, in the bedroom. And she encouraged him to do things he would never do to a woman. When he broke it off she pouted, claiming he just had cold feet and performed her job even more efficiently. His officers picked her up several times for speeding and reckless driving and brought her before him. The third time, he warned her. "Learn to control yourself or you are gone from this job. I won't tolerate it and will not give you special treatment." Her face had turned red and angry.

A few minutes later, she laid a stack of folders cradled in her arms onto his desk. "Will that be all, sir?"

"Yes, that's it, Darlene. Go home. Do some shopping. I'll see you in the morning. Close the door when you leave." He tried to temper his ricocheting emotions.

"Yes, sir."

"Did you cancel the charity dinner and send the check?"

"Yes. Sir." If it were possible, she made the two words even shorter than they were. Turning, she marched out the door, closing it softly.

Alone in his office, Brad focused on the job at hand. He expected Bob to arrive soon to review the evidence. He wanted to be sure he had enough to issue search warrants on George's body shop and home. He had a lot of circumstantial evidence and feared there wasn't enough hard evidence to make an arrest.

The light tap on his door interrupted his thoughts. Ken stepped in. "You okay, boss? Where's Darlene?" Ken studied Brad.

"I'm fine. I sent her home. Suddenly I can't stand to be around her. When I came in this morning, Judy was here. I thought there was going to be a catfight. I'm sure Darlene prodded her, but Judy had her tail feathers up, too. She was kind of cute. I wonder what would have happened if I hadn't walked in when I did."

"That would have made for some nice headlines. Did you talk to Judy?"

"We have a dinner date tonight. I'll do it then."

"Nothing like an interrogation by candlelight."

"I can handle it."

"I'm not so sure." Ken gave Brad's shoulder a slap as Bob entered the room.

Brad reached out and shook Bob's hand. "All right. Let's get to work."

After a couple of hours, Bob shook his head. "You're right, Brad. There's a lot here but all your witnesses are dead. We need more to connect the dots. We need a rat, someone pissed off enough to talk, and we haven't got that. There seems to be a connection with Judy, but until we get more, we don't know what it is. She knows more than she's telling. I definitely picked that up Sunday night."

Brad slumped. He had a case that was snagged and a snagged relationship with a woman he loved whom he wanted to love blindly and passionately. Both had to be untangled before he could have peace. He was returning the reports to their folders when another rap on the door came and John stuck his head in. "You wanted me, Chief?"

"Come on in, John. I got a job for you."

John gave a strong handshake to Bob, and then in his laid-back fashion, plopped down onto the leather couch. His long legs spread and fingers shoved into the pockets of his tattered jeans as he half lay on the sofa. "What's up?"

"I want you to spread the rumor we know who Pit Bull is. Let it be known that someone fingered him, that he's going down. Maybe he'll get nervous and make a mistake. Put some eyes on the body shop and his house."

"You got it, Chief. Hey, where's Darlene?" Brad locked eyes with John, but said nothing. John jumped off the couch with a limberness that belied his age and shifted back to the subject at hand. "Okay, then. I'll get my boys on it."

Bob followed John out. "Keep us updated. I'll make sure the judge has the warrants signed and ready."

After they closed the door, Brad sat still, gazing out the window at the Capitol building. He thought how history molds the future.

Chapter Twenty-Nine

I tossed the details of my visit around in my head as I drove back to my rig. Brad was bothered by something. Probably the case. Perhaps dinner would reveal the mystery. Back at the campground, I returned the rental car, stowed items away, unplugged, and unhooked so I could move over to Dad's. Sportster evaluated my movements and perched on the dash, anticipating a day on the road.

"Not yet, little buddy. We're only going across town. You have to meet your grandpa." I thought I heard Cowboy Jack mumble that we ought to be heading home.

"What's your problem? You want to go back to California?" I asked the doll. I guessed he thought I was wasting my time on foolish dreams. He discounted my feelings about the accident on the road, about George's attack, and reminded me I was not in the same league as Darlene. I wondered why I had brought him. He was becoming a burden and a disappointment. On a whim, I punched him in his polyester gut and he doubled over in his seat. I felt better.

Neither Bob nor Alice was around when I pulled out. I would miss the river atmosphere and Alice's cheery disposition. When I arrived, Dad laid down the water hose and waved me into the spot alongside the garage. The spring to his step showed his excitement for my company.

With my set-up chores completed, I drove Dad's Jeep to the store. I passed the Lincoln Log Motel and noticed a couple leaning against a convertible in the parking lot. The man pressed against a woman who sat on the hood, her arms wrapped around his neck. I would not have noticed, but a flash of yellow caught my eye. A bright canary-colored scarf billowed in the breeze from her shoulder. Her long hair hung loose, flowing with the scarf. I slowed almost to a stop and stared. It was Darlene. But it wasn't Brad she was with. The man wore a white shirt with sleeves rolled up, and a tie. A suit jacket slung over his shoulder and he smiled as he leaned into Darlene's flirting. His long tanned face sported a wide grin as her hands slid down from his shoulders, cupping his buttocks while her legs wrapped and locked around him. Laughing, he grabbed her from the car's hood. They disappeared into the motel room, with him carrying her.

A horn blared behind me. I realized I had stopped in the middle of the street. I gunned the accelerator and sped down the road, my mind swirling. If she was so possessive of Brad, what was she doing with that man? And who was he? Just what kind of relationship did she and Brad have? I sensed the answers would come that night at dinner. Whatever they were, I would handle them. I was tired of the unknown. I didn't want to play games and I was certain Brad didn't, either.

Chapter Thirty

For Carrie, the morning was surreal. George left early. Where he went or what he did now was of no consequence—a new attitude for her. How could she feel so numb and burn with anger at the same time?

Grabbing armfuls of clothes from the closet, she trudged outside and threw them into her car's trunk. Back inside, with a sweep of her arm, she shoveled the makeup and trinkets littering her dresser into a trash bag. Deep below the numbness was an urgency to hurry. George always threatened, "You never know where I'll show up or when." Finished in the bedroom, she stood at his office door, the room she was never allowed to enter. She checked the door. So sure of her obedience, George hadn't even locked it. Her anger blazed like the fire in the devil's eyes. She shoved open the door and charged into the room. Sharp pains from the beating fueled an internal inferno, jabbing her head and stabbing her torso. The agony threatened to bring her to her knees. Screaming in protest, her body urged her on, as if it too wanted revenge. She yanked the snaking cords from the computer and lugged the tower out to the car, dropping it on top of the clothes. She looked up and watched a black car moving along the road and approaching the driveway. The trees lined the street like a picket fence, showing only slats of blackness as the vehicle crept along. Her heart hammered, as she was unable to identify the sedan. Perhaps it was only her imagination when it appeared to slow at the entrance because, praise the Lord, it drove on past the driveway and out of sight.

Whimpering in relief, she rushed back into the house and, finding the set of keys George hid in Magnum's dog bed, she unlocked the file cabinet and desk drawers. Her hands shook so badly she used one hand to hold the other one steady. Sweat ran down her temple, slid down her neck, and nestled in her cleavage. She wondered how she could feel that sensation but feel nothing else. She stuffed two more trash bags. After hauling them to the car, she went back into his office one final time.

Pulling back the braided rug, she used the last key to open the trapdoor. Why had she never done this before? She knew the answer. She didn't want to know, could not have handled what she guessed all these years—that she was married to a monster. She reasoned he could perform horrific acts with her, but to know that he did the same to others…she could not have lived with that knowledge. How was she going to live with it now? She placed the photo albums carefully into her knitting bag, along with a thick address book and a laptop computer. She didn't open the albums. She never had, but she instinctively knew the stories they told. She thought of her friend Jackie in Crosby's cornfield. It was too late for her, but she would make sure there would be justice for Jackie and Judy. The thought made her feel better.

She rose from the floor, paused, and reached back down for the .38 snub nose, the only item left in the secret compartment. Shoving the gun securely into her jeans pocket, she rushed out of the room, not bothering to cover the evidence of her invasion. Grabbing her purse and car keys, she left without closing the front door.

Chapter Thirty-One

Brad studied the report from CSI. He heard the footsteps before the door opened. When he looked up, Carrie burst into the room like the explosion from a backdraft. She said nothing as she approached his desk, her face full of bruises. Her mouth drooped and her bottom lip hung loose. Her left eye was swollen shut, giving her the appearance of someone beaten both physically and emotionally. But in contrast, her anger flared, making her appear taller and confident. She slammed down her bulging knitting bag. Upending the bag, she spilled out the contents. Not yarn. George's laptop slid onto Brad's mahogany desktop, followed by several bundled paper packages. The last items to slide out, two photo albums and the address book came to rest on top of the computer. The title, "Our Family Memories," shouted from the top album's cover.

"The rest is downstairs with the officer in the lobby. Don't forget to look in the boat shed." She pointed to brown bricks of paper. "There's more where that came from." She turned to exit. At the door she paused, turned slowly, and, with tears in her eyes, said, "Tell Judy I'm sorry." Before he could respond, she vanished down the hall.

Brad's adrenaline raced as his mind quickly evaluated what Carrie had dumped in his lap. It was enough evidence to send George away for a lifetime. He radioed Ken and John ordered them to come back in. Next he called CSI to send up their electronic forensics specialist. "Hell, send the whole team up here!" Next, he called the front desk. "Stop the woman who left the evidence." He described her as a small woman with a big attitude. "She's not under arrest. Put her in protective custody immediately. She's dead if we don't."

Then he leaned back in his chair and opened the first album.

His stomach lurched. The first photos were of Jackie in various positions. She was not bound or even gagged, but the terror captured in her vacant stare proved she could not run or scream. The pages told of Jackie's final moments. Brad coughed then choked back tears. He slammed the book shut. CSI could examine the rest. He didn't have the stomach for it.

Chapter Thirty-Two

When I arrived back at Dad's, I unloaded the groceries, my mind still working the scene with Darlene and the stranger.

"Thanks for going to the store, Pumpkin. What would you like for dinner? Your old dad will cook for you tonight."

"Brad and I are going out. I forgot to tell you."

"Well, well. Somethin's already cookin' on the fire." He chuckled as he restocked the pantry.

"It is nothing like that, Dad." I felt my face flush. My heart still hoped for the best, even as I tried to pooh-pooh the seriousness of the dinner.

"In fact, I'll bet it's near the boiling point after forty years on simmer." Again he chuckled at his own metaphor.

"Dad, can I borrow your vacuum? I want to do a little housecleaning in my motor home. The cat hair's beginning to form a rug. I'll run it in here after I'm done. That should earn me privileges to a long hot soak in your bathtub, right?"

"Sure, Pumpkin. Make yourself at home."

I spent the afternoon vacuuming, polishing windows, straightening drawers, and stripping my bed. While I vacuumed in the house, I mentally made a list of chores. Tomorrow I would put new batteries in the smoke detectors and clean the furnace filter. The afternoon's chill reminded me the window screens needed to be changed out for storm windows. I enjoyed doing what I called "mindless work." Cleaning did not require much mental effort, but demanded enough to distract my brain from more serious problems. I soaked in the tub, calmed and satisfied with the afternoon's activities. I dressed in jeans and my USC sweatshirt. A thought intruded. Had my past been different, would I be donning the colors of the University of Illinois? I forced my mind away from the "what ifs" and joined Dad in the living room. The TV blared an old rerun of *Seinfeld*.

The time passed pleasantly and when I looked over at Dad, his chin was to his chest and his slight snore was muffled by the television's volume. I checked my phone and realized it was seven thirty. I had a missed call. I panicked. The TV had been so loud I hadn't heard my phone, and at that moment I realized I had told no one I had moved to my dad's. Brad must have gone to the campground and found me gone. I quickly pecked in the numbers but got only his voice mail.

"I'm sorry, Brad. I forgot to let you know I moved to my dad's. Give me a call?" *Boy, how stupid. Cowboy Jack will have fun with this one.*

I waited for his call back, becoming more depressed as an hour ticked by. Dad still dozed in his chair. I didn't want to disturb him, so I quietly slipped into the kitchen and called my cousin, John. He answered on the first ring. "Oh, I'm so glad you're home. Could you and Kate use some company?"

"Sure, Judy. We were just talking about you. Come on over."

I grabbed my purse and hurried to the car. When I parked in front of John's, he had the porch light on. When I was halfway to the front steps, Kate opened the door, flooding the flagstone walk with warm light. We embraced. "It's so good to see you, Judy. Come on in. John's in putting the kids down. Kristi and Eric left the kids with us for the week while they went to a retreat." She ushered me into the family room. "Would you like coffee?"

"If you have it made." Toys were scattered around the room and a diaper bag cluttered the coffee table. I scooted over a stuffed bunny and sat down on the couch.

"Hey, Judy. How's it going?" I stood up and almost knocked John over as I wrapped my arms around him. I began to cry.

"Why do you always make me cry?" I slobbered, trying to joke, but the tears didn't stop.

"Tell me about it." He waved Kate and the coffee away and she retreated to the kitchen, busying herself with the dinner dishes, giving John and me some privacy.

"Brad and I were supposed to have dinner, but I forgot to tell him I was at my dad's. He called and I missed his call and now he won't return my call. Oh, John, what should I do?"

"I'm sure he'll call you. Something probably came up. Is that all that's wrong?" He rubbed my back as I continued to sob.

"John, I know who raped me. I know who did it!" I pulled away from his embrace as his and Kate's eyes met. "It was George! I know it was him. I can't prove it but I know, John. I know." I paced the room, wringing my hands while John stood silent, with the calmness and patience that made confessions easy.

"Go on, Judy."

"Sunday night, he came to the campground while I was watching it for Bob and Alice. I wondered why he came. He said he was there to keep me company. Then he attacked me. He came around the counter, and before I knew what was happening, tried to rape me...and I remembered everything. It opened up the floodgates. It was like I was sixteen again, only this time I wasn't drugged. He shoved me down on the floor. It was awful, but then it was like...like I was a superwoman. I had a knife in my hand and I stabbed him. I stabbed him in the back." Kate's hand jerked and glass shattered on the floor.

"Oh, dear." Her head bobbed down behind the counter as she tended to the broken pieces. John stood still, unwavering in his attention to my story.

"But it didn't stop him. He raised up to hit me just when Bob and Alice pulled up out front. So he stopped, pulled on his jacket, the knife still in his back—well, the blade. The handle broke off. I still have it." I began to dig through my purse for the evidence I felt was so important. Holding out the handle, I showed John then Kate, as if they wouldn't believe me without it. "He made it clear that if I told, I would pay. He told me what he did to Jackie." I collapsed onto the couch, covering my eyes, my lungs gasping for air. "Oh, God, John. He killed Jackie. He told me! He bragged about it."

Telling John made it all so horribly real. "I was afraid to tell you and Brad, afraid what Brad might do, of what you might do. And what will happen to me? I stabbed him! What should I do?" John gathered me in his arms and held me so closely I heard his heart pounding. His outward demeanor belied the rage that I felt beating in his chest. *Oh, God, I shouldn't have told him. He'll tell Brad.*

"But I told. I told Carrie. She needed to know. She ran away. And I've tried to call her and she doesn't return my calls, either. I'm worried about her."

"Judy, don't worry. It'll all be okay. Everything's going to be fine. Kate and I are going to drive you back to your dad's. You just try to get some rest. Things'll look better in the morning."

It felt as if I had dumped a truckload of misery at John and Brad's feet. I knew they would take care of it. I even felt safe.

When John and Kate dropped me off and put the Jeep in the garage, I went in the house to check on Dad.

"How was your date with Brad?"

"He couldn't make it. I went over to John and Kate's for a while instead."

"So the pot still simmers?"

"I'll see you in the morning, Dad." I leaned down and kissed him.

"Good night, Pumpkin. Don't let the bed bugs bite."

Back at my motor home, I slipped into my pjs and made a cup of tea. Sportster purred and rubbed my arm as I stretched out on the couch. I checked my phone for messages. None.

Chapter Thirty-Three

Brad noticed that the Winnebago was gone as soon as he pulled into the campground. Fists tight with panic gripped the handlebars. What could have happened to her? Then anger. Where the hell did she go? Was she running from something? So much for taking her on a motorcycle ride. Revving the Triumph, he spun it around. A quarter of a mile down, the speed brought him to his senses and he slowed, pulling off into a clearing. He fished his cell from his pocket and in his haste, pounded out the wrong number, then redialed. His blood throbbed against his temples as he heard the voice-mail message. "Please listen to the music while your party is being reached." The first few bars of Elvis's "Are You Lonesome Tonight?" played in his ear. After listening to the ridiculous music, the digital voice instructed him to leave a message. What was going on? Slamming the phone shut without leaving a message, he straddled his bike, stewing over his situation before he eased his bike back onto the road. Finally, Brad twisted the throttle and the bike lunged, thrusting his body back. Pushing the iron horse to its max, he sped toward town. The cool night wind burned his eyes as tears streaked into his helmet, soaking his hair. He didn't hear his cell ring.

Brad passed the city-limit sign. Letting up on the throttle, he maintained a legal speed the rest of the way. At home, he cut the engine and coasted into the barn. Bridgette and Charlie approached, tails wagging. Dismounting, he crouched down and encircled an arm around each dog, pulling them close. He recalled reading somewhere that when someone pets a dog, his blood pressure goes down several points. He was exhausted from no sleep and forced to wait for the evidence against George to be processed. Then he could make a good arrest. Until then, he had to wait.

"How's the family?"

He rose and entered the stall Bridgette and Charlie had made the nursery, as four fur balls ambled toward him. He glanced around to reassure himself no one was witness, and then, on a whim, he lay down in the straw as Roy had done, allowing the innocent energy and puppy breath to renew him. Hours later, he woke to darkness under a blanket of bodies sprawled across his chest. Allowing exhaustion and lack of sleep to overtake him, he rolled to his side, toppling the warm brown shapes onto the floor, and slept with his head on Charlie as a pillow. He woke at daybreak to wet kisses washing his face and golden bars of sunlight streaming through the barn's slats.

He stretched, feeling rested. Heading into the house, he pulled out his phone and looked at his messages. One from Judy, three from John. By the time he reached the bathroom, he'd stripped off his clothes. After shucking his boots off, his bare feet hit the cold tiles of the shower. Thirty minutes later, he was back astride his bike and heading for the precinct. Before he reached the front door, he had John on the line. "What's up?"

"Where are you?"

"I'm at the front door. You?" Brad tipped his hat to the officer at the front desk as he passed.

"I'm here. We need to talk. I'll meet you in your office. Call in Ken, too."

Darlene was at her desk, a smile pasted on her face. "Ken and Bob are waiting in your office, sir.'

"Send John in when he gets here and hold the calls."

"Yes, sir." Her full lips formed a thin red line.

When they were all present, John began the meeting. "For now, what I am about to tell you stays in this room. At least until we know what to do." He locked eyes with each man until they nodded in agreement. "Judy came to see me last night when you didn't call her back." He focused accusingly on Brad. "She was upset."

Brad took a breath and opened his mouth.

John held up his hand to hush Brad. "She told me George tried to rape her Sunday night." John looked at Bob. "That's what had gone on that night, but when he attacked her, she wasn't the drugged-up teen he remembered. Our girl has balls now. She stabbed him in the back, but it didn't slow him down. The handle broke off in her hand and he was ready to beat her senseless when you and Alice pulled up. Of course he threatened her to silence."

Brad started for the door. How could this have happened on his watch? He had to see Judy.

John stepped in front of Brad. "Hold on, Chief. There's more. Judy's memory not only came flooding back, but our scumbag friend, George, admitted to killing Jackie. Judy was afraid to tell us. Afraid of what we might do, worried about the consequences of her actions. But she told Carrie. She felt her old friend needed to know."

"That's why Carrie did what she did. That's why she wanted me to tell Judy she was sorry." Brad looked around the room. "By now George knows what Carrie's done, but we have her in protective custody."

"No, we don't, boss. I checked this morning. Somehow she slipped out of here yesterday. I put out an APB, but nothing yet. She's disappeared."

"I saw George cruising through the campground last night. He was looking for Judy. It was a good thing she was gone. Let's get him. We got enough." Brad's breath was short as his neck muscles flexed and his jaw clenched.

"I'm already on it. The SWAT team is in the squad room waiting for you." Ken looked at Bob. "How soon can you get the search warrants?"

"I'm on it." Bob was already out the door, John at his heels.

"I'll be in the squad room in five." Brad gathered up the reports and flung them on Darlene's desk. "Get these written up for the DA. We got ourselves a solid case and a drug dealer." The elevator doors closed behind John, Ken, and Bob before Brad's quick strides covered the distance. He watched Darlene as the lights over the elevator scrolled to the first floor, then reversed their track back to the fifth. She held the phone to her ear. That woman was always on the phone. He wondered how she ever got work done, but she was efficient, he'd give her that. Which was probably why he would keep her on, even though in the past couple of weeks he had grown intolerant of her pouting personality.

As he rode down alone, his mind focused on Judy. He wanted to hold her, tell her everything was going to be okay. That he never wanted to leave her alone again. Never let anyone hurt her ever again. But then he smiled as he recalled John's words: "Our girl has balls." *I guess she can handle herself*. But this was Pit Bull she was dealing with. The photos from the album lit up in his mind's vision. The elevator doors swished open, and instead of heading for the squad room, he reversed directions. At the front desk, he ordered, "Send a message to the deputy chief to handle the meeting. I'll catch up later." He mounted the Triumph and bulleted away, his bike torqued to its limit.

Chapter Thirty-Four

Kneeling, I pounded the lid resealing the paint can. Dad was cleaning brushes, the part of the job I detested. I leaned back on my ankles, looked up, and surveyed our work. The front porch looked perfect. I had the satisfaction of a job well done and helping Dad felt good, too. The physical work occupied my mind and prevented me from pushing around the bothersome puzzle pieces of my life.

In the light of this new day, watching Dad, and just being here where I had begun, I felt the puzzle come together. The pieces found their places as if I watched a video of a shattering window in reverse. I could see clearly. Whatever happened with Brad I knew would be okay. When George pinned me to the floor, I faced my fears and passed the test. I no longer felt guilty, and no doubts about misdirected responsibility clouded my judgment. I would never again apologize for my existence.

Everything made sense. All the complexities in my life were now simple. Why I hadn't seen or understood before now, I would never know. I once heard it said that the universe reveals the answers when we are ready to hear them. So there I sat, the autumn air warmed by the morning sun as a sparrow lit upon the porch step and marveled at its improvement. Dad was in the garage without a drop of paint on his person. He too exuded an aura of peace. The morning light slanted in and spotlighted him. He meticulously lined up the clean brushes on the workbench and then, wiping his hands, he motioned with his cane. "I'll get us something for lunch."

I nodded and returned to my task when I heard the motorcycle's whine. It spit into a downshift as it neared, and finally putt-putted into the drive. I didn't need to see the face sealed inside the heavily tinted bubble with lightning-bolt decals to know who it was. Still on my knees, I observed every movement in total appreciation as Brad swung his leg over, peeled off his gloves, and flipped up the helmet's visor. In three long strides Brad stood before me.

He reached his hand down and I took it. As he pulled me up from the ground, our eyes locked. He drew me toward him. With arms of leather and muscle, he encircled me and I smelled only him. All that I had accomplished all that I had overcome—this made me feel complete.

We stood, embracing. The entire world was mine, if only for this instant, this megabyte in time. When we stepped back, he said, "John told me. Are you okay? Last night, when I saw you weren't at the campground, I thought you had left without even a good-bye. I didn't know what to think. And when Bob told me you were with George Sunday night...I should never have doubted you, Judy. I would have loved you anyway. I'm shameless with you, Judy. It scares me."

I laid my finger to his lips. The touch made my tummy flutter and my knees go weak. "It's okay. I'm okay. I know there's nothing you can do about George. I can't prove anything, but it's okay anyway."

"There's where you're wrong. Carrie came by to see me and she brought George's entire life with her and dumped it on my desk—computer files, drug money, scrapbooks, everything to send him away for a long time. We might not be able to prove what he did to you, but he will go down for Jackie's murder and all the others. Have you seen Carrie? We need to keep her safe."

"I haven't seen her since I had lunch with her. I guess she made her decision about George. I'm proud of her."

"I have to get back to the station. Everything's coming together. I'm posting an officer in front until we have George. Be careful."

"I'm fine. If I hear from Carrie, I'll let you know, but if I were her, I'd be putting as much distance as I could between me and that monster. I don't have anything going on. I'm just helping Dad with things around here."

"I'm going to be strapped for time until George is under lock and key, but I'm not breaking our date for the Get Together Dance on Friday. So I'll pick you up at six. We'll do dinner then the dance."

"I'll see you Friday." After he straddled his bike, he barked orders into his cell phone over the bike's rumble. Moments later, an unmarked car parked at the curb.

Back in the squad room, two teams prepared to hit the body shop simultaneously with George's residence on the river.

"I don't want any mistakes. Everyone watch your backs. This guy knows he's hot. He's got nothing to lose." His men were pumped. He saw the fire in their eyes, the determined line of their jaws. No one joked. The scraping and scrambling of men and equipment moved out the door. Brad stayed back in the now-silent empty room. He trusted his men to pull off a perfect raid, but with so many factors, he feared for their safety.

The radio in his office chattered as the clock ticked off the minutes, then the hours. Brad waited, staring out at the Capitol building. Darlene sat at her desk. They'd exchanged only a few words since his return from New Orleans.

He scribbled on a notepad. Waiting. Waiting. The clock ticked.

"Clear!" The radio squawked.

"We're clear, too. Shit!"

Pit Bull was gone. Somehow he had slipped under their radar. He tensed. He wouldn't rest until they had him. He reached for the mike. "Come on in."

Back in the squad room, Ken and John filled him in as the men stood by, quiet. "When we hit the house, no one was there," Ken reported. "The closet was half empty of clothes, Carrie's clothes. The cat was crying to be fed. No one's been there since Tuesday. Pit Bull probably went underground when he came home and discovered Carrie's deed. I'll bet he wants her as bad as we want him."

"That's bad." Brad thumbed through the preliminary reports.

"The body shop was like a bankruptcy sale. All the equipment and cars, just no principals." Ken handed over his prelims. "We have undercover listening for chatter and sweeping the known hangouts. It's going to take a while, but I'll bet if he wants Carrie bad enough, he won't stay hidden for long. Rage always influences a guy's judgment. He'll slip up. It's just a matter of time."

Brad nodded. "Good job, men. You're all on alert. No one goes home until this is done." As the team moved out of the room, John and Ken stayed behind.

"How's Judy?" John's forehead creased.

"She's good. We're good. I have a man at her house. I gave the job to McNalley. He was feeling left out."

Chapter Thirty-Five

Pit Bull woke to the building's creaking, as birds tracked on the tin roof like mice scurrying to infested holes. He rolled off the army cot that almost upended as he stood. Magnum, who lay curled in the corner, raised his head but didn't get up. A dusty shelf held a stash of groceries, five cans of ravioli, and a box of dry cereal. Beside the Cheerios, ten brick-size paper packages concealing over five hundred grand were stacked. He grinned. A half million dollars and his ticket out of the country. He lit the propane camping stove, heating water for coffee. He winced from the knife wound when he pulled the tattered curtain back, dragging it across the green carpet black with dirt. He peered out the only window without plywood covering it. Outside, a crumpled newspaper floated by like a ghost animal haunting the barren parking lot. He focused on a space on the asphalt where white lines once marked his favorite parking space that lay hidden from the main entrance.

Pit Bull's career had begun there. He could see the purple Mercury. He was eighteen, in the backseat with Judy, who was fresh, drugged, and ready. No one could say he hadn't been successful: the cars, the women, and the money. And he'd still be flying high if it hadn't been for Carrie. He wondered why he kept her around, but he knew. She was convenient, good for the in-between times. Like the punching bag at the gym, she absorbed the blows and swung in silence, always bouncing back for more, just like his mom. As the years passed, George became convinced she liked it.

So why'd the bitch rat him out? Women. Always changing their minds. If Judy hadn't come to town and put ideas in her stupid head, he'd still have everything. But she had and now it was over. Almost over.

He'd be dammed if he left the country without a little payback. He had feelers out for Carrie. Finding her should be easy. He hadn't figured her to be smart, and he was surprised she hadn't surfaced yet.

And Brad. He'd been an aggravation since high school, always winning with the faster car, always taking home the best in show. "You can bet Brad ain't going to win this one, Magnum," he said out loud. The dog perked up his head and gazed as Pit Bull yanked the curtain back. Dust motes danced in the air. Judy had been his ticket into the wonderful world of drugs and sex, and now she'll be his ticket out. Everyone knew Brad was a fool for the woman. He laughed out loud; the contempt echoed through the empty rink's arena. Magnum remained at a safe distance in the corner.

He'd been lucky for a long time. Smart-lucky. No one got this far in the business without good contacts and keeping his cool. With the help of Dirty McNalley and his bitch girlfriend, Darlene, soon he'd be sucking the worm from the bottom of his margarita while a bronze-bodied beauty on the beach of Mexico did the same to his dick. He laughed again, enjoying the echo. The image made him hard, and he paced, becoming more agitated in the small enclosure.

Everything was set. The FBI agent, McNalley, stopped by last night with updates and flight arrangements for two. The Feeb was proof that one man's weakness is another man's strength. The dirtbag Fed got addicted to Pit Bull's payoffs a few years back when the agent lost big at the track down in Florida. The mob wanted their money. McNalley had a wife and kids, making him a good candidate to become dirty. Pit Bull shared a joint and a brew with the guy many times in his own kitchen. In the bars, he marveled how the guy could work the women. Any bitch in the bar was easy prey. He'd rein her in with his cop stories, slip her Ecstasy, and the three made a night to remember. Darlene, the Chief of Police's main squeeze until Judy came to town, had her own addictions: dirty sex and dirty cops. That was going to give him a clean getaway and fresh start on the shoreline of old Mexico.

On Friday night, McNalley told Pit Bull where he parked the car and that Judy had left for the dance. "Don't you think about sampling any of that, McNalley," Pit Bull warned. "She's got a retirement plan in Mexico. She just doesn't know it yet."

The drug kingpin ferreted out his stash of weed from his jeans pocket and lay back down on the cot. Taking a deep hit, he closed his eyes and floated off to Mexico.

When the sun dipped into the horizon, he donned his hoodie and jogged through the twilight two blocks to the car parked at the Dublin Pub. He rubbed his stubble, pulled his hoodie low over his forehead, and slipped into the car. He turned on the ignition and the engine hummed in the darkness. "Good ole McNalley. A full tank of gas. That will get me to the airport, but first, The Meet and Greet Dance. How could I miss out on a last dance with Judy?"

Chapter Thirty-Six

I arrived at the dance early. Alice was working the registration, checking in the alumni as they arrived with their nerves and finery, trying, like me, to hide fifty years of life under elastic waistbands and hair dye. I wore my one full-length dress from my cramped closet. The black satin, perfect for funerals, was dotted with delicate lavender flowers for a classy look. The V-neck displayed enough cleavage to entice, but not enough to reveal the landslide that had occurred years earlier.

Alice lit up like a Christmas ornament when she spotted me. Jumping up, she rushed over and pulled me into a huge hug. "Bob and Brad promised not to be too late."

"Brad called me. He told me to meet him at the café across the street in thirty minutes. I'll mingle around, see if I remember anyone."

The gym was decorated in the school's colors of red and black. The DJ played "Alley Cat" and wore a red bow tie and white dress shirt. I made my way to the bar, keeping my hand on my small purse. Reassured by its weight, I straightened my shoulders and took a deep breath.

"Can you guys make a mean margarita?"

"You bet. We'll get you an early start." He flashed a warm smile and turned to the task at hand.

I scanned the gym. I thought of Jackie and our times in gym class. The bartender set the salted glass in front of me and I checked my watch. The gym filled up with squeals of recognition, handshakes and hugs, mixed with laughter and friendly banter. I was sure there were people I knew but they were masquerading as persons over fifty and I couldn't break their disguise. I wondered if they felt the same. I downed my drink, grabbed a handful of peanuts, and headed for the fire-escape exit leading to the alley.

Outside, autumn leaves rustled beneath the Dumpsters. A plastic bag fluttered and snagged on a renegade clump of dried dandelions pushing up through a crevice in the blacktop. As the door sealed itself shut, the noise of reunion gaiety was sucked back inside. I checked the alley both ways, trying to peer into the shadows. Spooked by the quiet, I headed toward the café across the street.

My hand clutched my purse. Streetlights lit up the small diner that had survived over the years on the support of delinquent teens ditching classes. The restaurant's sign didn't intrude on the alley's darkness. When I passed the last Dumpster and my foot reached the yellow pool of light on the sidewalk, a musky hand covered my mouth, jerking me backward while a strong arm encircled me. I felt a stinging pain on my neck and smelled my own blood.

"Fight me, bitch, and I'll have you bleed out right here."

I froze. "That's right, Judy. I never took you for a stupid bitch." He pulled me, dragging me toward a green sedan. "You and me are going to have our own dance, and then you're going to call that cop boyfriend of yours and he and I are going to make a deal."

Every nerve jerked alert. I calculated my options. I could do nothing but go along and appear terrified. I was terrified, but also an overwhelming anger burned like fire in my chest.

He shoved me into the driver's seat and ordered me to drive. When I passed the café, my foot pressed the high-beam button on the floorboard several times. I prayed Brad was inside and noticed and that George didn't.

George directed me toward Wabash Road. "Turn in."

I drove into the skating rink parking lot. The old abandoned building rested at the rear of the property, its patchy tin roof sinking from the weight of years of disrepair. In the dusk, tufts of yellowed grasses poked up irregularly in the dirt of dead flowerbeds. Only the bones of the rink's structure remained, wrapped in its rusted tin skin.

"Pull up by the door. That's right. You were always good at following orders." He laughed. His breath came fast. "Get out."

With one hand, he opened the boarded-up door, while his other arm grabbed me around the waist and restricted my movements. I felt the tightness of the dried blood on my skin, and the blade, no longer cold, burned against my neck. He smelled of Old Spice, the scent that had haunted me for a lifetime. Pushing through the door, he shoved me into a room that occupied the rink's office and skate rentals. In the dimness, an old vinyl couch lay sunken in one corner and a brown army blanket shrouded a cot that crouched low in the other. A crisp ironed shirt and pressed jeans hung on a rusty coat hanger from the arm of an old floor lamp. The clothes, lit by the filthy light, appeared expectant, waiting.

Chapter Thirty-Seven

Brad glanced out the diner's window, catching a glimpse of a familiar sedan driving past. He remembered he had seen George driving it occasionally around town. He tensed. It was George.

As the car passed the diner, Brad saw the headlights flash high beams three times. The car's windshield, the only glass not tinted, revealed Judy's shadow behind the wheel and George in the passenger seat.

His chair scraped loudly, crashing to the floor as he jumped up. Grabbing his jacket, he shrugged it on, and fished out his keys while barking into the radio's remote on his lapel. "The suspect's been spotted heading north on Lewis. Hold back! He has a hostage. I repeat. Hold back!"

George was a hunted man, yet the vehicle moved easily with the flow of traffic. The car turned onto Wabash Road, heading out of town past old man Crosby's place. Brad's neck stiffened and his jaw clamped at the memory of his first homicide. He'd been a rookie, on the force for a week, when he and his partner Ken had found Jackie's body in that cornfield.

With her murder scene in his mind, Brad drew on all of his training to control his urge to take up the chase. He held back, knowing how volatile the situation was. Knowing the wrong move would mean a death warrant for Judy.

The SWAT team and every officer on duty gathered at the Wal-Mart. Brad followed the sedan to the old building, then doubled back to rally his troops. In minutes, Brad barked out his strategy and his men exploded like shrapnel in different directions to surround the old skating rink.

He and Ken drove their cars close to the rink's door, parked, and waited. The night was quiet, but Brad saw the shadows of his officers stealing like assassins in the night, taking positions at the rink's back door and windows. Two flashes from a penlight signaled everyone was in position.

He exited his car. Ken followed his lead. The chief knew no one questioned his presence at this operation. He had overheard the talk in the rank and file. He was aware every officer knew this was personal. He figured the entire force knew Judy was never *just* an old high school friend before he ever admitted it to himself.

The SWAT team was poised, frozen in full gear, everyone's individuality hidden under armor and helmets. But Brad knew each and every officer. John stood closest to the door. When he was tense, John tilted his head, brushing his cheek on his wife's scarf tied to his shoulder strap. This had to be hard on him, too, restraining himself, Brad thought. And Joe. He stood to the left of John. He demonstrated his mark of identity by constantly wiping his palm on his thigh. Only twenty-two with a wife and three kids. The rest of the team had their personal stories, all important. Brad took a moment and asked his Higher Power for guidance. He hoped when the dust settled, Judy would be safe and all would go home to their families. Every fiber of nerve and muscle screamed to rush the building. But he held back.

Keep it slow. Stay controlled. It's so hard. My adrenaline's pumping. I want to get in there. Fix it. But I gotta take it slow. Trust my instincts. It's different every time. I have to go in, sweep every inch. Keep everyone together. Stay alive. Keep the others alive.

The chief picked up the bullhorn. "George! It's time to come out! Let's end this so no one gets hurt!" Only the quiet of the night answered.

Chapter Thirty-Eight

George shoved me onto the couch. The cushions sank from my weight, swallowing me. The dog in the corner did not rise, but tilted his head and studied me, ears up then back, then up again as if he did not understand. But his tail remained tucked between his legs.

"What's the matter, Magnum? Yeah, another cunt, just like Carrie. You just stay in your corner and watch the action. I don't need your help." George grabbed a gallon jug of water and took a long drink. The dog rose and faced him. George ignored the dog and leered at me.

"Like old times, right? Do you remember how good it was? No? Let me refresh your memory." He strode across the room, almost stumbling over the dog. He kicked it sharply out of his path. The dog yelped and I flinched. As perilous as my situation was, I jumped up to comfort the dog. Dropping to my knees, I hugged his big head. I felt the muscular body melt in my arms and the dog began licking my face.

"What we got here, Magnum? A dog lover?" His laugh sounded like a hyena, echoing throughout the building. He reached down and jerked me up. The dog scrambled to its corner. Again that smell, as he pressed his body against me. With both hands, I pushed against his chest and he laughed harder and louder. He removed one hand's grasp from my buttocks, reached up, and grabbed my hair, wrenching my head back. Cobwebs hung from a light fixture on the ceiling. A large black spider scurried around behind the globe. George kneed me in my crotch, shoving me toward the cot that smelled like wet wool.

I did not whimper. I did not cry. Fiery adrenaline raged through me like a wildfire but I kept it in check. I was in control as I appeared to surrender. I felt the weight of my purse dangling by its flimsy strap. One final yank of my hair sent me falling backward onto the cot. The metal legs scraped the floor and screeched as my weight landed.

George's crushing weight dove upon me like a pillow crushing my face. I couldn't breathe and I began to panic. White light blinded my sight. My arms flailed against his back. He jerked in pain as I pounded on the raw knife wound from Sunday. Still, his laughter rang in my ears so loudly I heard nothing else. My hand fell upon my purse and my vision cleared. I saw the spider above busily wrapping a large bug in its silk. I felt George's hot breath like a torch on my neck. I had been struggling but now my body went limp.

"That's right, bitch. Just relax and enjoy it. Or would you like to take something? It makes it so much better. I want it to be good for you. By the time we get to Mexico, you'll discover you can't get enough of this."

My hand fumbled with the purse's clasp. While George fantasized about his future, my fingers touched the cold steel inside the soft pocket of my purse. George's body tensed and twisted and once again the knife braced against my throat. "What have you got, bitch?" Reaching down, he pried the gun from my fingers, said, "You won't be needing that," and flung it across the room.

The thud of the piece against the drywall triggered an explosion within me. I twisted, screaming, and fought against him without fear. I would not lie down and die. The pressure of his blade increased and I felt it slice my skin.

"George! It's time to come out." Brad's voice penetrated my frenzy just as a roar of muscle and slobber streaked through the air.

Magnum propelled through the air. I felt George's body rammed by a hundred and twenty pounds of mastiff. In slow motion, my eyes caught George's wide-eyed expression and I heard the knife fall to the floor. For an instant, I thought the dog was after me, then realized the dog had not attacked his master, either, but instead wanted somehow to participate in our game. The dog used his massive form only to interject himself between us, and in the process slammed George against the wall.

The crushing weight removed, I rolled off the cot, dove across the room. Sliding on my belly, I grabbed the gun, rolled, and, in one fluid movement, I sprang to my feet. Legs spread, arms locked, my finger trembled on the trigger. "Don't move!"

The dog, as if following my command, froze, too, in a prone position on the bed like a sphinx of marbled muscle. George sat on the floor between the bed and the wall, draped by the curtain ripped from its rod. Although an amusing sight, George wasn't laughing.

"We're coming in, George. There's no way out." Brad's presence outside the room loomed like a bad storm.

George said nothing. I said nothing. The dog glanced back at me. He seemed to ask, What are you going to do? My finger flexed. It would be easy. Just a little more pressure.

George read my indecision. "Aren't you going to answer your boyfriend?" I heard the fear in his voice. He wasn't laughing.

"How about you, George? Why don't you answer? He's coming for you. Are you afraid he'll come in shooting? I'm not sure I want him to have the pleasure." I laughed. I felt good. "In fact, the more I think about it, I'm sure I don't want to share this experience. Like you said, George, 'I want it to be good for me.'" I laughed again. Nothing could stop me. I was invincible. My finger muscle twitched.

I heard footsteps in the arena. Magnum heard them, too, and jumped from the bed to check out the intruders. For a few seconds, my focus shifted to the door. George lunged for the gun, whose aim had followed my eyes.

He grabbed my gun as easily as if I'd given it to him. His quickness stunned me as he swung me around and again bound me to his chest. This time not a knife, but a gun's cold metal burned my neck.

"Why don't we invite the Chief to come on in and join the party?" He stabbed the muzzle deep against my throat. I coughed. "Go ahead. Tell him to come on in."

"Brad, we're in here. Don't come in; he has a gun."

"Don't listen to your bitch, Brad. This is better than any car show competition or drag race. The trophy will be your girlfriend. I know you'd like to win that." He didn't laugh. His tenseness made his body rigid.

The door's handle turned. "Okay, George. I'm coming in. Stay calm. We'll talk."

Chapter Thirty-Nine

The team crept into the rink, soundless like a smoke bomb, moving through the area. Only a whispering tink from their gear and a hint of rustling uniforms broke the stillness. They took it slow, so slow Brad's muscles ached. The area was clear. Except for the room.

The SWAT team crouched in front, while behind the counter the private door to the office remained closed.

"I'm coming in, George. I'm not armed."

"No! Don't come in. He'll kill you." He had dealt with hostage situations before, but none whose outcome had such a personal investment. He motioned for his officers to stay down, but nodded to John to move outside and around to a position by the window.

Brad turned the knob, pushing the door open ever so slowly. Brad stood facing Judy, whose body blocked Pit Bull's. Magnum took his stance between the two forces, his head swiveling back and forth from Judy to Brad. The chief did not see what he expected in a hostage's eyes. There were no tears.

Standing proud and angry, she was ready for the outcome, whatever it may be. His stare shifted up to the drug dealer, who kept his position behind Judy.

"You can't get far, George. We have you in our sights. There's a red bead dancing on the back of your head. Put the gun down and maybe we can make a deal."

"The only deal I'll make is a police escort to the airport. Your girlfriend and I got tickets to Mexico. I'd invite you but a three-way with you doesn't excite me. You always were a tight ass, Brad."

Brad didn't react to the taunting. He smiled and focused on Judy. "Judy could always do the moves, that's for sure. Right, Judy?" He looked into her brave eyes. "All that roller-skating made you as limber as a rag doll. Remember?" Her brows creased, then widened in recognition.

A faint nod from Brad and Judy's body dropped, folding forward as if she collapsed. When George's hold faltered, the chief swung his leg up in a karate kick, sending the gun flying. Judy dove for the gun as Brad reached behind his back for his own.

"Hit the ground, asshole!" Brad hoped he wouldn't. Hoped he'd make a move, but George dropped. Together Brad and Judy stood poised, guns aimed at the drug dealer.

"You go on outside, Judy. I'll wrap things up here." Brad didn't take his focus off Pit Bull but realized she hadn't moved. "Go on, I said." Still no movement. When she did, only her arm shifted to target her rapist's head. Brad didn't hesitate. Following her lead, he adjusted his aim as well. The drug dealer stared up, his eyes pinched in hate.

"Looks like Judy and I are on the same page. What do you say, George?"

"You won't kill me." Defiant to the end, Brad thought.

"Did you hear that, Judy? We can't do this. Shall we prove him wrong? What d'ya say?" He raised his voice. "What do you say, men? Are you with me on this?"

Five officers in full gear crowded into the doorway. A boom of voices answered, "Yes, sir, Chief."

"I'll bet Carrie would like to share in the fun. Right, Judy? Maybe we should call her."

"And there's Jackie's folks, too. They told me if they ever found out who killed their daughter before the cops did... well, I think you can fill in the blanks."

"Carrie's a bitch just like you." George spat at Judy. "And Jackie was the biggest cunt of all. That's why she's dead." Brad's leg delivered a sharp kick to Pit Bull's ribs that caused the kingpin to writhe in pain. Brad swept down, grabbed the man by his shirt, and slammed his weapon against Pit Bull's face. Pit Bull's body went limp.

Brad looked over at Judy. "Won't be much fun to finish him off now, huh?" He smiled.

"Damn, guess not." Judy turned, snatched up her purse, and slid her weapon inside.

Brad rolled the kingpin over, cuffed him, and then looked back at Ken. "All yours, Detective." Brad slid his arm around Judy's waist and they walked out of the building. Magnum trailed at their heels. "Do you think I can get you back in time to have the last dance?"

Chapter Forty

After dumping George's career onto the Chief of Police's desk, Carrie slipped out the side door of the station and headed for old man Crosby's place. She figured she would have a few days before being forced to find another hideout.

She had always planned—dreamed, really—of what she would do if she ever got away.

First, she would get a place of her own, something not much different than the cottage on the river. A quiet place, serene. A place where she would have a garden. She would grow fresh vegetables, and black raspberries. She loved black raspberries. And she would cook. During the few good days of her miserable life, she experimented with herbs and spices, creating new dishes. She accumulated boxes of cookbooks over the years. Escaping her depressing, lonely existence, she would become absorbed, studying the ingredients of a particular recipe.

She fantasized about being a writer, too. She saw herself in a cozy room at her humble cottage, gazing up from the manuscript she crafted to view a scenic landscape, a river, or sometimes she imagined a mountain view. There she would write cookbooks and the stories inside her head that abuse prevented her from telling.

But she had to bide her time. Wait. She had been waiting for forty years. She could wait a few more days. Crosby's farm was perfect. George would never look in his own backyard. She felt safe. It was quiet in the barn's loft. An old, paint-blistered rocker remained by the loft's partially open bay doors. The antique chair swayed with the help of the breeze drifting into the loft. She recalled Judy and Jackie hefting the piece up the ladder. They spent many Saturday afternoons up there dreaming about their futures. When she sat in the chair and looked out, the world promised her everything. Funny how things turned out.

She lay back in the loft, the hay brushing her cheek, and she slept, exhausted from the pain of her injuries, which had not yet healed, some she knew never would. For a while she slept soundly, satisfied with her first day of freedom.

"Carrie! Carrie! Over here." The young female voice came from deep in the cornfield.

"Where are you?" Carrie left the road and ventured into the forest of corn. The silken tassels were ripe with yellow dust that sprinkled into her hair and onto lashes. "Where are you, Jackie?"

"Right here. I can see you." The voice of her friend was pleading, urgent.

She veered right, crossing a couple rows, bringing her closer. When she crossed the third row, the field of maize opened up into a lush green meadow.

"Carrie!" A red convertible, its top down, was parked under a tree. The girl waved again. "Over here."

It was a short distance but Carrie walked slowly, passing images.

She saw her friends, Judy and Jackie. They sat in the Cozy Dog. Jackie motioned for her to join them. But it was as if their greeting, like the sweep of a wand, caused the dreamer to vanish. Poof!

Another image along the path showed a woman in a hospital bed. Carrie saw herself, cuddling a newborn in her arms. The reflection, too, bid her to approach, but as she did, mother and child evaporated.

Everything seemed out of reach.

She walked on, determined, with a quickened pace toward the car. Jackie was still seventeen, her thick hair flowing over the seat. Dark sunglasses hid her eyes that everyone called "sparkling." Jackie fiddled with the radio knobs and "Teen Angel" scratched the quiet of the meadow. At last Carrie was able to approach the illusion. "Jackie, I've missed you. Where have you been?"

Jackie looked up from the instrument panel and turned to her. The sunglasses fell to her lap. The woman in the car had no eyes, her head only a skull with strands of blood-soaked tresses that smeared her blouse. "What happened to you, Jackie?"

"You know, Carrie."

Carrie woke to her own shrieks and slapped her hand over her mouth. She held her breath, listening for stray sounds. Nothing. No voices in the fields. She let out the air in her lungs and lay back in the straw. Daylight pried through the slits from the warped lumber that tried to pull away from its restraining nails. She knew what the dream meant. She felt responsible for so many deaths. If she were going to have any peace in her new life, she was going to have to make it right.

She reached over to her duffel bag. Her hand dug down to the bottom; her fingers felt past the cold metal and rested on the paper packages. The paper was like velvet. She had wrapped them with the most expensive paper she could find and topped them off with satin bows.

She rose, walked over to the bay doors, pushed them open wider, and sank into the chair. From the loft she had a clear view of the road and the surrounding fields. She thought about her life, where it had gone, where it was going.

She would miss the dance tonight, she mused. Judy was going with Brad. Carrie smiled, thinking of her friend. Out of the Threesome, maybe one of them would find happiness. As she gazed out on the landscape, Carrie thought of her day. She wished she could have seen the look on George's face when he came home. It proved wishing someone dead didn't make it so, because she knew he was plotting her death at this moment. Sooner or later George would find her if the cops didn't get him, and even if they did, he had connections.

The afternoon wore on. She read from her favorite cookbook and jotted ideas in her notebook, nursing her fantasy of freedom.

The setting sun peaked over the rows of corn. It was twilight when headlights beamed unnecessarily, yet being without them would have been risky. She saw the beams first, then the car as it made its way down Wabash Road to the old abandoned skating rink. A considerable distance behind, a second car she recognized as Brad's Chevy followed suit with no lights. Brad should be at the dance with Judy, she thought.

Carrie's pulse quickened. Was fate handing her an opportunity? Grabbing her car keys and bag, she hurried down the ladder.

Chapter Forty-One

Carrie scrambled down the ladder, duffel bag in tow. She pulled open the barn doors, tossed the bag into the passenger seat, and followed it in. Her pulse raced as she fired up the engine. She kept her eagerness in check, driving slowly to avoid a dust cloud, though dusk was quickly turning to darkness. She, too, stayed within the speed limit, without headlights.

Two blocks before she reached the skating rink, she passed an army of patrol cars converging at the Walmart, but she crept on past. She hung back and watched Brad pull to the side of the road. The green sedan Brad tailed was already parked in the rink's lot. George must have already been inside. When Brad made a U-turn, heading back to Walmart, she turned right, ducking down a side street, and parked. She felt for the cold steel of her gun's barrel and yanked it out of the canvas. Jumping from the car, she sprinted down the road darkened by a canopy of trees. She felt her pulse throbbing in her temple. When she reached the green sedan, she dropped to the ground and rolled under the car. Her hands shook as she hugged the gun to her chest. She dragged her legs of lead under the belly of the car. And waited.

Hours passed. She looked at her watch. Thirty-seven minutes. Brad's Chevy, shadowed by a patrol car, crawled up to the rink's entrance. Carrie watched as Brad's and Ken's boots lowered to the ground and took a solid stance behind their car doors. A dozen pair of black boots attached to blue legs scattered like centipedes infesting the parking lot. Similar to the pests of darkness, they made no sound. She could touch Brad's pant leg, he stood so close. She held her breath.

"George, we're coming in." The blast from the bullhorn made her jump, hitting her head on the undercarriage. The two pairs of boots moved slowly toward the door and took their turns disappearing inside. Five more pairs trailed the two.

"Don't come in! He's got a gun." Judy's voice sent a chill down Carrie's stiff aching spine.

The ridiculous segment from the Disney movie *Dumbo*, called "Pink Elephants on Parade," flashed into her mind. The tune from her childhood played in her head. '*Look out! Look out! Pink elephants on parade. Here they come. They're here. They're coming around the bend.*' *Da dump, da dump, da dumpety-dump.* But this was not a hallucination. The boots tramped inches past her head. When the last pair disappeared inside, the boarded door slammed shut and silence settled under the sedan again.

Hours passed. She looked at her watch. Twenty-eight minutes. Needles pricked at her muscles. Her neck bones crackled if she moved.

A rush of feet, confident in their destination, burst through the door, now opened wide. Gear rattled on belts, voices were lighter, but words were still clipped. Next she saw low heels, followed by Brad's boots. Carrie let out her breath. A tear leaked down her cheek. "Thank God," she whispered. But still she lay there, not moving.

Another hour passed. Again she looked at her watch. Only twelve minutes. George's large tennis shoes stumbled by next, accompanied by another pair of police-issued boots. They moved to the squad car that blocked the sedan. His spicy scent snaked down and slid under the car. Her stomach lurched at the smell that clung to everything she owned and saturated every thought she ever had.

The parade of black boots tramped back by and reassembled around the other squad cars. Leather creaked and equipment thudded into car trunks. Voices became louder, words easier.

Time was running out. George's sneakers stood by her face. If she scooted up, she could point the .38 at his crotch. If she was going to do this, she'd better do it now. Could she do it?

"We'll take it from here." Carrie jerked her head around. She rolled onto her belly to get a better view.

"Hey, Chief." The words came from the detective standing beside George. They were now joined by a pair of wingtips in plain clothes. She scooted forward. It was the FBI guy, McNalley. The creep had been to her house, drinking and popping pills with George so many nights she couldn't count. She remembered how his musk cologne mingled with the Old Spice and left a stink in her kitchen worse than garbage.

McNalley handed the chief papers as two plainclothes men stepped in, encircling George, Brad, and his chief detective, Ken. Carrie had seen the two with George, but didn't know their names.

Ken and the chief exchanged muffled words. Ken flailed his arms and Brad shook his head. One of the men moved behind George and began to uncuff him. From Carrie's angle, she observed the man slip an automatic into George's hands.

"Oh, no!" Carrie thrust her body out from under the sedan and leaped to her feet. "Don't move! Anybody! Brad! McNalley's one of them."

McNalley reached inside his jacket as Brad drew on him. "Listen to the lady."

Ken aimed at the other suits. "Like he said, listen to the lady." When the detective reached to grab George, the drug dealer slammed his body against Ken. The detective, knocked to the ground, squeezed off two shots as the suits reached for their weapons. Brad grabbed the automatic from McNalley's jacket and shoved him over to his officers. "Cuff him." Both Brad and Ken swung around as George brought the automatic from behind his back and aimed at Carrie.

The series of shots that followed lit up the night. Carrie saw every detail of George's expression as he watched the bullet from her gun smash deep into his groin. He remained standing. "You fucking bitch!" She smiled and then saw Brad's bullet hit its mark. Pit Bull's face exploded while Ken's bullet tore open his throat. His legs buckled and he dropped to his knees. His arms extended but bloody hands clasped no weapon. He wavered a moment. Ridiculous, she thought, it looked like he was praying. He then toppled over, face first onto the ground.

Everything went still. Carrie stood and watched Brad turn toward Judy, whose arm pointed her .38 to the ground. It must have been her bullet that shot the gun from Pit Bull's hands. She looked one more time at George. He lay face down in the dirt, arms still extended in Carrie's direction. Magnum approached from the shadows, sniffed his master, and caught Carrie's scent floating in the gun powdered air. He bounded to her. Everyone moved at once as the parking lot came alive with activity. Judy rushed to Carrie as Brad approached Pit Bull's body.

"Are you okay?" Carrie dropped her weapon and fell into her friend's arms. The embrace released every needle of tension, and Carrie wondered if she had been cold all her life, because now she felt warm. Warm and safe.

Chapter Forty-Two

After hours of grueling questions, Brad and the FBI reached an agreement, and Carrie and I were allowed to go home. I hugged Carrie outside the station. "How are you doing? Are you going to be okay going home alone?"

"I've never felt better in my life."

"Will I see you at the dance tomorrow night? I hope so."

"I'm going with Kate and John, since you already have a date."

"I'll see you there." I gave her one more huge hug and climbed into Dad's Jeep.

"What kind of meet-and-greet dance ends up at the police station?" Dad's brows wrinkled as he reached across to embrace me.

"I'll tell you all about it, but first let's stop at Den's Chili. We'll eat chili and talk 'til dawn."

At home, I invited Dad into my rig. After I covered every detail of my ordeal, he asked, "Where did you learn to shoot like that? Not from my lessons with you and your sister at the river."

"I got robbed at gunpoint at my grooming shop once. The guy shot my dog. After that I bought the gun and went to target practice regularly. I never told you. I didn't want you to worry. What I want to know is, where did Carrie learn to shoot like she did?" We both laughed. "She'll never live that down."

"I can't wait to see the paper in the morning." Dad started to rise. "It's been a long day for you, Pumpkin. I'll let you get to bed." Sportster jumped onto the table, purring and rubbing my hand. "You take care of her, Sportster." Dad ruffled the cat's fur and kissed me on top of my head.

After Dad left, I stood in the hot shower, washing away the filth, mental and physical. I scrubbed until my skin turned red. Satisfied, I slipped into my soft kitten pjs. Sportster beat me to the bed, lying in the middle and refusing to move over. I crawled around him and slipped under the covers, hugging the edge.

As I lay snug in my motor home, Sportster making muffins on my neck, I heard Cowboy Jack mutter, *I knew it was him.* I laughed out loud. It didn't matter anymore what the doll thought. "Did you hear that, Sportster? He always has to have the last word. This is going to be Cowboy Jack's last trip." The cat tilted his head at me.

"Not you. You have a permanent position." I dozed off with Sportster nuzzled by my side.

I dreamt of puppies and kittens, green grass and four-leaf clovers. Rivers floated colorful leaves in their currents. Couples danced jitterbugs and waltzes, dressed in gowns and blue jeans. In the center of these images, Roy hugged a dog as a prison guard looked on.

The visions faded and I finished the night in a deep, dreamless slumber.

In the morning I lay in bed, enjoying that peaceful time between sleep and being awake. The sun had made its appearance hours ago. I heard Dad's knock.

"Hey, sleepy head. How about some breakfast?"

I sprang out of bed and swung open the door. "Good morning."

"Breakfast will be served in the dining hall, madam." Dad held up a rose and then took a long low bow.

I snatched the rose and placed it behind my ear. "Thank you, sir. I will be right in." I did a sweeping curtsy.

Sausage and waffles were on the menu as we ate Dad read the front-page account to me.

When he finished I said, "Internal affairs had an eye on McNalley for a long time. With George's record, it looks like he'll be spending a long time on the other side of the tracks. Brad's going to be earning a few more commendations for all this."

"I'm just glad you are okay, Pumpkin. I don't know what I would have done if something happened to you. Which brings me back to the question, have you thought anymore about moving here?"

"It's not that I don't want to, Dad. It is wonderful being here, but I would have so much to wrap up back in California. And the winters here—they can be so harsh."

"I handle them. And anyway, now you have more than a cat to keep you warm...if that's what you want." Raising his brow, he gave me a mischievous grin and refilled my coffee.

"Oh, Dad. I never knew you to be such a matchmaker."

"I just want what's best for my little girl."

"I'm not a little girl anymore, Dad."

The morning hours rolled by as we covered every subject from the care of rosebushes to politics. My mind wandered around the kitchen, and I saw my sis and me huddled by the furnace grate on winter mornings, waiting for the radio to announce school closures. My hand moved over the yellow Formica on the kitchen table where it was rubbed white from wear. I remembered Mom's excitement when Dad installed the gold and green linoleum, its pattern featured in the magazine McCall's. The memories pulled at me and the idea of moving home settled comfortably in my head. While I drifted back into the pleasantries of the past, Dad excused himself and moments later reappeared.

"I wanted to show you this." Dad held up a dress that I recognized as Mom's, a cotton halter dress with purple and yellow flowers. Although a casual design for its time, the T-straps and wide belt and big buckle gave it an elegant look.

I saw my parents laughing and cooing, just home from a night out, Dad with his arm around Mom as they sat in the swing on a summer night.

"This was her favorite. I wondered if you might want to wear it tonight."

"It would be perfect. I always loved that dress." I swept it from his hands and pressed it to me, swirling around. "It will be perfect."

Chapter Forty-Three

Four hours of sleep was okay. He couldn't sleep longer anyway. Catching the sunrise, Brad sipped coffee as Bridgette lay on the porch beside him, watching her puppies race in circles around the yard. Charlie lay at the bottom of the porch steps. Brad had watched the dog decide it was not worth the pain to his hips to make the climb. A stab of sadness made Brad squeeze his eyes closed.

He reviewed yesterday's events. Pit Bull was dead. The drug ring was falling apart. The mounds of information and data collected and still being processed was going to impact the drug scene for years.

And the miracle was, he had not lost one man. Judy was safe. The mysteries of her past were solved and he knew she would have closure. The grayness of the dawn began to fade as the cirrus clouds blended into pinks and blues. It was going to be a beautiful morning.

He reached down and scratched Bridgette's ears. Charlie lifted his head, watching with envy. "Okay, buddy." He swung his legs off the railing and came down the steps to sit on the last one. "I know, old boy. Life is hard sometimes." he old dog leaned his head into his hand and closed his eyes as he enjoyed Brad's attention. Bridgette looked on from her spot on the porch. Brad thought she looked grateful he was comforting her friend.

"Tonight's the night, Charlie." He sang softly to the dog, *"Tonight, tonight. I'll see my love tonight..."* The soundtrack from *West Side Story* played in his head. Very few knew he loved musicals; *Oklahoma, South Pacific,* and *Grease* were some of his favorites. *"Tonight, tonight..."* He hummed the tune and made his way into the yard. Four racing puppies shot a look in his direction and put on their brakes. Tumbling over one another, they reversed direction and stampeded toward him. Brad squatted down as the fur balls climbed all over him and leaped to kiss his nose and nip his ears. Puppies cancel evil with only a look, Brad thought.

Before Judy left for California, he intended to ask her if she would consider moving to Springfield. He would offer her a job to motivate her if his vow of love wasn't enough.

He had been reading about a new program in New York that raised puppies and sent them to live with prisoners. The inmates were taught to train the puppies to become service dogs for Iraq veterans who suffered from post-traumatic stress syndrome. The curriculum was highly successful, not only in the rehabilitation of the prisoners but also in enabling the veterans to live with their disabilities. After watching Roy relate with Bridgette's puppies, Brad considered starting a program at the state prison. Judy would be the perfect candidate to run it.

He tossed the last bit of coffee with grounds into the rosebushes and headed into the house. He picked up the paper and sat in the recliner. His eyes fell on the small envelope that lay next to the reunion tickets. Late last night, Bob had rushed into his office just as he was leaving.

"We found this in the Mercury, Chief. I thought you would like to have it." Bob left quickly, not waiting for Brad to reveal the contents. When he opened it, Brad was glad he was alone. A mixture of emotions, hot and cold, rushed through him. He slid the contents back into the envelope and tucked it in his pocket.

Brad scanned the front page of the *State Journal–Register* and two other newspapers he read every day. "Woman Finds Revenge." Another was bolder. "Drug Kingpin Loses His Life and His Balls." And the last quoted him: *"This puts an end to an era of drug-related crime. I'm proud of each and every officer for his teamwork, and the FBI for its cooperation,"* stated the chief. Brad folded the papers and set them aside. *Now we have to stay vigilant for the vermin trying to scurry into the hole Pit Bull left.*

Brad laid out his sports jacket and jeans for the night even though it was early. He sang, *"Something's coming, something good. I don't know what it is, but something's coming, something good. If I can wait..."*

Chapter Forty-Four

We walked through the gym doors, Brad's hand resting firmly against my back. I tried not to think of his touch, because it made me shiver and covered me in goose bumps. I wanted to do a happy dance, jump up and down, and shout.

I walked calm and steady beside him, as if I'd made this entrance a hundred times before with the Chief of Police. The locals turned to look but pretended not to. Brad's blue jacket picked up the blue in my dress as if the two were dyed to match. I smelled my corsage's perfume and wanted to swoon like a southern belle. Brad made his way past friends and acquaintances as if we were in a receiving line. He paused to shake a hand, clap a shoulder, or ask about family. I felt proud, no, humble, yes, proud, definitely proud to be by his side. What if things had been different, would we have done this forty years ago? Would our children be here to help us celebrate? All the "what ifs," the "should haves," and "shouldn't haves" swirled in my head. I felt dizzy.

I saw Carrie waving from across the room. I nudged Brad and nodded toward Carrie. We made our way through the crowd of alumni.

"They're playing 'Jailhouse Rock.' What could be more appropriate?" Carrie shouted above the band and grabbed my arm. "Let's dance. Do you remember how?" She dragged me into the crowd. I felt foolish, but her energy and the music spurred me, sweeping me into the frenzy. I laughed so hard tears wet my cheeks. Brad watched from the sideline, still the bystander, but he stood confident, dignified, and magnificent. Again I shivered, the goose bumps tingled, and my knees went weak. What a night.

The time passed quickly. I danced the slow dances with John, Ken, and Bob. The wives joined Carrie and me as we did the Chicken, the Twist, the Hand Jive, and the Locomotion. John, never afraid to embarrass himself, joined in, too.

The lights dimmed, signaling the last dance. The band's lead singer, who looked like Patti Page herself, began to sing as violins played "Tennessee Waltz." Couples moved onto the dance floor. I felt Brad take my arm. I looked up and he nodded toward the floor. "May I have this dance?"

My heart stuck in my throat and I wondered, "Had I used enough deodorant?" He pulled me close and impressed me with his skill on the floor. We glided through the crowd as if we were the only couple. Our cheeks touched and our hips melded, and we danced as if we were one...as if we had danced together for forty years.

Can I have this dance for the rest of your life?

The woman sang and the music continued but Brad paused, releasing me, and stepped back. Had I stepped on his foot? From his pocket he held up a golden locket. My eyes widened and I stopped breathing. I reached up. My fingers touched it as if it were a feather. I looked up at Brad. He studied my reaction. His intensity stunned me. I looked back at the locket, unable to believe what I saw. It was the same locket he had given me forty years ago at the fair. Brad moved around behind me and fastened the clasp and then kissed the back of my neck. The tears ran freely down my cheeks. I cradled the locket in my hand. He came back around in front of me. His finger lifted my chin and his intense blue eyes aligned with mine.

The kiss was long, tender, yet ended too soon. The world was mine and yet there was nothing else, nothing but the kiss. I didn't think, but whispers raced in my head. Weak and wobbly, I had to lean into him, but my heart swelled so large I had the strength of Atlas. A roaring in my ears confused me, and then whistles and cheers drew me down from my cloud.

When I opened my eyes, we were alone on the dance floor. The crowd encircled us, cheering and shouting. My face flushed and Brad smiled down at me. I was home.

Look for Judy Howard's
new book in 2013

Invisible Heroes

The memoir of an American service dog

My name is Masada and I am an American Service Dog.
I slept in the dark on the floor next to the bed of Marine
Corps Sargent Bud March. An odor I named *Panic* drifted
down and invaded my nostrils like smelling salts. I lay still
with my eyes open. The bedside clock cast shadows across
the hardwood floor and the green glow from the numbers
made me squint. Long before Bud's flailing arms and legs
rustled the bed sheets and his penetrating cries reached
my sensitive ears, my two years of intensive training kicked
in triggered by the Panic smell. It was my signal for action
and I jerked my head up.
The Sargent stared into the darkness unaware of the
eager wag of my tail so I jumped onto the bed and pushed
my head under his thrashing arms. Only after I lay my head
solidly on his chest did my distraction cause the sweeping
motion of his arms to slow and his trance broken by my
enthusiasm to comfort. I shivered from the thrill of his touch
when he brought his hands around and he cradled my
head. When he returned to the present, I convinced him
how much I needed him to be okay by nuzzling deep into
the crook of his neck. I felt his tenseness fade.

These events unfolded like a choreographed dance whose steps I had practiced over and over in my training classes. The performance became a demonstration of anxiety that transformed into a ballet of tender caresses. I executed the steps weekly, many times nightly even several times a night, because I am an American Service Dog. I am a professional. I stand ready and I will never quit. I will never leave my comrade's side.

Whatever demons that stole into our apartment and caused Bud's *Panic*, vanished like villainous ghosts. They would be back, though. They lurked like vultures, perched in the ceiling's corners, waiting for sleep to come. Three months ago when I first arrived they had been brazen and relentless, not waiting for the advantage of unconsciousness. They came no matter how often I challenged them. As time passed I wore them down with my constant nurturing and they began to tire of their hostilities.

Wide awake, Bud sat up and swung his legs to the floor. I shifted my body and placed my head on his thigh. The rhythm of his breathing slowed and he rubbed his hand over his shaved head. Outside our apartment's barred windows and triple locked doors, the world slept in peace, safe from the terrors Bud began to reveal to me. I sensed another wave of Panic as he began to talk so I jumped down from the bed and sat at attention facing him.

With hands that hummed with nervous energy he lifted my head. I looked, unblinking into his moist blue eyes hoping to soothe him. "Masada, I am supposed to tell you my experiences," he began, "but it is difficult even though I know you won't tell a soul."

Unwavering I wagged my tail and met his gaze feeling his despair. Trying to comfort, I pushed my nose against his arm and licked his hand while my tail thumped the wooden floor.

"I was walking with Eddie. It wasn't like the walks you and I take, down the tree-lined streets here, dodging skate boarders and joggers." Bud massaged my ears as he rocked back and forth. "There was only sand and rubble. It was Eddie's first day and we swapped stories about the States and Iraq.

"Eddie bragged about his high school sweetheart from Indiana who became his wife and had just borne him a son.

"Eddie's son was only two months old. They'd named him Ethan, after his grandpa. Before he was deployed Eddie and his wife stayed with his folks to save money. They were going to get a place of their own when he finished his tour. I remember his excitement as he spoke of his family.

"But my job was to train Eddie, keep him safe. As I described life in Iraq, I watched the kid's homegrown color drain from his face."

Bud's trembling fingers dug deep into my fur and I listened to his voice drone on.

"I told Eddie, 'Don't trust anyone. Watch everyone. See that guy over on the corner waving at us? He was in a group of insurgents shooting at us yesterday.' As I explained the dangers of the streets the look on Eddie's face shot through me like a piece of shrapnel. I had seen the look on others. It was the look of fear you feel when you have everything to live for."

Bud continued sitting on the edge of the bed, scratching my head. In the dark I listened and felt the dampness of his tears soak my fur as he buried his face into my neck.

"We patrolled streets lined with concrete buildings, every complex decorated by the war, displaying gaping holes in the roofs and walls chewed off by the bombings. I pointed to a soda can laying in the gutter. You have to be careful of soda cans, they can be IEDs."

Releasing me, Bud stood to pace the small room. The bed's blankets absorbed his words that had faded to a whisper. "I told Eddie, 'We'll cross here. Proceed on the other side,' you know, to avoid the can. Eddie didn't question why, and stepped out in front of me. When we crossed the street I waved to a young boy of ten who came running up.

"'Don't panic. Just be ready,'

"'He's just a boy,'

"When the boy neared, I noticed the kid's thinness and unruly black hair for the first time. His name was Yusuf and he came around every day selling us movies or bringing us fresh baked bread. His folks had been killed in the bombings. I took a stance aiming at the boy. 'Sorry Yusuf, no closer.' The boy stopped and waited unconcerned by the weapon aimed at his small chest because he had done the drill before. I remember vowing that Eddie's boy will never have to live like this if I had anything to do with it."

Bud stopped his pacing and sat down. I nuzzled and licked his arm. His arms encircled me tightly as he pulled me close. His knee moved up and down with a nervous rhythm.

"I ordered Yusuf to open his shirt. War had become a lifestyle and he obeyed the order. He had no bomb strapped to his chest. Only then did I dig into my pocket for the candy. Our hands touched his small fingers as he grabbed the sweets.

"Nothing happened that day, which made me even more hyper-vigilant. A week passed. We patrolled, shared stories from home, and watched the Iraqi shuffle through the rubble that was now their daily lives. We dined with Yusuf's family and visited his school, handing out more candy.

"I remember it was a Sunday, as if the day of the week made it more unconscionable when he ran up and again stood before us.

"'Hello, Yusuf.' Eddie smiled as he greeted the boy and then reached in his jacket pocket. I should have stopped Eddie when he omitted the search routine and began to approach the boy.

The Panic odor smoldered from Bud's body and in response I nudged his arm with my nose, again reminding him I was there, listening. I felt him relax, come back to me and the darkened room. He rubbed my back.

"The boy just exploded. Eddie went down. I was thrown back from the blast but staggered and stood my ground.

Do you smell that Masada? To this day I still smell the burning flesh and see the pink mist. I rushed to Eddie who lay face down. Before I rolled him over I had to shove a charred body part off Eddie's back. I don't know what body part it was, maybe one of Yusuf's small fingers.

"Eddie groaned and began to stand, miraculously only stunned. I offered him my hand that shook badly and I was embarrassed. *I am an American Soldier. I am disciplined, physically and mentally tough.* I wiped sweat from my brow, but when I looked down at my glove it was smeared with the boy's blood. Yusuf's blood."

Follow Masada, an American service dog, who grows from a bumbling golden retriever puppy into a serious, philosophical dog whose only desire is serve the people she loves.

On Masada's journey through life, she touches the souls of two desperate men: Mike, a prisoner doing a life sentence with nothing to live for, and Bud, who has lost everything he had to live for, as an Iraqi veteran struggling with his own life sentence of PTSD.

This is an inspiring story of invisible heroes, American service dogs and our veterans as they cope with the "invisible disease," post-traumatic stress syndrome.

At the writing of this book, eighteen veterans a day are committing suicide because of PTSD. Those figures are expected to increase dramatically as our young men return home.

Don't forget to update your reading with Judy Howard's first book.

Coast To Coast With
A Cat And *A Ghost*

Coast To Coast with A Cat And a Ghost

An engaging novel about overcoming loss and picking up the pieces.

When Judy's husband, Jack, dies of cancer, she takes off in her RV in hopes of piecing together her shattered heart piece by piece and state by state as she travels across the country. She tem-porarily leaves her home and grooming business behind in sunny California and makes her way out to a friend in Florida. In addition to the radio, she's joined by her new cat and a man-sized doll she made (whom she refers to as Jack Incarnate) for the 5,000 miles to Florida and back. In between new places and new faces, Judy thinks back to the relationship she had with Jack: when they first met at an AA meeting while drinking coffee, the time he was almost put behind bars for spousal abuse, etc. Though rough-around-the-edges Jack certainly had his fair share of baggage, he truly loved Judy, and she loved him back. Now that he's gone, Judy has to make her way without him and count up all the good and bad that came with their relationship. In her debut novel, Howard conveys piti-less reality with beauty and eloquence. "I felt like a dried leaf clinging to a branch, hoping to hang on as the cold harsh wind blew cruelly against my brittle spine," she writes. Despite the numerous brutal, intense battles between Judy and Jack, it's nearly impossible not to relate to her on some level, as she's so real and vulnerable. Most of all, she's a sur-vivor who manages to move on from the relationship that dictated much of her life. Though it could be easy to write off Jack as a villain, Howard portrays in him the many layers that each of us contend with—it's what makes us all so com-plex. She doesn't make excuses for his behavior, but there's a sense of sadness in everything he himself suffered, which, to a certain degree, made him who he was. The frivolous title doesn't capture the mature spirit of Judy's mindset.

Beautifully written and real to the core.

-Kirkus Review

Made in the USA
Charleston, SC
16 November 2012